D1329894

THE DECEPTION

GILLIAN JACKSON

www.bloodhoundbooks.com

Print ISBN 978-1-914614-77-4

ALSO BY GILLIAN JACKSON

The Pharmacist

The Victim

While all deception requires secrecy, all secrecy is not meant to deceive.
— Sissela Bok

CHAPTER ONE

Samantha – 2010

Alison Ashby lay motionless on a hospital bed, hovering on the edge of life. It was late June, a night too warm for comfort, and quite airless in the hospital ICU unit. Ali's sister, Samantha, sat as close as possible to the bedside, clinging to her hand, willing her to recover. Tubes snaked into Ali's nose and mouth and a grotesque ventilator assisted her breathing.

The rhythmic whoosh of the machine sounded almost otherworldly, an ugly reminder of how serious the injuries were.

An emergency operation hadn't been entirely successful as the pressure on her brain was severe. The doctor had explained that if Ali did recover, the injury would almost certainly impact future brain function. She was out of theatre – but not out of danger.

Sam stroked her sister's hair and whispered words of encouragement, reminding her of how much there was to live for.

'Don't leave me, Ali, please! I'm sorry I've let you down but I'll make it up to you – promise. We can find that flat we talked about buying for next year, and maybe have a holiday together. I need you, Ali, there's no future for me without you in it – please, please get better...' She didn't know if Ali heard her words but they were all she had to offer, she'd never felt so alone or helpless.

Samantha rubbed the tears from her eyes and shuffled her chair closer to Ali. The bruising and swelling made her sister barely recognisable and compounded Sam's feelings of guilt and regret. *The beating should have been mine,* she thought, *it's all my fault.*

Samantha and Alison Ashby were born in June 1991, twins arriving ten minutes apart, who grew closer to each other with every passing year. Their parents, Veronica and Phillip, adored their girls as did their paternal grandmother, Doreen Ashby.

There have probably never been identical twins who didn't play tricks on family and friends and Sam and Ali were no different. As soon as they realised those around them couldn't always tell them apart, they used their new-found knowledge to have fun, targeting anyone within sight. They could rarely fool their parents, but Granny Ashby was another matter – she roared with laughter at their tricks even if she wasn't always taken in.

At school, Sam and Ali quickly learned that their alikeness was an exception rather than the norm. It had never occurred to them that other children couldn't communicate without words, hold a conversation with their eyes, or constantly have someone beside them who could second-guess their every thought. To the twins it was natural to see an image of themselves across the kitchen table as well as in the mirror; they knew no different and wouldn't change it if they could.

In each other, Ali and Sam achieved security, companionship and understanding without ever having to try. Their bond was tangible, irrepressible and neither wished for life to be any other way. Veronica often declared it impossible to tell where one of them ended and the other began, an observation which dissolved the pair into fits of giggles.

With blonde curls and wide blue eyes, the twins earned the nickname, the sunshine girls, an apt description not only of their looks but their apparent sunny dispositions and charmed life. Yet it's impossible to remain untouched by tragedy; to encounter pain and loss is the unavoidable path of life and unbeknown to them their lives were about to change forever.

The tender age of sixteen is far too young to be confronted with the stark reality of death – too soon to be robbed of the security of a comfortable, carefree life. But Ali and Sam were unexpectedly thrust into a new and alarmingly different world from the one they'd known and possibly even taken for granted.

Veronica Ashby rarely accompanied her husband on work trips but made an exception when Phillip, an up-and-coming architect, was to receive an award and she was included in the invitation to witness the accolade.

'Be good for Granny – I love you both.' These were the last words Veronica spoke to her children – it was a celebration fated to end in tragedy when the couple were killed in a horrific car accident.

If they hadn't been so keen to get home to their daughters, they may not have ventured out so late at night and in such adverse conditions. But the truth died with them, as freezing fog and a treacherous country lane conspired to rob Samantha and Alison of their beloved parents. Shocked and heartbroken they mourned their loss bitterly, leaning heavily on each other and their grandmother for support, attempting to understand how and why the accident happened, yet finding no consoling answers.

And so, Sam and Ali moved in with Granny Ashby, and their second home became their only one, their world shrinking at a time when it should have been expanding.

The loss of their parents took away the girls' security, structure and the unconditional love which perhaps they'd taken for granted. Feeling adrift, Ali and Sam clung to each other for support, robbed of the adults who'd been their compass and guiding lights. Doreen Ashby did her best for her granddaughters but she too was grieving, and the untimely death of her only son took its toll on her health.

Exams were looming at school adding more pressure to Sam and Ali but they worked hard, determined to do well in memory of their parents who'd been passionate about education, and encouraged them to be the best people they could possibly be. University was their ultimate goal and over the following two years the twins worked towards their A levels. But another blow was to leave Sam and Ali reeling when their much-loved granny died.

Another funeral and another loss brought with it the familiar heartache as their world shrank yet again. On the cusp of adult life, the twins found themselves bereft of family other than each other.

CHAPTER TWO

'Will you be okay on your own, Ali?' Samantha dropped the last box of her sister's possessions in her room at the halls of residence and rolled her shoulders to ease the aches and pains.

'Stop fussing, I'll be fine and I'm hardly alone – the halls are literally crawling with students.' Alison hugged her sister. 'Off you go and get your own stuff sorted – we'll meet up in the morning as planned.'

Sam reluctantly said goodbye, feeling years older than her sister, not just the ten minutes it actually was. It was the first time they'd been separated and it felt strange, as if a part of herself was missing.

'Ring me if you need anything, won't you? I can be back in twenty minutes.' A towel whizzed past her ears as Ali waved her away.

It was the beginning of a new era – the sisters needed the comfort of being geographically close if not on the same course, and Liverpool John Moores University offered the opportunity to do just that. Samantha had enrolled for a BSC honours in adult nursing while Ali plumped for a BSC in biochemistry.

Wishing to experience living among other students, the girls opted to reside in separate halls of residence yet on the same campus. Looking ahead, they planned to find somewhere together during the second year, a flat perhaps, using the money from the sale of their grandmother's house rather than the trust fund left to them by their parents, but education was the first year's priority.

Both the academic and social sides of student life proved hectic yet exciting with the consequence that for the first time in their lives, Ali and Sam didn't see each other every day, a strange unnatural feeling eased only by daily phone calls.

The first weeks of term flew by and as Christmas approached Sam and Ali were at a loss to know what to do.

'I don't feel like celebrating.' Samantha flopped down on her sister's bed one day. 'Half the students have already left for home and I can't help being envious of their perfect family Christmases. What shall we do, Ali?' Sam was painfully aware of this being the first year without their grandmother, a hard-hitting reality which brought home precisely how alone they were.

'If we do nothing, we'll be miserable and I don't want to mope. Why don't we book ourselves into a posh hotel somewhere?' Ali's eyes sparkled. 'We don't have a home to go to and it'll be like a ghost town if we hang around here. I know it's an extravagance but we'll be together and it'll be fun to be pampered for a change.'

Samantha didn't take much winning over. 'Great idea and I know just the place!'

It proved a strange and different way to celebrate Christmas, yet the break from studies and the opportunity of being together was enjoyable. Making new memories rather than living in the past became a mantra for both girls.

Early January of 2010 found Samantha and Alison back in their student accommodation throwing themselves into studying, yet missing the daily contact which had previously marked the whole of their lives. Although not entirely the same, video calls were a tolerable substitute, although Samantha felt the loss of face-to-face contact with her twin keenly – until she met Gary Drake.

'I've got a date!' Sam laughed at her sister's startled expression on the small screen of her phone.

'Fantastic, who is he? Where did you meet him?' Ali's questions were no more than Sam expected.

'Hey, slow down.' She laughed at her sister's enthusiasm. 'His name's Gary Drake and we met in a pub. He's not a student; he works behind the bar and I've seen him a few times before but we only started chatting last night.'

'When do you have time to go to pubs?'

'You have to experience the social side of uni – all work and no play...'

'So, where are you going and what's he like?'

'Just for a bar meal, nothing formal, and he's gorgeous – tall with dark brown hair and such dreamy eyes, like melted chocolate – and judging by his body he must work out often. He's fit!'

'Okay, so I want a photo and a full account of the evening.'

'I can't take a photo of him on a first date. What will he think?'

'Course you can, just get him in a selfie and send it straight to me. He's a man, he'll be flattered!' Ali laughed.

'I'll see how it goes. No promises though. Gary might be hunky but we've only just met and it might end up being a one-time thing, we'll see.' Sam was already looking forward to the date and the occasional distraction from her studies which having a boyfriend would offer.

The first date went well. Gary took her to a small country pub, quiet enough to allow conversation yet busy enough to have a convivial atmosphere.

Sam looked around the room. 'Wow, this place is fantastic!'

'Glad you approve – and the food's great too. I can recommend the fish, it's their speciality.' Gary was undeniably attractive and appeared so much more mature than most of the students Sam had met since coming to Liverpool. He was at ease with himself, a quality she admired, and those eyes – they were almost hypnotic.

'I'd like to see you again, Sam,' Gary said as he drove her home in his old Ford Focus. Samantha smiled – it was what she wanted too.

A second date progressed to a third and soon they were seeing each other three or four times a week which wasn't always easy with Gary's unsocial working hours, and Sam's commitment to study.

'I know you have a sister but what about your parents? Do you see them much?' Gary asked one evening.

'They were killed in an accident when I was sixteen.' Sam swallowed hard, the pain still very real, dulled only slightly by the passing of time.

'I'm so sorry, I didn't mean to upset you.' Gary reached out to hug her and Samantha relaxed into his hold.

'Do you want to talk about it?' he asked as they pulled apart, and Samantha found herself pouring out the awful events of the last two years, sharing the details of her parents' accident and the more-recent death of her grandmother.

Most people were embarrassed about her loss and avoided the subject entirely so it was a relief to unburden herself to someone other than Ali. Cathartic even. Perhaps not seeing her sister every day prompted Sam's uncharacteristic openness. She craved the closeness she'd always known with Ali and missed so much. Gary proved to be a good listener.

'We've always tried to cling to the positives, the happy memories we have, and at least I still have Alison.' Sam thought perhaps she was talking too much but Gary appeared interested and sympathetic, so she continued. 'We were fortunate in Dad's forward thinking too. He set up a trust fund years before they died which eased the practical side of our loss and allowed us to enrol at university. His forethought certainly solved our practical problems, but I miss them so much.'

The dates continued but over the next few weeks, Samantha saw another side to Gary as things started to change. Occasionally he would turn up on campus, surprising Sam in between lectures, trying to persuade her to grab a quick coffee – to play hooky. Sometimes she refused, reluctantly so at first but when the surprise visits became a regular occurrence, his persistence and constant wheedling grew irritating.

When Gary worked evenings, he expected Sam to visit the pub, and although keen at first the novelty soon wore off. She felt like a groupie sitting at the bar waiting for whatever crumbs of attention he could throw her way.

In short, Gary very quickly appeared to think Samantha should put him before her studies, regularly suggesting she skipped lectures when he was free and wanted to see her, and showing little regard for her need to set aside time to study. He was also displaying a moody side to his character which she'd not noticed before.

By the time Alison met Gary, Sam was already having doubts about the relationship and considering ending it.

'But he's gorgeous!' Ali declared. 'Why would you not want a man as sexy as Gary?' She took Sam's face between her hands and pinched her cheeks, teasing her as she'd done so often when they were children.

'I know but he thinks I should put him before my studies. He doesn't realise how important nursing is to me and how much time I need to keep up. Twice last week he turned up as I was going to a lecture and tried to persuade me to skip it because he was at a loose end.'

'You could take it as a compliment that he wants to spend so much time with you.'

'It's not just that – at times he's animated and a good laugh, but he can be morose and even sullen on occasions when we're alone. Gary's moody and difficult to read at times, and I'm not sure I want to try anymore.'

'Why not talk to him and explain how you feel?' Ali suggested. 'A man like him doesn't come along every day you know!'

The sisters laughed about it and Sam agreed that perhaps Gary was worth a second chance – she couldn't deny the physical attraction, Ali was right about him being gorgeous.

Sam rang Gary the next day and invited him to her room for a serious discussion. He arrived late afternoon just as she was getting back from her last lecture of the day.

'Hi, beautiful! Were you missing me?' Gary kissed her

lightly and followed her into her room where he lounged on her bed and smiled at her.

Sam decided to get straight to the point. 'I have to say something, Gary. Things are moving too quickly for me.' Gary swung his legs off the bed and sat upright, his smile gone.

'I mean, I enjoy being with you and we've had some great times together but I need to spend more time on my studies. I can't skip lectures when you fancy a day out – nursing's important to me...'

'Yes, I know. Oh hell, Sam, I'm sorry. Have I messed things up between us?'

The little boy lost look on his face made Sam feel guilty. 'No, I just need you to slow down a bit and not expect so much of my time.'

'I've been inconsiderate, Sam, and I'm sorry – it's just that I think I'm falling in love with you. I know it's early days and I promise to slow down and not rush you. But you're right, your studies are important and must come first. I can see that now. Forgiven?' Gary looked at her with that lopsided smile she found so endearing. Flattered by his declaration of love and encouraged by his understanding, Sam could hardly refuse.

'Of course. Let's just enjoy seeing each other when we can, shall we? No strings, okay?'

'Great, so is it to be McDonald's or Kentucky Fried – my treat to say sorry?'

It was a relief to have reached an understanding so readily, Ali had been right.

A pattern developed over the next few weeks which seemed to satisfy them both. Meeting only twice a week enabled Sam to concentrate on her studies and the couple talked frequently on the phone at the end of the day.

It appeared they were both content – or so Samantha thought.

CHAPTER THREE

At the beginning of April most students returned home for the Easter break but Ali and Sam remained at the university. Barring another hotel stay there was nowhere else to go. At such times the ache of missing her parents and grandmother was palpable, and although pushed deep into the recesses of her mind, the pain of their loss threatened on occasions to overwhelm Samantha. Yet she resolved to be pragmatic, and as the halls were quiet with only a few other students, mainly from overseas, remaining for the holidays it was an excellent opportunity to knuckle down to some studying.

On a rare Saturday off, Gary called Sam. 'Hey, it's a lovely morning and I hate the thought of you cooped up in that stuffy little room. Let me take you out for the day?'

Samantha visualised his crooked smile and the twinkle in his eyes. It would be a welcome diversion from a rather heavy assignment with which she was grappling. 'Why not, I'd love to get out for some fresh air. Where are we going?'

'It's a surprise, but I promise you'll enjoy yourself.'

The morning was bright with a watery sun heralding better things to come and lifting her mood. Samantha wrapped up in her favourite orange wool coat, and as she hurried downstairs to meet Gary a positive feeling about the future filled her mind. It was too easy to become maudlin, which had been the case of late and she refused to allow self-pity to define her. Work gave Sam focus and motivation, but a day out with her handsome boyfriend was precisely what she needed to lift her flagging spirits.

The campus, always a fantastic place to live, was looking good that morning. Daffodils added a welcome splash of colour to the borders which had been bare for so long, reminding Sam that spring was upon them. Although she envied the students who went home for holidays and weekends, she still had Alison and Gary and decided to look for the positives in life and not dwell on the negatives.

Gary's old Ford Focus pulled up beside her spot-on time and Sam jumped in, kissing him on the cheek as he drove away.

'Okay, so where are we going?' she asked. 'And am I dressed okay?'

'Lovely as ever but you'll have to wait and see or it won't be a surprise, will it? Don't worry it's not far.' His confident smile reassured her that their destination would be one she'd enjoy.

It certainly wasn't far as in less than ten minutes they turned into Albert Dock, a place Sam had only visited a couple of times before and always intended to go again. Gary parked the car in an already-busy car park and took Sam's hand as they walked towards the docks.

'Coffee first?'

'Please.'

They made their way to the Gallery café and ordered lattes and doughnuts, sitting outside to enjoy the sun's warmth which was gaining strength as the morning aged. A companionable silence settled over the couple as they enjoyed the bustling atmosphere.

'This day's just for you, Sam, so you can choose where you'd like to go first. Tate Liverpool or the Beatles Magical Mystery Tour?' Gary offered.

'Oh, the tour, I think. I've been to the Tate with Ali and as it's such a lovely morning the bus tour will be fantastic.' The day was already proving enjoyable and Gary was going out of his way to be good company.

The tour certainly lived up to expectations with piped music, Beatles songs of course, playing in the background as they drove to all the sites associated with the rise of the Fab Four.

Two hours later Samantha felt more relaxed than she'd been in weeks, with her workload forgotten in the delight of a day out with Gary. It was time for lunch and they settled on a small independent café, ordering toasted paninis and salad, followed by ice cream with warm cherry sauce.

'This is just what I needed today, thanks.' Sam smiled, enjoying his company.

'It's not over yet.' Gary winked mysteriously and Sam wondered what else he had planned.

Strolling around the docks after lunch, hand in hand, with sunshine on their faces, they admired how the old buildings had been sympathetically renovated.

Gary suddenly halted outside The Colonnades, a large warehouse residential development and turned to look at Sam. 'What do you think?'

'Amazing!' She looked up at the vast building beautifully re-purposed as modern luxury apartments. 'Do you know someone who lives here?'

'No, but let's have a nosey around anyway.' He took her hand and headed through the doors towards the lift.

'We can't just go wandering about!' Sam protested trying to drag him back outside. 'These are people's homes.' But the lift arrived and Gary steered her inside and pressed the button for the tenth floor, silencing her with a kiss and refusing to answer any questions. The lift stopped and they stepped out into a spacious hallway.

'Ah, Mr Drake!' A young smartly dressed man walked towards them, hand outstretched to shake Gary's. He introduced himself as Jason Urquhart and hugging his briefcase to his chest asked them to follow him.

'Hang on – Gary, what's going on?' Sam whispered, confused and a little annoyed.

'This is your surprise!' Gary pressed his finger to her lips to silence her and would say no more as he followed Jason into the apartment he was unlocking, dragging her reluctantly behind him.

The tenth-floor apartment was nothing short of stunning; exposed brick walls, steel pillars and an open tread metal staircase enhanced the rustic, warehouse feel. The room into which they entered was a spacious lounge with high ceilings, floor-to-ceiling windows and concealed lighting in the alcoves at either end of the room. It was furnished beautifully with huge cream sofas, glass and chrome tables and enormous colourful prints positioned to catch the light – and the room boasted plenty of natural light from the windows where so much glass elicited the feeling of being outside. A balcony, the length of one wall, provided space to sit outside to watch the boats bobbing on the water and experience the bustle of the Albert Dock; a fantastic vantage point with an unrivalled view.

Jason, whom Samantha realised by then was an estate agent, was pointing out the high specification of the kitchen appliances, an endless patter designed to impress when his words were unnecessary, the apartment spoke for itself.

They moved from the high-quality bespoke kitchen to the

staircase and as the agent ascended first, Sam hissed in Gary's ear, 'What are we doing here?'

'Just looking. Relax, sweetheart, and enjoy the ride!' He beamed, ignoring her discomfort. They followed the estate agent upstairs into two huge bedrooms both immaculately presented with luxurious soft furnishings enhancing the expensive décor. The bathroom was next, a large family bathroom as beautifully finished as the en suite in the master bedroom.

The tour was over, leaving Samantha stunned. The apartment was undoubtedly impressive but she was angry and hated wasting the agent's time simply so they could be entertained by mooching around someone's luxury home. It smacked of voyeurism.

As they left the apartment and returned to the corridor Gary said a few words to Jason which Sam didn't quite catch before Jason went down in the lift. The couple were alone together, standing on plush springy carpeting which looked far too expensive to be in a communal corridor.

Sam turned angrily to Gary. 'Are you going to explain what that was all about?'

He snaked his arm protectively around her. 'Let's find somewhere to talk, love.' He steered her to the lift, a self-satisfied smile across his face.

CHAPTER FOUR

S am and Gary walked in silence beside the quay, eventually finding a low wall on which to sit and talk over the last hour.

'Why did you think I'd enjoy noseying around someone's apartment – it's just mean, giving false hope to the vendor and the estate agent?' Samantha couldn't understand Gary's reasoning.

'It wasn't idle curiosity. It's a glimpse of what our life could be like. Didn't you just love it?' He was clearly excited and Sam, shocked by what he might be implying, remained silent to allow him chance to explain.

'Look, seeing you only a couple of times a week isn't enough for me. I thought it would be, but it's not. I miss you, Sam, and want to be with you. If we moved in together, we'd have the opportunity to see more of each other. The university's near enough to walk from here and we'd be together every day.' Gary's voice was high, animated, but Sam was stunned.

In a way it was flattering that he thought so much of her, but she wasn't yet nineteen and still in the first year at uni. It was far too soon to make such a huge commitment. And why show her such an expensive apartment? Gary lived in a tiny terraced house near the pub where he worked. Sam had visited once, which was enough, it left much to be desired. He rented the house and said he only stayed there because it was cheap.

'But how could you afford somewhere like The Colonnades? You work in a pub and I'm at uni; it's impossible.'

'No, it's not. Think about it, Sam. You're well off, and if you use that trust fund of yours, we could easily afford such a place. It's £345,000 and they'd probably take an offer for cash.' He looked at her, eyes sparkling. Gary was eager, like a child at Christmas, and showed none of the maturity she'd thought he possessed.

Sam was suddenly furious. 'How dare you think you can decide how to use my trust fund! We've only known each other three months, it's far too soon to be making any such commitment – and I'm not even sure I want to be with you anymore!' She stood to go.

'Wait, Sam, why don't you just think about it? It would be our own little love nest. We'll see each other every night and you'll still have plenty of time for your studies. Come on, be reasonable!' A scowl was spreading across his face and she could tell his mood, although imploring, was darkening.

Sam was speechless – had he simply expected her to be wowed with the apartment and buy it outright? It was Gary who was being unreasonable. The money was for her and Ali's future. How dare he decide how she should spend it? Unable to think of anything else to say and wanting to be as far away from Gary Drake as possible, Sam set off to walk back to the university.

'Sam! Don't be stupid. At least think about it!' He ran after her, grabbing at her shoulder to pull her back. A few people stared at them as she shrugged him off and quickened her pace. 'Come on, come back to the car!' he hissed.

Sam couldn't even look at him, she was so angry and didn't trust herself to reply.

Gary didn't persist in following and Sam was glad of the walk, the time alone to clear her head and think over what had just occurred.

Arriving back at the halls she headed to her room, for the first time pleased that the place was almost deserted. Flopping down on the bed, the angry frustrated tears she'd been holding back were released. Her mind whirred at the day's events; it was almost unreal and she wondered if she'd imagined it all.

Half an hour later and feeling more than a little sorry for herself, Sam rang her sister.

'Hey, I thought you were on a date. Is something wrong?' Ali asked.

'Everything! Can I come over?' Sam knew she sounded pitiful.

'Of course. I'll put the kettle on.'

Alison's halls were fifteen minutes' walk away and soon Sam was sobbing in her twin's arms, pouring out what had happened. Alison listened quietly, her eyes wide.

'Wow, Sam. What did you say?'

'I told him we were finished. I thought he understood I didn't want to get too serious and was okay about meeting only a couple of times a week, but it seems not – and to suggest using the trust fund! How dare he?' Samantha was clenching and unclenching her fists as she spoke.

'I didn't know you'd told him about the trust fund.'

'Yes and I wish I hadn't, it was stupid but I never expected this.'

'Perhaps he wasn't thinking of moving in there but somewhere else, his house, maybe?'

'No way. His place is a dump, he meant The Colonnades all

right, and he wanted to use our trust fund to buy it. It makes me wonder if it's me Gary wants or just the money.'

'Oh come on, sis. I've not had chance to get to know him well but he seems keen on you, and why not? You're a catch, Sam!'

'Because I've got money?' The words sounded rather more bitter than she intended.

'So, what are you going to do? Do you want to see him again?' Ali stroked Sam's hair as their mother used to do when they were small and upset.

'No, never! He doesn't seem to have got the message that I want to keep things light, so the best thing for us both is to break up. I don't need the pressure and certainly don't feel the same way about him as he *says* he does about me. It's clear our relationship isn't going to work out and the sooner I tell him the better. But I'll have to see him again to tell him, sending a text or email's the coward's way out, isn't it?' She glanced at Ali for advice.

'There's nothing wrong with being a coward here. If you really don't want to see him then say so—' They were interrupted by Sam's phone ringing and guessed who it would be. Slowly pulling the phone from her pocket, Sam's face paled.

'It's him!' Suddenly fearful of confrontation she was tempted not to accept the call, but telling Gary when Ali was with her would be so much easier, so she answered, a cold shudder passing through her body as she heard his voice.

'Sam, I'm so sorry. I've put my foot in it again, haven't I?' Sam said nothing as he continued. 'Where are you? I'm at your halls waiting for you. We need to talk.'

'No, Gary. I don't feel the same way as you do so it's not fair to continue seeing each other.'

'Sam, please at least let me explain. I made a mistake and

I'm sorry. Come back here, or I can come and pick you up. Tell me where you are?'

'It doesn't matter. I don't want to talk so please just go home.'

'Look, I'll ring you tomorrow. Perhaps we can go out for Sunday lunch?' Gary's persistence was unsettling.

'I don't want to see you anymore – it's for the best, really it is, so goodbye.' Sam ended the call, disturbed by events and Gary's resolve to continue their relationship.

Ali watched her closely and reached out to hug her again. 'You were clear enough, sis. I know it wasn't easy.' Her embrace was welcome.

Grateful for her sister's support and understanding, Sam stayed with her for another couple of hours, reluctant to go back to the halls on her own, but eventually she stood to leave.

'You can stay over if you like. I can easily put a duvet on the floor, or you can have the bed seeing as how you're older than me!' Ali teased.

'Yes, by ten minutes.' Sam appreciated the attempt to cheer her up. 'No, I'll get off. There's an assignment waiting for me to finish tomorrow and I should get an early start. Thanks for listening to my moaning, you're a star.'

Sam took a deep breath and set off, suddenly weary. An early night and getting her head down to study the following day would take her mind off Gary – it would be better if she could simply forget about him and put her studies first.

But events were to conspire against Samantha and her life was about to spiral out of control.

CHAPTER FIVE

A peaceful sensation descended on Sam after the decision to finish her relationship with Gary. There were no sleepless nights or bitter regrets, which she took as a sign that she was right in her decision, he wasn't the man for her. Despite his declaration of love there was an element of doubt in her mind as to whether he was attracted to her or her money. Sam felt she'd learned her lesson and would never tell another boyfriend about the trust fund until she was absolutely sure of him.

The peace, however, didn't last long. Catching up with work and even getting ahead of herself instilled a good feeling, so she indulged in some 'me' time to relax and unwind. Although not going far from campus, using the gym and the pool, or meeting Ali or a friend for coffee, Sam experienced an uncomfortable sense of being watched each time she ventured outside. At first, she shrugged it off as paranoia – when she looked around, no one was there, and she concluded she was simply obsessing. The whole Gary thing had shaken her more than she cared to admit, yet it was three weeks since she'd seen him, and with the passing days he occupied less and less of her thoughts.

One day as Sam returned to her room, she was surprised to see the door standing ajar. She was always careful about locking it, paranoid even since the Gary fiasco. Running a couple of doors down to Yetta's room, she dragged her back to check no one was inside waiting for her. Yetta was a tall athletic girl from Romania, and a down-to-earth person. She pushed straight inside, sweeping the small space with her eyes and declaring,

'No one here. You forgotten to lock door.'

Sam felt rather foolish yet was convinced it had been locked, she'd been extra cautious since the feeling of being watched had haunted her.

'Thank you, Yetta, you're probably right.' Yetta left and Sam searched the room to see if anything had been taken. Nothing was missing but an uneasy feeling lingered in her mind and glancing around she suspected some of her books had been rearranged. The room wasn't quite how she'd left it, not that Sam was the tidiest of people but the notion refused to go away. In an attempt at distraction, she switched on the radio which stood on the windowsill. Strangely, it was no longer tuned to the local station she favoured, but thinking nothing of it she told herself it was all in her mind.

It was only later when Sam decided on an early night and pulled back the duvet that she found the dead mouse on her sheets. Her scream brought Yetta and another girl from down the corridor banging on the door. She let them in, shaken and feeling rather foolish.

'Practical joker,' Yetta announced as she lifted the mouse by the tail and calmly dropped it in the waste paper bin. 'You don't like mouse?' Her matter-of-fact common sense was comforting, her accent endearing.

'No, it's silly but I've always hated them.'

'No worries, he be more scared than you.'

Sam's friends left and the next hour was spent in telling herself it was stupid to let such a silly incident rattle her. She could hardly call the police – it was only someone's stupid idea of a practical joke. Sam changed the bedding and took the bin downstairs to empty it outside, unable to bear the thought of sharing her room with a mouse, even a dead one.

Eventually, crawling into bed, sleep refused to come and the silent dark hours dragged by, feeding her paranoia and self-pity. Having agreed with her friends that the incident was a joke, it seemed a particularly cruel one by someone who apparently wanted to spook Sam, and Gary Drake was the first person to come to mind as a possible culprit. He'd been strangely quiet since she'd ended their relationship, not quite what she'd expected from someone who was usually so determined. But would he be so petty as to place a dead mouse in her bed? And what could he gain from such a stunt?

The next day was busy – back-to-back lectures and a tutorial kept Sam's mind from dwelling on those silly minor incidents which were probably insignificant and hopefully wouldn't be repeated. When evening finally came, she rang Ali to catch up with her news but the phone went to voicemail.

'Hey, where are you, sis? Ring me back when you get this. I need a chat.' Disappointment descended like a fog. Sam had been looking forward to talking to her sister, sharing those weird events and getting them out of her system. They would laugh about them together and the laughter would be cathartic. When Ali didn't return her call that evening, Sam left another message.

'Sorry not to have caught up with you. I'm around until ten tomorrow morning if you're free to call – love you!'

It wasn't like Alison not to ring straight back but Sam was confident the morning would bring an apologetic call and they'd catch up then. Her sister would likely think the mouse incident a hoot; Ali loved practical jokes yet it still unsettled Sam. Had she forgotten to lock her door? If so, it was a strange coincidence that it happened on the same day someone decided to play such a tasteless prank.

Alison didn't ring before it was time for Sam to leave for lectures so she gave her another quick try. This time her phone was switched off so she couldn't even leave a message. If Sam didn't hear from her during the day, she resolved to walk over to her halls that evening, but before she had the chance to do so, Alison rang.

'Ali, hi! I was getting worried when you didn't reply.'

'No need. I was out last night, that's all.' Ali sounded unusually snappy and was breathless as if she was running.

'Oh, okay, did you go anywhere exciting?'

'Nowhere special. Look, Sam, is there anything particular you wanted, only I'm in a hurry?'

'Well, no, just a chat, really.'

'Can we do it another time then? Got to dash, bye.' Ali ended the brief call leaving Sam puzzled. If she hadn't recognised the voice she wouldn't have known it was her sister, it was unlike her to be so abrupt. It wasn't as if they lived in each other's pockets but they talked about everything, there were no secrets between them, yet she sounded secretive now. Deciding to give her the benefit of the doubt Sam put her sister's mood down to her simply being in a hurry, late for a lecture maybe.

Over the next few days the sisters exchanged more similar phone conversations; Ali claiming she was busy yet not saying with what, until Sam felt as if she was harassing her. It was so out of character for Ali, and Sam's worries multiplied. Needing to see her in person to check everything was all right, Sam set off after lectures one day on the off-chance Ali would be in her room.

She was.

Ali opened her door a crack, hair mussed and in her underwear.

'Oops, am I disturbing something?' Smiling at her obvious embarrassment, Sam's expression quickly changed when a familiar voice shouted from inside.

'Tell whoever it is to go away!'

She didn't need telling. Horrified, Sam ran from the building as if it were on fire, unable to believe her sister was sleeping with *him*! Tears blurred her vision as she hurried back to halls, her head spinning as to why Ali would do such a thing, Sam's heart pounded as she ran. Perhaps it was none of her business who she saw but Ali knew what Gary had done to her – if she was so attracted to him surely she could have told her – warned her.

Sam needed to put distance between them. The more she thought about it the angrier she became; not with Ali but with Gary. Was he playing games with her, using her twin to get at her as some sick payback? Or, an even more sinister thought, was he going after Ali to get at their trust fund? Whatever his motives Sam couldn't believe they were innocent and suddenly she was deeply afraid for Alison. Was this why she'd been avoiding her; why she wasn't returning her calls and had no time to see her? Sam suddenly felt very alone, yet the only person she had left in the world to turn to was in bed with Gary bloody Drake!

CHAPTER SIX

'Sam, let me in!' Alison knocked persistently. Her voice didn't bring Sam the comfort it usually did as she opened the door.

'Can I come in?' Ali asked. 'To explain.'

Sam nodded and stood aside – from her window she could see Gary's car parked nearby – he sat in the driver's seat, watching, waiting. She was lost for words to say.

Ali's eyes searched her sister's face. 'Sam. I'm so sorry. I was going to tell you but it seemed too soon. I wasn't sure how you'd react.'

Sam eventually found her voice. 'It's only four weeks since we split up. Did he come running to you for comfort?' The words sounded petty, but she was upset and angry to have been kept in the dark, made a fool of even.

'It's not what you think. Yes, Gary did come to see me to talk about you – he cared for you, Sam and was devastated when you finished with him.'

'Not too devastated it appears. He made a move on you soon enough!' Sam sounded like a petulant child, her voice shrill, yet she couldn't seem to help herself.

'It just sort of happened. It wasn't as if you still wanted him, did you?' Ali's beautiful eyes glistened with tears.

'Oh, Ali, you know what happened to me – what he wanted. Has he tried to get at the trust fund through you?'

Alison winced. 'No, he hasn't. Gary realises his mistake and he's learned from it. The money's never been mentioned between us.'

'But it *will* be, don't you see? He can't have one twin so he'll have the other?' Sam knew it was a cruel thing to say and probably didn't come out quite as intended. Still, Ali needed to know, to be aware of what this man was like.

'What a vile thing to say! Do you think he could only want me for my money? This is why I didn't tell you, Sam. Gary's a sweet man you just didn't give him the chance to prove it.' Ali's eyes sparkled with angry tears. They'd never argued so bitterly.

'He's a chancer, Ali, out for what he can get. Please don't get involved with him!' Sam was almost begging, afraid of how this would play out and fearful that it was already too late.

'But I am involved! We've become close and I want to go on seeing him. I've met his mum and sister – they're lovely people, Sam.'

'Maybe his family are lovely but it's Gary who concerns me, he's simply not to be trusted.'

Alison's face hardened at her sister's words. Sam had never seen her like that before and half expected her to put her hands over her ears, close her eyes and shake her head as they'd done as little girls when they didn't want to listen to something.

'Look, I love him, so don't make me choose between you. If you don't like me seeing him then you know what to do!' Alison almost spat the words out.

Samantha was stunned. Would Ali really dismiss her twin sister for a man she'd only known for a few weeks – and she couldn't possibly know she loved him – it was far too soon; she was too young.

'You don't have to choose, Ali. I'll always be here for you, you know that.' She moved to hug her, determined not to let a man come between them but Ali stepped back and a lump caught in Sam's throat at the rejection. The pain was almost tangible but that awful man was not going to take her sister away from her. Sam would remain in her life and be there to pick up the pieces when things went wrong, which was inevitable.

There was no chance to say more, to repair the rift between them. Sam stiffened at the sound of a loud knock on the door, knowing it would be Gary, afraid she'd persuade her sister to leave him. Ali opened the door. Gary stood in the corridor, craning his neck to see inside.

'Everything all right?' he asked, an innocent smile playing on his lips. Sam couldn't bring herself to speak to him, to even look at him, convinced he was enjoying the awful situation he'd created.

'Yes, I'm ready now.' Ali smiled up at him, the look in her eyes confirming she was already under his spell. 'We'll speak later, Sam, okay?' She barely glanced over her shoulder and hurried off down the corridor. Gary remained leaning against the door jamb and smiled lazily. His eyes swept the little room and he nodded towards a packet of biscuits on the windowsill.

'I wouldn't leave them lying around. You're likely to get mice.' The man then had the audacity to wink at Sam as he turned to follow her sister down the stairs.

The next few days passed in a blur. Sam was livid, bitter at a man who didn't deserve her beautiful sister and confused as to the best way to proceed. If she tried to turn Ali against Gary it would look like sour grapes. Even though Ali must surely know she didn't want him for herself, it would probably push her closer to him. It would be the same if she told her about the mouse. There was no doubt in Sam's mind that Gary had been in her room but would Ali believe her?

The sisters continued to speak on the phone, although not every day as was the norm, and their conversations were stilted, unnatural, talking only about their studies and avoiding any personal issues. Neither of them mentioned Gary, the subject taboo, and Ali's silence shouted loud and clear that she was still involved with him. Sam's stomach churned at the thought.

Determined not to give up, Sam rang her sister. 'Hi, Ali. I wondered if you had time to meet me at the mall on Saturday? We could have coffee or lunch if you like, and I'd like your help in choosing a new dress...' She knew she was trying too hard, rambling even, but to her surprise, Ali agreed.

They met in Costa Coffee, both wary and unsure what to say. Ali broke the ice. 'Is the dress for a special occasion?'

Sam smiled a little too brightly. 'An end of term party for one of the girls in my study group.' An awkward silence followed as they both tried to think of things to say without mentioning Gary.

'Let's try Oasis first,' Sam suggested when they'd finished their coffee and Ali followed on with little enthusiasm.

Sam chose a dress she didn't particularly like. Having always enjoyed shopping together, the excitement and frivolity was noticeably absent. Gary may not have been with them in person but he hung over them like a cloud, dogging their relationship and driving a massive wedge between them. Sam felt a deep sadness but remained uncertain how to put things right.

June rolled around and once again many students were

leaving for the long summer break. Sam stayed on for lack of anywhere else to go, as did Ali, presumably to be near *him*.

The time was quickly approaching to consider accommodation for their second year at uni and Sam wondered if Ali would still wish to share with her. How it would work she had no idea; it would inevitably mean accepting Gary as part of the package – an appalling thought which made her feel sick. But she missed her twin more than she could ever have thought possible and as each day passed, Sam felt increasingly alone as if time was widening the gulf between them.

CHAPTER SEVEN

I t was over a week since their difficult coffee date and Sam wanted to see Ali again to discuss the next term's accommodation. Their infrequent phone calls remained awkward, initiated by Sam and cut short by Ali, yet Sam refused to let her sister drift out of her life – she'd make a nuisance of herself before losing her.

There were still times when Ali didn't answer her calls; times she assumed her sister was with Gary, and she didn't always return her messages but there was no way she was going to stop trying.

After several unanswered calls one week, Sam decided to visit and made her way to Ali's halls of residence hoping to find her alone. There was no answer to her first knock so she knocked again louder, willing her to be in.

A familiar-looking girl appeared from the room next door. 'Are you looking for your sister?'

'Yes, do you know where she is?' They'd met before but Sam couldn't remember the girl's name.

'No. She moved out last week and didn't say where she was going. That boyfriend of hers helped to move her stuff, you know, the fit one?' The girl shrugged and returned to her room leaving Sam standing with her mouth open, incredulous. Pulling out her phone she rang Ali's number, praying she would answer.

She did.

'Sam?' Ali's voice was barely a whisper.

'Ali! Where are you? Your neighbour said you've moved out – why didn't you let me know?' A sob at the other end of the phone tore at Sam's heart. 'What is it? Where are you? I'll come and get you...'

'Sam, I've been so stupid – I've done something terrible.' Her sobs muffled her voice.

'Tell me where you are, please! Is Gary with you?'

'No, he's out. I'm at his house on Grainger Street... I love you, Sam, and I'm so sorry!' Ali's voice sounded strange as if she was talking with a mouth full of stones.

'You don't need to apologise for anything. I'm on my way.' Sam was already running, ending the call to ring for a taxi, telling them it was an emergency, begging them to hurry.

A dreadful feeling washed over her, an awful premonition that if her sister had moved in with Gary, she was vulnerable.

Sam shivered – that awful sense of someone walking across her grave. Grainger Street wasn't a particularly salubrious area; what had possessed Ali to move there?

The taxi arrived at the university and Sam asked the driver to hurry. It took an endless twenty minutes.

'You all right, love?' the driver asked as he took her money.

'Yes, thanks.' Sam barely glanced at him, already scanning the row for number twenty-five. Having only visited once before, which was enough, she didn't know how Gary or anyone else could live there. The terrace of houses was horribly run down, many of them empty with boarded-up windows. Number twenty-five was one of the better residences, although the paint on the wooden door was peeling with dirt ingrained into it. Surely, Sam thought, Ali couldn't be living there voluntarily.

There was no answer when Sam banged on the door. Her heart raced and she could hear the blood pulsing through her ears. She tried the handle and it opened – a portal into the worst nightmare of her life.

At the bottom of the stairs lay Ali, barely recognisable in a heap of bruised and broken limbs, her phone still in her hand, her only lifeline.

'Ali!' Sam knelt beside her smoothing the hair from her face – a face swollen and bleeding, hair matted with blood.

Sam's hands trembled as she fumbled with her phone to ring for an ambulance. She left Ali for a minute to dash back into the street.

'Help me, someone, please help!'

A middle-aged man was riding up the street on a bicycle and Sam jumped out in front of him almost knocking him off.

'Please, my sister needs help!' As she grabbed at his arm with the phone still in her hand, the operator was asking which service was required and she garbled the address for the ambulance. The man dropped his bike at the side of the road and followed her inside.

'She's still breathing!' he said – news Sam relayed to the operator. 'Don't move her, love. Let's wait for the paramedics.' This kind stranger made sense but Sam wanted to hold her sister, to cradle her in her arms and tell her everything would be fine.

Alison's eyes fluttered.

'Who did this?' Sam asked almost rhetorically, not expecting an answer.

'Gary,' Ali whispered and her jaw dropped open, revealing a missing front tooth. A trickle of blood ran from the side of her mouth. Sam gasped, trembling with fear and anger.

The man took over the phone call and Sam heard him tell the operator to send the police as well as an ambulance. Ali drifted back into unconsciousness; all her sister could do was to hold her hand and whisper how much she loved her, to tell her everything would be all right and they'd get through this together as they'd done so many times before.

Dazed, Sam had no idea how long it was before help arrived. She was held back and watched horrified as paramedics worked on her sister. Then they were in an ambulance, sirens blaring as they rushed through the streets where people walked around without a care in the world.

Within minutes of arriving at the hospital Ali was taken for a CT scan, the doctors concerned about her head injuries.

The scan revealed a significant skull fracture and severe intra-cranial pressure which needed immediate surgery. Ali was wheeled into theatre while Sam waited for what seemed an age, beside herself with worry and feeling so utterly alone.

At some point, a policeman approached her, asking if she was up to answering his questions. She nodded and spoke words to him which later she couldn't recall. Sam must have told him how she'd found Ali and what she'd said as he thanked her and squeezed her shoulder kindly before he left.

At 8pm, a solemn-looking doctor appeared at Sam's side. Startled, she turned to look hopefully at him.

'Alison's out of theatre. We did all we could but your sister's in a critical condition. She's in a coma now – the next twenty-four hours will be crucial.'

'Will she wake up then?'

'We can only hope – as I said, we'll know more in a day or so.'

'Can I see her?'

'Of course. Give the nurse a minute or two and then she'll come and get you.' The doctor turned and walked away. Sam's mind went into overdrive imagining terrible scenarios and she trembled with fear.

The nurse came and took her into a side room where Ali lay, pale and still. They allowed her to stay – to hold her sister's hand and whisper to her. They brought endless cups of coffee and a blanket to stop her from shivering, but Sam was aware only of the still figure on the bed. The coffee went cold, as did she.

Attempting to hold back her tears, to be braver than she felt, Sam talked of their childhood – of their mum, dad and granny, of happy times, sunshine-filled days and endless laughter. She spoke through her tears, willing Ali to wake up, to come back to her. Samantha prayed that night as she'd never prayed before.

At 11.44pm Alison Ashby, Sam's beautiful sister, her other half, took her last breath.

It was their nineteenth birthday.

CHAPTER EIGHT

The following days passed in a blur of pain and unfathomable sorrow. With nowhere else to go Sam returned to her little room in halls, knowing she'd have to vacate it soon. Once again Yetta came to her rescue. The Romanian girl was packed and ready to move into a flat near the campus and insisted Sam go with her, at least until she found an alternative place to stay. It was comforting and easy to allow someone else to take charge. Yetta was practical, kind and willing to help and Sam leaned heavily on her over the next few weeks.

The minutes bled into hours, the hours into days. Yetta reminded her to eat, to shower; Sam survived due to her kindness. It was hard to say what time of day Sam found the most painful. At night, as darkness descended, the pain was crushing, never-ending. The doctor prescribed medication to help her sleep which she took greedily but morning inevitably arrived – another day, another painful excruciating day to face up to. There was perhaps a moment or two when waking, in that grey zone of dawning reality – a precious instant when her world was normal, when she was still one half of a pair, still a sister, and Alison was alive. But reality nudged its way in. She railed against the injustice of it all, longed to die to be with Alison, but each morning she awoke, climbed out of bed and doggedly put one foot in front of the other.

The police arrested Drake; the man on the bike who'd helped her on that awful night confirmed that Alison had spoken his name. Gary had moved Alison into the house in Grainger Street, whether willingly or not Sam would never know, after which their relationship spiralled rapidly downwards. Neighbours attested to the violence Ali suffered at his hands but it wasn't uncommon to hear fighting in that particular neighbourhood and no one intervened.

Gary admitted to a fight with her earlier in the day yet maintained that Ali was okay when he left the house. He suggested she'd fallen down the stairs, a fact which could be neither proved nor disproved. Without witnesses, the most the CPS could charge him with was aggravated assault – even Ali's accusation didn't count as evidence – she'd only spoken his name.

Considered to be a flight risk, Drake was remanded until sentencing, a small comfort for Sam. At the back of her mind was the fear he might come looking for revenge.

The image of her sister's bruised and broken body haunted Sam's every waking hour. She tortured herself thinking of what Ali must have suffered at Gary's hands, and was reasonably sure the violence was because she'd refused to give him the money from their trust fund. It was conjecture but if it was the case then it appeared Sam had had a lucky escape, yet how she wished it was her rather than Ali who'd endured those beatings.

Ten days after the attack Sam received another visit from the police. A uniformed officer filled Yetta's tiny flat, shuffling his feet as if wanting to impart his news quickly and leave.

'The man we arrested for the attack on your sister has been killed at the remand centre.' His words were almost impossible to process. Gary Drake was dead.

'He was involved in a fight with another inmate.' The officer mumbled something about the investigation being halted and a detective who would be visiting to explain, but Sam barely heard. The plethora of emotions this news prompted threw her completely; relief mingled with regret – she wanted the man to stand trial, to be convicted and go to prison for what he'd done to Ali – death was too easy an escape for him! Shame edged its way into her thoughts. When had she become such a bitter and hateful person?

When the officer left, Yetta tried to convince Sam that it was a good outcome and if Drake had gone to prison, at some point he'd be released, perhaps to hurt another young woman, or as she feared come looking for her. Sam leaned on her friend's common sense and cried her tears while alone late at night in the sanctuary of her bed.

One thing Sam didn't factor into her waking nightmare was the inordinate interest of the press in Ali's story. Even before her sister was laid to rest, the telephone rang constantly.

'Ms Ashby, is it true that you and your twin were in love with the same man? Did you fight over him?'

'Was your sister's death an accident or did her boyfriend push her?'

'I'm authorised to offer you a large sum of money if you're prepared to give us exclusive rights...'

Sam was hounded for information. Not answering her phone didn't help – if the press couldn't get information, they made it up.

Requests for photographs arrived regularly, but Sam refused, not wanting her or Ali's face spread across the papers.

Unfortunately, it didn't stop it from happening. It seemed as if people couldn't get enough of the *story*, and photographs from the twins' social media pages were copied and printed without permission, becoming public property and turning the knife in Samantha's heart. She closed all the accounts but it was too late, the images were out there in the public domain. Being identical twins appeared to add to the novelty; the journalists even used their old nickname of the *sunshine girls* to headline their lies.

One of the most persistent journalists was Frank Stokes from the *Liverpool Mercury* who rang at least once a day, often more. The *Mercury* ran a front-page article with barely any facts, featuring a photograph of Ali and Sam side by side smiling at the camera. But they doctored the image and depicted it as torn in two with Gary Drake's face between them – the headline – *Love Triangle*. Reporters dredged up their family history as if it were a narrative simply for entertainment and to sell papers – *poor little rich girls orphaned and alone, separated by loving the same man until Alison was killed in a crime of passion.* What utter rubbish, Sam groaned. Yet there was nothing to be done to dampen the interest; the storm raged, she would simply have to hang on to her sanity and sit it out.

The inordinate interest and speculation of the press made those days almost unbearable. Even the accident in which their parents died was dragged up again and questions asked as to whether Phillip Ashby had been drinking.

How dare they insinuate such vile untruths? Sam cried, frustrated at the constant lies.

Refuting the allegations only fuelled the flames. Aiming for a dignified silence, Sam longed to scream at them, to berate them for their falsehoods, to protest and deny everything, to burn every copy of a newspaper she came across.

After the trauma of Ali's funeral and when most of her anger at the injustice of life was spent, Sam knew the time had come to look to the future. She was still alive and the last thing Alison would want would be for her to stop living – to become a bitter and broken person. There were times when Ali's voice seemed almost audible, telling her to live for them both, dream for them both and try to be happy.

CHAPTER NINE

G oing back to uni wasn't an option for Sam. There were far too many memories, and she needed a complete change, an escape to start a new life.

The first step towards this goal involved a visit to Stroud to the family solicitor whose help Sam sought to wind up the trust fund. At least there was more than sufficient money to buy a property somewhere; a place where she was unknown, where she could breathe easily again and decide the course her life should take.

William Jenkinson had been a friend of Sam's father for many years and handled all the family business. He'd been the one to suggest a trust fund to Phillip and Veronica to secure their daughters' futures, a timely proposal for which Sam was now grateful.

She made an appointment and was in the Stroud office of Jenkinson and Willis in good time. Instead of the expected handshake, William greeted Sam with a hug and expressed his sorrow at the trials she'd been through of late. He knew everything; it wasn't only the local Liverpool papers who ran the story, the nationals jumped on the bandwagon too and the sunshine girls were quite famous. Sam thanked him for his condolences and took a seat on the other side of his large partners' desk.

'How can I help you, Samantha?' He smiled at her and after the horrendous time she'd been through his fatherly concern and the calm soothing atmosphere of his office was almost her undoing, but she was there to conduct business, so swallowing hard, she spoke.

'I'd like to dissolve the trust fund my parents set up. It's my intention to move away and use the money to begin a new life.' It was a simple enough request yet the words appeared to surprise William.

'But, Samantha, you closed the fund a couple of months ago. You sat in that very chair before signing the papers.'

'No, you're mistaken! I haven't been here since Gran died. The fund's intact, surely?' A few moments of silence hung in the air as they tried to make sense of what had happened. William tapped at the keyboard on his computer.

'It was on the 29th of April. You called me a couple of days before and said that you and Alison were buying a property and wished to dissolve the trust. I drew up the paperwork, and you agreed to come in to sign it.' William frowned, clearly expecting Sam to remember something she'd not done. Thinking through the shock and the pain of his words, Samantha knew there was only one logical answer, one she didn't want to be true.

'But surely it needed both Ali and me to sign?' Her voice was cracking, willing this to be some ghastly mistake.

'Well, yes, that's correct but you told me you couldn't make it together so you came on the 29th and Alison came to sign the following day.' William stood and moved to a filing cabinet, withdrawing a Manila folder and pulling out several sheets of paper.

'Here. Your signatures are on both documents; one to

release the funds and another authorising me to transfer them into this account.' He tapped the paper with his forefinger.

Sam could hardly read the words for the imminent tears; it certainly looked like her signature but they were well practised at writing each other's – it had been a game during their childhood, but this was not a game. Her sister had visited the solicitors twice, once as herself and once as Samantha.

Had Gary Drake threatened and coerced Ali? Was this what she'd meant when she said she'd done something stupid, and apologised on that fateful day?

'The account we transferred the money into is in Alison's name. It isn't uncommon for the monies to go to one place and for the trustees to divide up as they see fit.' William looked at Sam, his face drained of all colour. 'It wasn't you who signed, was it?'

The sadness Sam felt was overwhelming, yet her heart went out to William Jenkinson who also appeared to be reeling at the shock of Alison's betrayal. He'd been fooled by her too and shared a fraction of her pain.

'I don't blame Alison, she was very much under Drake's influence, probably intimidated too. We'll never fully know.' Sam's instinct remained protective; she truly didn't blame Ali and felt sad rather than angry. Although she hated the notion, it was becoming apparent that Gary Drake had won even in death.

'If the money's still in Alison's account it belongs to you now as her heir; her only surviving relative.' A spark of hope danced in William's eyes, a spark Sam was about to extinguish.

'I've already closed all her accounts. There was very little in them, certainly not the proceeds from the trust fund.'

'Then where is it?'

'I would guess it went straight to Gary Drake. He would

either have bullied her or sweet-talked her into handing it over with promises of a rosy future together.'

'Then we must go to the police – this is fraud!' William spoke passionately but Sam was about to disappoint him again.

'Drake's dead and I'm pretty certain wherever the money is we'll never see it again.'

The following day, and with William Jenkinson's backing, Sam did go to the police. They agreed to look into Gary's financial affairs yet found nothing other than a current account with very little in it. There was no evidence of his involvement in any fraud; they were only surmising. The simple fact was that Alison had been the one to perpetrate it, and with Gary dead, as far as the police were concerned the matter was closed.

Samantha imagined their money squirrelled away in an account in the Cayman Islands, her only comfort being in the knowledge that Drake was never going to have the pleasure of spending it. Maybe she could have looked at trying to trace the money by other means, but any such action would make Ali's part in the deception public and her memory was too precious for Sam to tarnish with allegations of fraud. It would provide the press with even more fodder for their stories.

She wasn't penniless; there was still the money from their grandmother's estate which they'd set aside for tuition fees for the next two years at uni. Sam took in a deep breath and stuck a pin in a map to find her new home.

CHAPTER TEN

Rosie – 2019

E arly morning had always been Rosie Cantrell's favourite
time of day. Even as a child she was invariably the first
one in the household to rise, escaping into the quiet solitude of
the garden to check on the frogs in the pond. Or to gather
daisies for her mother, still wet with dew, and pick up windfalls
from the gnarled old apple trees that drooped over their wall
from the neighbouring garden. It was her secret time before the
rest of the family rose and the day entered its familiar routine.
Now, grown with a family of her own, Rosie still loved the early
morning when the coming hours held undiscovered promise
and possibilities – when the day was a blank canvas.

But not today – today was different.

Rosie watched the sunrise from the kitchen window. A
majestic orange glow, the herald of another beautiful day,
outside at least. It was a sight of which she never tired. A heat
haze shimmered in the distance, burning off the dew from the

field in front of Hilltop Cottage, her Eden, but was the dream about to shatter before her eyes?

The arrival of the letter changed everything. With it, Samantha Ashby – the identity Rosie thought she'd buried nine years earlier – drew breath once again, rising to life to ruin everything Rosie had worked so hard to achieve. The letter, a simple inconsequential small white envelope, possessed the power to smash her carefully constructed life into a million fragments and rob her of everything she held dear.

Sleep had refused to come the previous night as Mike snored peacefully beside her, mouth open, oblivious to his wife's torment. Baby Noah slept contentedly for a full seven hours and even Ben their Border collie dog happily chased rabbits in his sleep, all of them unaware of the approaching storm. Rosie's mind, however, refused to shut down and allow respite from her fears. Familiar night-time sounds which usually brought such comfort failed to relax her body and with the dawn of a new day, the horrors of the past once again flooded her mind.

Would today be the day *he* came – here to her place of safety, her refuge? Would this be the day he would steal her new life and happiness away from her?

Bloody journalists, bloody Frank Stokes!

Like a leopard the man had hunted her down, alone and determined, the scent of a story meaning more to him than another human being's peace of mind. Yet perhaps she should have known it was impossible to leave the past entirely behind, to relax and enjoy the new existence she'd carved out for herself. Life was never easy, especially, it appeared, for her.

Lost in thought Rosie failed to hear Mike come downstairs, their baby cradled in the crook of his arm. She turned to take in the noticeable similarities between father and son; the unmistakable red hair, wiry on Mike, soft and fluffy on Noah. Two peas in a pod. The smile which the sight of her husband

and son usually elicited was an effort as her heart flipped with fear at the thought of losing them both.

'Hey, Rosie! Couldn't you sleep?' Mike kissed the top of her head and she attempted to return the warmth of his greeting.

'No. Sorry, I didn't hear him; shall I take him?' She reached out for her son, burying her face in the baby's neck to hide the tears welling in her eyes. 'I'll just go up to change him. Could you start the coffee?' Rosie couldn't meet her husband's eyes.

Noah chuckled as he lay on the mat to have his nappy changed. It was a customary game. Rosie blew raspberries on his tummy and he responded with a deep throaty laugh, a sound she never tired of hearing. Cleaning him up she sniffed back the tears and forced herself to smile at her son. What would Noah think if he knew the truth? What would Mike think – and why had she not told him before, trusted him to understand?

The smell of coffee wafted up the stairs, reminding her Mike was waiting. Rosie pulled herself up from the floor, lifted her son and headed back to the kitchen. Her husband was rummaging in the cupboard for cereal, bread already in the toaster, humming a cheery tune.

'A whole day to ourselves, whatever shall we do?' He grinned roguishly and wiggled his eyebrows. Rosie smiled, troubled that she was about to spoil his first Saturday off since Noah's birth, yet she must tell him first, today – before Frank Stokes arrived and Mike learned of her past from him.

It could at least wait until after breakfast, a few more minutes of playing happy families wasn't much to ask. Noah snuggled in his bouncer seat as his daddy rocked it in between pushing spoonfuls of baby rice into his mouth. Rosie breathed in the sight, wanting to imprint it in her mind's eye – Mike in his pyjamas chewing his bottom lip, concentrating on the task in hand – Noah blowing bubbles into the milky rice.

Usually, her husband would have left an hour earlier.

Running a market garden was demanding, always something to do, and with Saturday being market day an early start was the norm. Only in the last few months had they afforded the luxury of taking on extra help, hence the welcome day off. Lisa Edwards was doing the farmer's market that day.

'Will Lisa be okay alone?' Rosie asked absentmindedly.

'She'll be fine. She's proving to be quite a godsend, great work ethic and as strong as any man. She might even sell more than me with her pretty face.' He slathered butter on another piece of toast. They both appreciated Lisa who'd become a firm friend since coming to work for them six months earlier when a heavily pregnant Rosie had reluctantly hung up her gardening gloves. Rosie missed the physicality of being at the market garden but continued to do the book-keeping, an involvement which made her feel useful at a time she could do little else due to high blood pressure and a huge baby bump. After Noah's birth, Lisa became a willing babysitter, giving his parents the welcome opportunity of an occasional break, and the baby loved her.

'He's getting sleepy,' Mike announced, watching fascinated as his son struggled to keep his eyes open. Rosie lifted their baby, holding him close to climb the stairs and breathing in the unmistakable baby scent as she laid him in his cot. The little boy's rosebud mouth was blowing bubbles as his breathing slowed. For a few moments his mother gazed at her sleeping son, his long lashes flickering on his cheeks and her heart felt as if it would burst with love – and something less welcome, fear perhaps?

Mike followed her upstairs and stood close behind her, his arms wrapped around Rosie's waist as he kissed the warm spot on the back of her neck, the place which sent shivers down her spine. Taking her hand he led her back to their bed, making love to her so slowly and tenderly she needed to bite her lip to stop tears from flowing.

Afterwards they lay silently side by side, Mike thoughtfully curling a lock of her hair between his fingers. Rosie smiled sadly, untangled her legs from his and slid out of bed to shower.

'What's bothering you?' Mike asked when she came back into the bedroom with her hair wrapped in a towel and smelling deliciously of soap and shampoo.

'We need to talk.' She dropped the towel from her body and pulled on her underwear, jeans and a T-shirt.

'Sounds serious.' Mike's eyes followed her every move, a frown forming on his face.

'Have your shower and I'll make another coffee.' Kissing his stubbly cheek, she stroked the contours of his jawbone. 'I love you,' she added almost as an afterthought.

'Phew that's a relief! I was beginning to wonder.' He laughed and scrambled from the bed to head for the shower.

Ten minutes later Mike appeared, hair damp and in faded jeans and an ancient polo shirt, certainly not dressed for going out. Did he perhaps have an inkling of what was to come, Rosie wondered. He flopped down beside her on the battered old sofa they'd picked up in a charity shop, all they could afford for the time being, saying nothing, simply waiting expectantly for Rosie to speak.

'There are things you need to know about me, Mike. Things I should have told you before we married.'

CHAPTER ELEVEN

Over the next hour, Mike listened as Rosie shared the details of her past life with him, starting with revealing her real name as Samantha Ashby. She spoke haltingly at times, tearfully at others, asking him not to interrupt until she was finished, which he did with difficulty.

When Rosie's story was complete, Mike took her in his arms and held her close. Moved by her harrowing tale, it was one he would never have suspected. Yes, he knew Rosie could be reflective at times and she wouldn't be drawn into talking about her past – all she'd ever told him was that her parents died in a car crash when she was young.

Accepting how painful it must be to talk about, he hadn't pushed for details, assuming she'd confide when she was ready. But there'd been no mention of a twin sister or the awful circumstances surrounding Alison's death, and now Mike felt such love for his wife and an overwhelming desire to protect her from the horrors of the world.

'So why Bedale, Rosie? Did you really stick a pin in a map?'

'Yes, I did. I admit to being selective in the area. I loved North Yorkshire and wanted to get away from city life. It's fate,

I suppose, that I ended up in Bedale. Finding a job as a waitress in Bella's tea shop was a bonus. My predecessor had left without notice and Bella was short-staffed during the busiest time of the year. With only the briefest of interviews, I was thrown in at the deep end – precisely what I needed to take my mind off recent events. There was even the flat available upstairs should I want it.

'Those five years in Bedale with its slower pace of life, and the friendly Yorkshire people have gone a long way to easing my pain and restoring my faith in humanity. And I met you – for once in my life something good was working out for me.'

Mike nodded, not fully understanding but trying to. If he was truthful, he was experiencing a degree of hurt that his wife hadn't had enough faith in him to share her story.

'Why didn't you tell me about your past? Don't you know you can trust me?' It was painful to realise she'd held so much of herself back; that he'd never truly known her.

'I do trust you – but Samantha needed to go – to tell anyone, even you, would keep her alive. I'm sorry, Mike. I know how this must appear and I only kept quiet to preserve my sanity. The past had to stay buried – please try to understand. And I'd lived for almost five years as Rosie before we met – I was beginning to *be* her – to inhabit her skin, her persona. When you came along it seemed too good to be true and I was unsure if it would last. I'd never anticipated being happy, or daring to love again. Everyone I ever loved had been cruelly snatched away from me and I believed my destiny was to be alone. And then we met and now there's Noah – you'll never know how much you both mean to me.'

'So why tell me now? Has something happened, are you still keeping secrets?' Mike longed for her to share her pain and allow him to help if he could.

Silently Rosie handed over a letter.

'What's this?' He unfolded the paper and read the letter, his face growing darker as each word registered.

'Is this Frank Stokes the journalist who hounded you?'

'Yes, from the *Liverpool Mercury*. It appears he wants to do a follow-up to give me the chance to set the record straight. He's even hinted at a book. Can you believe the nerve of the man? I don't trust the bastard. It was because of him that people thought Ali and I fought over a man, a fight which ended in two deaths. Why the hell should he think he has a right to rake over all that grief again?' Rosie sniffed back the tears.

'More to the point, how did he find out your new name and address?'

'I changed my name legally by deed poll so there'll be a record somewhere and our marriage will be in the public record too. Stokes is an investigative journalist so finding me probably wasn't too demanding a task for him. I'd just not expected to still be of interest.'

Mike reread the letter, then looked at Rosie, his mind rapidly seeking a solution – the best way to handle this problem. 'Have you replied to him?'

'No. He didn't give a number or an address, probably deliberately. The letter just says he's coming here to Thursdale. I'm scared, Mike, terrified of my past being raked over again. What can we do?'

Mike looked at the envelope accompanying the letter. 'This was posted a couple of days ago and he doesn't say when he's coming. Perhaps we can get in touch with the editor at the paper to warn him off, threaten him with legal proceedings or something.' Mike's mind was already seeking a solution, processing the little information they possessed.

'We can't afford legal action; you know that, but maybe Stokes's editor will be more reasonable than him? It's worth a try. Will you ring for me?'

Mike googled the number for the *Liverpool Mercury* and jotted it on a scrap of paper. With Rosie at his side, he tapped in the number and asked to speak to the editor. Apparently, there were several and eventually he was connected to the feature's editor, a weary sounding lady who had better things to do than listen to a complaint. With a firm but reasonable voice, Mike told her about Frank Stokes's letter while Rosie listened to his end of the conversation. After a lengthy silence he rang off after only a brief discussion.

'Frank Stokes left the *Mercury* two years ago – that was his former editor who thinks he's working freelance now.'

The implication of the words hit them both like a physical blow. If Stokes was freelance, he wasn't accountable to an editor, they had no one to turn to for help, to call him off. Mike searched again for a phone number on the letter which they may have missed. There was none. He looked at Rosie who was close to tears, and a strong desire to protect her overcame him, to take charge of the situation and lift this burden from her shoulders. Mike could hardly imagine how alone she must have felt when the press harassed her at the lowest point of her life. He didn't want her to go through any more pain yet was unsure how to achieve that goal.

Rosie spoke again. 'He's not the sort of man you can reason with, Mike. If I don't give him a story, he'll make one up as he did before. I don't want to be identified as Samantha Ashby again; to have people look at me with pity or even suspicion as if I was somehow responsible for what happened to Ali – I can't go through all that again!'

Mike pulled her close and stroked her hair as she sobbed. They heard Noah waking and the couple drew apart, almost relieved to have another focus in their son.

'I'll go,' Mike offered and ran upstairs returning almost immediately with a sleepy baby in his arms. Noah smiled at his mother and waved his clenched fists in the air, conducting his own imaginary orchestra, as another silent tear trickled down her cheek.

In an attempt to restore a sense of much-needed normality Rosie made lunch, putting aside any thoughts of going out for the day. What they needed now was the comfort of their home and to simply be together. They made no attempt to form a plan; any strategy was pointless until Stokes contacted them which he most surely would and probably soon. It was a matter of finding out what the man wanted and then deciding how to dissuade him from disclosing Rosie's true identity.

Later in the day when Noah was sleeping peacefully in his cot the couple talked again. Mike was finding his wife's story hard to process and he needed answers to the endless questions which filled his mind.

'I know it's hypothetical, yet out of interest how much was in your trust fund?'

'About two million pounds.' Rosie smiled woefully.

'Two million! Hell, Rosie, that's a lot of money to lose – why didn't you try to find it?'

'The police weren't interested. They did a cursory check on Drake's finances but he appeared to have nothing, and as he was dead there was no way to pursue it. Ali's accounts were as expected too, the money seemed to disappear into thin air. William confirmed that Ali took the money but there was no trace of it.

'At the time I was so low that I wanted to forget about it and move on. I also didn't want to blacken Ali's name – she wasn't responsible – it was Gary Drake who made her do it, I'm sure. After a year in Bedale I did look into tracing the money but hadn't a clue where to start so I contacted a private investigator in Northallerton. He took the case on but his fees were £150 an hour.'

Mike gave a low whistle, wide-eyed as he listened.

'I agreed to employ him for an in initial six hours during which time he hoped to get a result, but he didn't. He was at a loss to know where to go after using his usual resources so I decided to drop it. It was foolish to throw money at a project which appeared impossible, and it was money I could ill afford.'

'Oh, Rosie, I don't know what to say. I wish I'd known before.' Mike wanted to comfort her but didn't wish to appear patronising. Again, Noah came to the rescue by demanding their attention and they happily lifted him from his cot.

'Let's take Ben for a walk – it's a beautiful afternoon and some fresh air will be good for us all.' Mike grabbed the excited dog's lead and they set out for a walk in the meadow, Ben barking enthusiastically at the prospect of some exercise.

Sunday was a working day for Mike and although reluctant to leave his wife alone, they decided it was unlikely Stokes would put in an appearance at the weekend and as the market garden was only a couple of miles away at the other end of the village, Mike could get home in a matter of minutes if Rosie rang.

It was almost impossible to concentrate fully on anything other than the story his wife had revealed the day before. Rosie had hidden depths – how brave and strong she'd been to cope with such tragedy at such a young age. Mike was deeply touched and if possible, loved her even more for all she'd been through. Now it was his turn to be strong for her, to ensure that Frank Stokes left Rosie alone for good, and he resolved to do whatever it took.

Arriving at the market garden Mike was surprised to find Lisa already there, in the little brick shed which served as an office. Officially it was her day off but as ever she couldn't keep away from the place, and loved the job almost as much as he did. Today, however, Lisa wasn't dressed for work, and wore a strappy cotton dress with a full skirt which skimmed her knees. It was yellow with a daisy pattern, quite the change from her usual dungarees and T-shirts, and she wore make-up too, again a look Mike hadn't seen before.

'Hi, how did the market go yesterday?' He smiled at the sight of her; she looked so young and pretty.

'Brill! Record takings and I could have sold half as much again if I'd had the stock. I've just put the takings in the safe. Did you have a good day off?' Lisa hitched herself onto the edge of the desk, seeming in no hurry to leave. Her fresh floral scent filled the little room.

'Okay, thanks. Look, do you think you could manage Helmsley market on Friday too? I'm sorry to ask but I want to stay around the garden this week if possible.'

'Sure, I'd love it. Anything wrong? You're usually up for the markets yourself?'

'Nothing really. Rosie's a bit under the weather so I'd like to be close at hand that's all.' He smiled to reassure Lisa.

'Oh, sorry. Shall I go over to the house now to see her? I've nothing special planned and could help out with Noah if she's not too well?'

'Thanks, but I think she'll probably try to rest when Noah does today so it's maybe best to leave her alone. Get yourself away and enjoy your day off. You spend too much time here as it is.'

'I don't mind. I'm making myself indispensable so my job will be secure.'

'No worries there, I already appreciate all you do.'

Lisa left and once alone again, Mike threw himself into his work. The summer had been busy and with the dry spell of late watering alone took up several hours of his day. Produce was ripening daily and needed to be picked and stored at precisely the right time to be at its best for market days.

The first task was to sort the deliveries, thankfully not many on a Sunday, just the local pubs and restaurants who all appreciated his fresh, organic produce. With his thoughts still firmly fixed on Rosie and the tale she'd told him, Mike rolled up his sleeves and began to load the van. The sooner he started the sooner he could get back home.

CHAPTER TWELVE

Frank Stokes loathed Monday mornings. Truthfully, he was beginning to hate every morning; dragging himself out of bed, usually contending with a hangover, his own fault of course, and having to apply himself to making a living was something he'd never enjoyed. Yet as Frank was born into a working-class family, work was the only way he knew to make money, legally at least.

Perhaps the daily grind fed his disdain for wealthy people, for those to whom life handed everything on a plate, a silver one at that, and he took every opportunity to have a dig at the wealthy classes, his job offering the perfect medium to do so. Reluctantly, Frank accepted that a certain amount of discipline was necessary, especially now he was no longer a salaried staff member on any paper and found himself in the unenviable position of making his way in an already overcrowded business.

Having left the *Liverpool Mercury* under something of a cloud, their fault and their loss naturally, Stokes found it almost impossible to secure a position with another newspaper. Excuses dogged him at every enquiry – sales of paper editions were down due to increased internet usage – downsizing was the order of the day – until eventually there was no option other than going freelance. If the national papers were getting rid of salaried staff it stood to reason they'd still have column inches to fill, and Frank assumed his copy was of a standard to be at the top of the pile on any editor's desk. Yet so far it hadn't been plain sailing and rejections were sadly becoming the norm. He was a man with a chip on his shoulder, an affliction he almost cherished and nurtured with regular bouts of self-pity.

Frank's brain was often befuddled by alcohol, the demon drink which he vowed so often to eradicate from his life, but his lack of success in doing so didn't help his career. It had cost him his job, or at the very least been a contributing factor, and his wife and daughter, leaving him on the long hard road of proving his worth once again.

It was nine years since his last big story – since he was the editor's golden boy and could do no wrong. Now he was reduced to trawling through the dozens of local presses which very occasionally proffered some undiscovered gem of a news item which he could dig into and discover a story worth his time and effort. Always looking for an angle, Frank allotted two hours to this task, two tedious hours each day which needed the assistance of several cups of coffee to keep him focused. Invariably all the good stuff was picked up by the nationals but he ploughed on. Human interest stories were what every editor wanted, extremely good news or devastatingly bad – they didn't care which, as long as it made good copy.

Taking a break from his laptop and pouring his first real drink of the day, the idea first occurred to him – why not revisit his last big story – do a follow-up? As he pondered the notion, the possibility of writing a book struck him. Could Samantha Ashby be persuaded to write the story of her life? Frank would be the ghostwriter of course, the professional, but that genre nearly always dominated the bestseller lists and were without fail lucrative ventures. Surely, she'd be interested. Everyone was interested in money, weren't they? The thoughts and ideas whirled in Stokes's head, spurring him on to find the surviving twin, to dig even deeper than before and write the book everyone would want to read.

Perhaps the key players were long forgotten by the public, yet with gentle reminders it would occur to them that they'd always wondered what happened to the girl with the murdered twin; the poor little rich girl who had and then lost everything. The story had the whole shebang too – glamorous identical twins, sex, a love triangle, two murders, revenge, love, hate – hell yes. Frank could throw everything at this book and all in time for the tenth anniversary of the event. He poured another drink, pleased with himself and excited at the prospect of the financial returns. His imagination raced ahead to interviews on television chat shows, being in demand to pen celebrity memoirs – the possibilities were endless. But there was work to be done, research, perhaps a few contacts to exploit; it would be just like the old days, real investigative journalism. There was the best part of a year until the tenth anniversary, time enough to get publishers interested, perhaps even secure an advance, and for the first time in years, Stokes was fired up about a project he was convinced couldn't fail.

A frenzy of activity infused the man. First, he would need to find out where Samantha Ashby was hiding and what she was doing these days. With a bit of luck there might even be more scandal to dig up; all sorts of angst could have befallen her during those intervening years. Trouble had a habit of following some people around which could be to his advantage. Then he'd have to find Gary Drake's family to get their take on what happened, confident they'd want to put forward their version of events. Everyone has an opinion, everyone wants their voice heard, truth is subjective. It was all taking shape in his mind, energising him as no other project had for years; could this be his way back into the fold of journalism, back to the top? Or could it even ignite a new career in ghostwriting?

It amazed Frank how just a few clicks with a computer mouse could reveal so much about a person in these days of data protection. Drake's family were the easiest to locate so he commenced his research with a visit to Gary's mother.

She was living in Huyton, an area of Liverpool with a reputation for crime, and one Frank had come across many times. He entered the estate with apprehension, parked his car near to what looked like a fly tipping hotspot and sighed with relief that it was daylight, this wasn't a safe place to visit at night.

Norma Drake opened the door two or three inches and stared suspiciously at her unexpected visitor. She was a small-boned, gaunt woman, mid-sixties he guessed, with grey ratty hair and pinched features. Frank introduced himself and stated his purpose as seeking her view on the tragedy of her son's death. Frank's dubious charm gained entry to the tiny house and soon he was listening to her version of the events of nearly a decade earlier.

'My Gary was innocent and if he'd lived, he'd have proved it!' Norma spat out the words while Frank nodded solemnly in agreement.

'If he hadn't got mixed up with those tarts, he'd have been with me today – he was a good boy, always looked after his mam.' She sniffed, wiped her eyes and blew her nose on a crumpled tissue. 'See what I've come to? Gary wouldn't have let me live in this dump, he'd have looked after me he would.'

'So, you were close to your son?'

'Oh, yes – he was my only son, my lovely boy.' Another sniff.

'Yet he didn't live at home but in... where was it again?'

'Erm, over near the university,' she hesitated. 'I lost everything when I lost him. So, what's this proposition you mentioned?' Norma leaned forward in her chair.

'I'm putting the events of those tragic few weeks together, as a book. Hopefully I'll have Samantha Ashby's point of view so I thought it only right to get your take on what happened.' Frank didn't wish to say too much, he was there to gather information, not give it.

'You won't be able to believe anything that bitch tells you. She was a scheming little madam who told the police my Gary killed her sister! It's a lie, Gary was a gentleman, I brought him up to respect women. He'd taken the girl in to live with him when she had nowhere else to go and that was all the thanks he got. And then he was killed, never had the chance to clear his name. Those twins were evil schemers who took advantage of my Gary.' The tissue came out again.

Frank was having difficulty imagining what the Ashby sisters would have wanted from Drake but he allowed the woman to ramble on.

'Are you going to use what I say in your book, Mr Stokes? I suppose it'll make you quite a bit of money, books about murder sell well, don't they?'

'I'm not sure you've given me much to go on. Did you ever meet Samantha Ashby?'

'No, but I met the other one... the one who fell down the stairs.'

'And is there anything else you can remember which might be relevant?'

Norma Drake screwed up her face in concentration. 'Well, after he was dead, that Samantha had the bloody cheek to send the police round. They said he'd stolen money from her but my Gary was no thief!'

Frank raised his eyebrows. 'Really? Tell me more about this accusation.'

Driving home, Frank mulled over his conversation with Mrs Drake. He would have to take her contribution with a large pinch of salt and any input from her would be minimal if included at all, and written with a considerable dollop of literary licence. She was clearly more interested in a fee for her co-operation and was undoubtedly an unreliable source – a bitter woman who'd say anything to turn a profit.

Reading between the lines Frank picked up that she hadn't been as close to her son as she made out, and rarely knew what he was up to. She didn't even know where he was living – Grainger Street was nowhere near the university.

Samantha was the one Frank needed. It was vital to win her over, talk her into co-operating yet first he must find her. The only interesting snippet from his morning's work was the mention of money. Had Drake stolen from the twins?

A call to an old police contact answered Stokes's question. He learned that after Drake's death, Samantha Ashby visited the station to claim Drake had stolen a rather large trust fund, almost two million, his contact said. It was an unexpected bonus for the journalist. Nothing sold stories better than sex and money so he appeared to have hit the jackpot. Stokes was unsure how he'd use this new information; it would depend on whether or not Samantha agreed to co-operate – time to ponder that one when he found her, he thought, as he added the new information to his copious notes.

When the name Samantha Ashby drew a blank in his initial research and the woman appeared to have dropped off the face of the earth, Stokes was confident she must have changed her name and reinvented herself. He would probably have done the same. But he was nothing if not persistent and allotted time each day to research, to finding the surviving sunshine girl – in fact that would be a great title for his book.

As Samantha's name was changed legally, Frank's hours of research paid off and he discovered a new name with which to work. Even a second name change when she married wasn't too difficult an obstacle to surmount – he was becoming adept at trawling the internet and knowing which sites to visit, and he wasn't averse to using old contacts if it suited his purpose. It proved harder to locate the woman yet not impossible, and after weeks of intensive research and planning Frank was ready to make his initial approach.

Stokes could have turned up on Rosie Cantrell's doorstep unannounced, taken her by surprise and possibly wrong-footed her into committing to his plan. But no. He decided to write a letter first, to make a civilised approach in the hope of gaining her trust. The journalist was proud of the final draft, which pointed out how assisting him would benefit her, whilst the tone was firm and authoritative. He decided not to give a contact address or phone number and simply wrote that he would be in touch very soon. Naturally he dropped hints that he would proceed with a feature or even a book with or without her permission. Surely that fact alone would make her see reason.

A sense of satisfaction gave him the kind of buzz he'd not experienced in a long time as he dropped the letter into the post box. The groundwork was complete and Frank Stokes couldn't wait to approach Rosie Cantrell and begin to write his book.

CHAPTER THIRTEEN

Rosie wandered around the house aimlessly after Mike left. The place felt eerily quiet without him even though she was used to his long hours. Before pregnancy curbed her activities, she'd enjoyed working with him, a labour of love as they built their business, anticipating a future of security when money wasn't so tight. A few difficult years were to be expected until they reached that happy position, yet what they hadn't planned for was their son, Noah. Maybe he wasn't planned but there couldn't be a more wanted or loved baby, and when they grew accustomed to the idea of a family, he brought nothing except joy.

The Cantrells' home in Thursdale, a village just a few miles from Bedale, was an eighteenth-century cottage, adored by the couple yet sadly in need of mountains of work to bring it up to modern-day standards, renovations they put on hold to prioritise getting the business up and running. It was situated on the edge of the village with their nearest neighbours being almost a hundred yards to the west with the rest of the village scattered beyond in a delightful higgledy-piggledy fashion. It offered peace and tranquillity without being entirely isolated.

Rosie loved so many of the village's characteristics, like being able to walk from one end to the other, and the primary school nestled at the heart of the village, where Noah would hopefully attend.

Thursdale was where Rosie wanted her future to be, a place to put down roots and feel at home. Mike loved village life too, and many residents were now his regular customers, appreciating the garden's organic produce and sustainable practices. The villagers befriended the young couple who, after five years were now accepted as locals and no longer considered incomers.

Although Rosie's life was near to perfect, there were times she wished things were different and the money from her trust fund was still in her possession. Yet by nature she was philosophical and daydreams of how useful such a sum would be for the cottage and the business were rare. If the past hadn't been what it was, she would never have met Mike and become a mother to Noah.

Giving birth was undoubtedly the very best of experiences. If Mike had brought happiness back to her life, Noah took it a step further, in some small measure making up for past pain. He was adorable, a true gift. Mike and Noah brought meaning and contentment back to Rosie. She was happy again, a happiness which was threatened when the letter from Frank Stokes arrived.

The plop on the mat of that one little envelope dragged her reluctantly back in time to relive events she'd tried so hard to obliterate from her memory. Having lived as Rosie Cantrell for so long, she fitted into her skin. She *was* her. But now Samantha Ashby was haunting her again. Those familiar insecurities which had hovered in her mind, the sense of loss and fear of being alone – all those emotions, so very real in the past, returned with the arrival of that one hateful letter and suddenly

Rosie no longer knew who she was. Even that awful feeling of being watched, an unpleasant sensation which dogged the days before Alison's death, had returned. Ridiculous though it was, Rosie thought someone had been in the house when she'd been out the previous week – how paranoid was she becoming?

Rosie was also developing a fear of leaving the house, painfully aware that if she ventured far she'd be looking at every stranger, searching faces for Frank Stokes, simultaneously wanting to see him to warn him off – to rid her life of the threat he posed – but also to hide from him, never to have to look at his face again.

Noah, sensing his mother's unsettled mood was unusually fractious. When there was a knock on the door after lunch Rosie was delighted to see Lisa's smile and invited their friend inside. 'Wow, you look lovely!'

Lisa gave a mock curtsey. 'Thank you.'

Noah continued to whine and Rosie apologised for her son's grizzles.

'Could it be teeth coming through?' Lisa asked.

'It's a bit early at four months although a possibility, I suppose.' Rosie felt guilty knowing Noah's anxiety was probably a reflection of her own but she could hardly tell Lisa what was happening in their lives.

'And what about you? Mike said you were a bit low today. I wasn't going to come and disturb you but thought you might welcome some company.'

'Oh, I'm fine, just lack of sleep catching up with me but I'm glad you're here. Let's sit in the garden, shall we?'

Rosie opened a bottle of wine, not something she'd normally do during the day but she felt in need of something to relax her, to take her mind off the letter.

'Do you think it's a late case of the baby blues?' Lisa's face was so serious that Rosie laughed.

'Goodness no! I didn't feel anything other than ecstatic after this little chap arrived – still don't. Tell me how you got on yesterday?' Talking about herself was the last thing she wanted to do. It was difficult enough to share her past with Mike and although she was sure Lisa would be understanding, Rosie had no intention of opening up to her friend. Fortunately, Lisa didn't pursue the subject and happily related anecdotes from her day at the market, an experience she'd enjoyed immensely and was keen to repeat.

'Mike's asked me to do Helmsley market on Friday. It'll be fun, it's always busy so takings should be good too and I love the banter with the customers. It's quite the day out, hardly like work at all.'

'Thanks, Lisa, we do appreciate all you do for us and this little man loves you too.' Noah was less fractious and happily cradled on Lisa's knee, twisting his fingers into her hair as she jiggled him up and down. She was good with him. Rosie thought she'd make a fantastic mother herself one day.

'He's adorable and you know I'm always happy to mind him for you when you need a break, don't you?'

Lisa stayed for another hour and left when Noah went down for his nap, allowing Rosie to try to rest too although she doubted sleep would come; her mind still reeled with thoughts of the impending visit from Frank Stokes.

CHAPTER FOURTEEN

It didn't happen until Wednesday. Mike was at work and Rosie was attempting to keep her mind occupied by making a batch of bread when she heard a car bumping up the track to their home. A glance out of the window confirmed it wasn't anyone she knew so immediately she grabbed her phone and rang her husband.

'There's a car pulling up with a man driving. I think it's him!'

'I'm on my way. Don't open the door until I get there!' Rosie could hear Mike's breathing quicken; he was already on the move. It would take only a few minutes and she had no intention of letting the man inside without her husband there.

Stokes appeared to be in no hurry. Rosie stood well back from the window and watched as he unfolded himself from the driving seat and stretched his limbs. He locked the car and turned almost full circle, taking in the cottage and the view before striding towards the front door. She could recall very little about the man's appearance from the past; he'd been one of a pack although usually at the front and the most vociferous, but he appeared shorter than she remembered and thinner too.

Ben lay on the stone flags and gave a low growl at the sound of their visitor; he never barked until someone knocked on the door – not much of a guard dog. Rosie willed him to remain silent. Noah was sleeping peacefully in his crib and Ben's bark would surely wake him, alerting Stokes to their presence inside. She found she was holding her breath, counting off the seconds in her head and longing for Mike to arrive.

The inevitable knock came; loud, intrusive. Ben jumped up barking excitedly at the sound, his tail wagging furiously as he commenced his usual ritual of chasing his tail until the door was opened. Noah woke with a sudden cry and his mother lifted him, holding him close and hurrying into the lounge, knowing Stokes would now be aware she was inside. A second knock came a couple of minutes later followed by shouting through the letterbox.

'I know you're in there, Mrs Cantrell. Please open the door so we can talk. I'm not going away until you give me at least a couple of minutes of your time!'

The welcome sound of another car pulling up behind Stokes's brought Rosie's heart rate down and tiptoeing back into the kitchen she watched her husband talking to the journalist, an animated discussion the words of which she couldn't hear but could guess. They seemed to reach an impasse and Mike moved towards the door, opening it and stepping inside. Frank Stokes followed. Rosie wasn't surprised when Mike allowed the man inside their home; they'd discussed how to handle the meeting and both accepted that Stokes was unlikely to go away without speaking to her.

For a moment Rosie stared at the unwelcome visitor, transported back to that awful time in her life when he'd pestered her for quotes and persistently remained on her doorstep for hours on end. He looked older; it was nearly ten years on, years which hadn't been kind to him. His round shaved head seemed too large for his now-skinny body and a bulbous nose appeared more prominent than she remembered. An odour of stale beer and tobacco clung to his clothing which was crumpled, even stained.

Stokes smiled at her, revealing crooked nicotine-stained teeth. 'Hello, Samantha.'

'It's Rosie.' Her voice was curt.

'Yes, of course, sorry.' He took a step nearer and she could smell alcohol on his breath – it wasn't even midday. She desperately wanted this man out of her house.

'You're wasting your time here, Mr Stokes. I have no intention of giving you an interview or discussing events of the past whatever you say.' Rosie felt braver with Mike by her side and held Noah close. He'd stopped crying and was watching his mother intently. His little starfish hand tapped her cheek and she hugged him even tighter, her arms a shield protecting her son.

Stokes shifted his weight from one foot to the other. 'Look, I know we didn't hit it off last time we met but things are different now and I have an idea which could benefit you. I'm not working for the *Mercury* any longer. I'm freelance and am planning a book...'

'If the book includes anything about me then you can forget it – there's no way I'll give permission to have my past dragged up again purely for entertainment and for you to make money.' Rosie was trembling.

Mike squeezed her shoulder his hand reassuring. 'Okay, Mr Stokes, you've heard it directly from my wife. She doesn't want any part in your scheme so I think it's time you left; we have things to do.' Mike moved forward to edge the journalist backwards towards the door. They were still in the hallway. This wasn't a social visit so they hadn't invited the man into the lounge. Stokes held his ground, not quite finished, and looked at Rosie again.

'You do know I can write this without your co-operation? Your story is in the public domain and people are interested in what happened to you. Do I need to point out that if I go ahead without you, there'll be nothing in it for you?' The man smiled again and Rosie's stomach roiled.

'Is that a threat, Mr Stokes?' Mike asked.

'No, it's just a fact. It's what will probably happen if you refuse to talk to me.'

'And if you go down that road, we'll take out an injunction to stop you so you might as well forget about your book.'

'An injunction would only delay the inevitable, Mr Cantrell, and cost you five hundred quid or more for the privilege. I'm offering you the chance to make some serious money here and if you don't mind me saying so, it looks as if it would be welcome.' Stokes cast his eyes around the downstairs rooms, able to see into both the kitchen and lounge from where they stood. Rosie was embarrassingly aware of the shabby furnishings, the crack in the plaster beside the fireplace, the ill-fitting windows.

Stokes continued. 'We can discuss the angle of the book – the hook is the tenth anniversary which is coming up soon – it's entirely possible we'll be ready to publish by then as I've already done much of the groundwork. It'll be a sympathetic account, nothing salacious I promise.'

'The answer is no whatever angle or hook you're thinking of. I want nothing to do with your book and we'll fight you all the way if you proceed with its publication.' Rosie's voice was raised, anxious. She was close to tears yet refused to break down in front of this awful man. How dare he intend to profit from her life, from the misery and loss suffered in the past; the man had no ethics, no moral fibre. Why would he think she'd want to work with him?

Mike stepped forward, forcing the man back out of the open door. 'You have your answer, Mr Stokes, and that's final so please respect our privacy and don't call or write to my wife again.'

'At least sleep on it and discuss how the money could help you. Samantha's story has the potential to be a bestseller. Look, I'm staying at The Green Dragon in Bedale and I've another appointment in the area so I'll call back tomorrow to see if you've changed your minds.' The journalist wasn't going to admit defeat.

'Please don't bother, the answer will be the same.' Mike moved to close the door but Stokes wasn't quite finished.

'It would make up for the loss of your nice little trust fund, don't you think?' He threw that golden nugget in as a last resort before the door was firmly closed on him.

After a few minutes they heard his car start up and drive slowly away.

'Are you okay?' Mike asked as he took Noah from his wife's arms and laid him back in his crib.

'I'll be fine. I just hate confrontation of any kind and he was certainly persistent. Do you think he'll come back?' Rosie was trembling and sank down on the sofa drawing in several deep breaths.

'Probably. He's likely to have another go before he returns under whichever stone he crept out of. You don't have to see him again though. If he turns up tomorrow ring me again and I'll be here in no time. Don't even open the door.'

Rosie thought they'd been reasonably polite to the man but if he turned up again the next day she knew Mike would be angry. 'How did he know about the trust fund?' Rosie spoke to herself as much as her husband. 'I didn't even find out about it until Drake was dead by which time the papers had more or less given up on the story.'

'I don't know, love, but don't worry about it, we're not getting involved. Look I'm going to make you a cup of tea, you stay there.'

Rosie did as he said. Leaning her head back and closing her eyes, her breathing returned to normal.

'Feeling better now?' Mike handed her a steaming mug.

'Yes, thank you. If you need to get back to work, I'll be okay, honestly.' She forced a smile knowing Mike was on his own in the garden and there was always work to do. She shouldn't keep him.

He leaned close to kiss her goodbye. 'Okay but just ring if you need me.'

Locking the door after Mike left, Rosie intended to keep it locked the next day and the one after that too. If Stokes had travelled from Liverpool, he'd probably not leave before trying to see her at least one more time but she wouldn't let him inside her home again.

Rosie's mood swung between raw fear and anger during the remainder of the day. Stokes's insensitivity was incredible. To view her life as simply a story to entertain was unbelievable – to have Alison's memory besmirched, and to once again be reminded of Gary Drake – however did the journalist imagine she'd want any part of his book?

The hours dragged by and Rosie achieved very little other than conjuring up every conceivable scenario, at least every negative one, and gaining a headache in the process. When Mike returned, concern in every inch of his being, she almost knocked him off his feet greeting him; breathing in the scent of fresh air, the lingering smell of the market garden in his hair, his clothes. His presence brought comfort and a little envy as she hugged him wishing she'd been with him working outside, exhausting herself physically and having no time to think.

Rosie served a cold meal of leftover meat and salad and was unusually pensive as they ate in reflective silence talking only to their son. Mike bathed Noah after the meal and then put him to bed while Rosie cleared the dishes. Mike then poured his wife a glass of wine and took it into the garden where she sat, lost in thought.

'Don't worry, love. If he does come back we'll threaten to report him to the police for harassment. That should see him off.' Mike attempted a smile. They both knew how unlikely it was that such a threat would deter Stokes.

'I hope so but he strikes me as a man who doesn't give up easily.'

'Neither do I, so leave Frank Stokes to me.'

CHAPTER FIFTEEN

To Rosie's surprise they didn't hear from Stokes the following day nor the next one. As the weekend loomed, she finally relaxed, hoping the journalist had thought better of his plans and gone home thwarted, although deep inside she doubted it would be quite so simple.

Despite the relief of not seeing him again, Rosie still experienced an unsettling feeling of being watched which she put down to paranoia and resolutely stopped herself from looking out of the window quite so often.

It was the same uneasy sensation she'd felt during the weeks prior to Ali's death. At times, generally through the long hours of the night when sleep refused to come, Rosie even imagined Gary Drake was still alive. Since the arrival of Stokes's letter, Drake's ghost seemed to haunt her every thought, encroaching on her peace. His face inhabited her mind, those eyes laughing at her discomfort, images she could not readily shake off. It was a crazy thought which Rosie couldn't get out of her head, even though she knew Drake was dead.

For some reason Rosie was unable to share these thoughts

with Mike. Perhaps he'd think her unstable after her recent revelations. To his credit, since she'd told him the truth about her past he hadn't pushed for more information or asked the many questions which must surely be in his mind. It concerned her somewhat that his perception of her might have changed but if so, it certainly wasn't showing in the way he treated her. If anything, Mike was even more loving and attentive so she told herself to stop obsessing and continue life as Rosie Cantrell, consigning Samantha Ashby to the past.

Early on Saturday morning as Mike dashed about upstairs getting ready for work and Rosie was in the kitchen giving Noah his bottle, a car pulled up outside. Rosie's heart raced – could it be Stokes? But it was only 7.30am. She stood to look out of the window and was even more surprised to see a police car with two uniformed officers climbing out.

'Mike!' she shouted, needing her husband's support. Clattering downstairs, he was just in time to open the door. After scrutinising the officers' ID Mike stepped aside to allow them into their home where Rosie hovered nervously.

A young PC addressed her. 'Mrs Cantrell?'

'Yes?'

'I'm PC Jenna Bowman and this is my colleague, PC David Wilson. Would you mind answering a few questions, please?' She smiled. If it was an attempt at reassurance, Rosie thought, it failed miserably.

'About what?' Rosie sat down and put the bottle back into a grizzling Noah's mouth.

'Do you know Mr Frank Stokes?'

'Yes, we've met.' Rosie's heart rate was increasing. Anything to do with Stokes wasn't going to be good news. Was that man still going to rob her of her peace?

'And could you tell us when you last saw him?' PC Bowman asked.

'He visited us here on Wednesday, late morning sometime and left about eleven, eleven thirty, I'm not entirely sure.' She looked at her husband for confirmation.

Mike obliged. 'Yes, that's right. Mr Stokes was with us for about twenty minutes or so and then left.'

'Are you personal friends of his?' PC Bowman continued while her colleague wrote everything down in his notebook.

'No, not at all. I knew him briefly many years ago when he was a journalist in Liverpool. I hadn't seen him since then.' She wondered why the police should be looking for him.

'And have you seen him since his visit on Wednesday?'

'No. As I said, he left after only a short while and we haven't seen him since.' Rosie was curious yet almost afraid to know why they were asking these questions.

The officer persisted. 'So why did Mr Stokes visit you on Wednesday?'

'Just hang on a minute here,' Mike interrupted. 'Why all these questions? We've told you all we know; the man was here for only a few minutes and then left, why the third degree?'

'I'm sorry, Mr Cantrell, but it appears Mr Stokes has gone missing. He stayed at The Green Dragon in Bedale on Tuesday and didn't return as expected on Wednesday evening. His belongings are still in the room and among them we found your wife's name and address.' PC Bowman turned back to Rosie. 'So, can you tell me the purpose of his visit, please?' She smiled again, a tight, false smile.

Rosie was anxious, not wishing to appear evasive yet also not prepared to discuss her past connection. 'As I said, Mr Stokes was a journalist. He approached me recently about a book he intended to write with which he wanted my co-operation. I declined to help with the book and that's about all there is to it.'

Mike took over. 'And Stokes left then. He did say he had

another appointment in the area and would call back before leaving the following day, but he didn't. Have you tried his home address in Liverpool?'

The officers looked at him as if he was stupid and PC Bowman drew in a deep breath before answering. 'Yes, Mr Cantrell, we have and it appears he's not there and no one has heard from him since Tuesday. Thank you both for your help. If you do think of anything else could you give me a ring?' She handed him a card and the pair left.

Rosie looked at her husband, stunned. 'What do you think's happened?'

'I don't know. Perhaps he's gone on a bender? He was clearly disappointed when you wouldn't play ball so maybe he's holed up somewhere. He looked like a drinker.'

Remembering the smell of alcohol on Stokes's breath she thought perhaps her husband was right but the visit from the police rattled her. Irrationally she wanted to beg Mike not to go to work, to take a day off which would be unfair of her. It was a beautiful day. She would push Noah down to the market garden in his buggy instead, and as it was less than an hour's walk it would do her good. They could spend a little time there and see Lisa too. Rosie needed to get out of the house; to do something other than mope and worry.

Mike left shortly after the police and Rosie settled Noah down for his morning sleep while she tidied the kitchen debris, all the time wondering about Frank Stokes while trying not to.

The walk proved to be precisely what she needed. Noah was awake and propped up in his buggy so he could see his mother as she chatted and sang to him throughout their journey.

Lisa was the first to see her and greeted them both enthusiastically. 'Hi, Rosie! Mike's in the greenhouse; honestly, those tomatoes are ripening faster than we can harvest them.' She was busy packing mixed fruit and vegetable boxes into the van, a new venture which was proving popular with the locals. 'I'm off on a delivery run with this lot soon. Will you still be around in an hour or so when I get back?'

'That depends on this little chap. I'll see how busy Mike is too. I don't want to be in the way.'

'Nonsense, I'm sure you'll be welcome. See you later!' Lisa jumped in the van and set off on her round and Rosie went to find her husband.

Mike stopped work and looked up when she found him in the greenhouse, sweat was trickling down the back of his shirt and he looked exhausted. He grinned and reached out to hug his wife. 'Well, if it isn't my two favourite people.'

'Are we in the way?' she asked, it appeared he had a long way to go.

'Never, but you can grab a bucket and help if you like?'

Rosie was only too happy to do so, and balanced an empty bucket on the buggy and began to pick ripe tomatoes. Noah chuckled at the new game.

'That's right, get him started early on,' Mike joked and for half an hour they worked happily together, a reminder of the life she loved and the future they'd planned.

This life was worth fighting for; she was Rosie Cantrell now, not Samantha Ashby.

When it became too hot in the greenhouse for Noah, she pushed him outside and went into the brick shed to get them all some water. Mike came to join her, in need of a break.

'I suppose I should be getting back.' Rosie sounded reluctant and felt guilty at escaping the house for no good reason, a feeling she confessed to her husband.

'You don't need a reason to come and visit, especially when the weather's as glorious as today. It's good for Noah to see me at work too. He'll be wanting to help as soon as he can walk.'

'And he'll want to stop as soon as he gets to an age where

he'll be useful!' Rosie added. 'Say goodbye to Lisa for me, it's too hot to hang around.' She kissed her husband and set off on the walk home, deciding to buy something nice for tea in the village on the way. They deserved a treat after the strange goings-on of late.

CHAPTER SIXTEEN

In all her fifty-eight years, Florence Smith had never seen a dead body and it was worse than she could have imagined. Sandy found it first. The inquisitive golden Labrador ran into the trees sniffing around as usual but failed to come back after a few minutes when generally he rarely wandered out of her sight. Initially the dog didn't respond to her calls and then the urgent barking began.

Florence followed the sound into the wooded area to discover her much-loved pet excitedly digging at something she first mistook to be a bundle of rags. It was only on closer inspection that Florence noticed the flesh, hardly recognisable as such, not flesh coloured at all but a dull grey. Leaves and soil partially obscured the man's head, but a head it was, and Florence immediately hoped Sandy hadn't been responsible for covering it. The body too was partly covered, as if someone had made a half-hearted attempt to conceal it and either failed or given up.

Florence wished she'd not indulged in that extra slice of toast for breakfast as her stomach churned and she turned away to be sick. Such a hideous sight marred the beauty of the spot she loved so much; it was doubtful she'd ever wish to walk Sandy there again.

'Sandy, Sandy here boy!' Florence called out and the reluctant dog eventually left his new plaything to return to his mistress, tail wagging and tongue lolling, waiting for praise for being a good boy. His trembling mistress clipped him on his lead, propped herself up against a sturdy tree trunk for support, called the police and in a very shaky voice told them of the body in the woods.

'Are you sure the patient isn't breathing?' The voice on the other end asked. Florence reluctantly glanced again at the heap of a man and noted blood on the body parts Sandy had uncovered – dried up pools of blood which again had her retching. She could see the man's eyes too, open and staring, eyes she knew would haunt her dreams for a long time to come. She almost laughed – he could hardly be called a patient; it was far too late for that. After giving her considered opinion that the man was way beyond help, and her location, Florence stepped well back, outside of the woods and back on the track, keeping Sandy from returning to his find as the woman had asked. The whole scene was an incongruous sight for such a beautiful day and Florence knew she'd never think of the woods again without seeing the man's body.

It seemed an age until sirens could be heard in the distance. Florence assumed they'd be coming from Bedale, the nearest police station and felt a rush of relief to be able to pass on the responsibility of the body – for that was how it felt – her responsibility. After all it was her dog who'd found the poor soul.

Three police cars bounced along the track beside the wood coming to a halt when they saw Florence waving wildly at them. A female PC approached her first, gently asking what she'd found while her colleagues dashed into the trees to discover the body for themselves.

'Is it anyone you recognise?' the PC asked after establishing that Florence lived locally in the village of Thursdale.

'No. At least I don't think so although I didn't get a good look.' She'd not considered it would be someone local, but then all she'd seen of his face were those eyes. Florence comforted herself with the thought that nothing like this happened in a sleepy little village like theirs so it must be a stranger, a tourist perhaps – although she most certainly wasn't going to offer to take another peek. An unmarked car joined the others and two detectives jumped out and hurried off into the woods.

'Will you be all right to talk to the detectives now or would you rather we take you home and call for a statement later?' The young officer was very considerate, Florence thought for a moment before choosing the latter option; she needed to sit down and ring her husband at work, and then perhaps have a cup of tea or maybe a glass of something stronger...

Rosie hadn't been home above five minutes when she heard the sound of sirens at the bottom of the hill. Her heart leapt, initially assuming the police were about to return to ask more questions. Yet why the sirens, the urgency?

From the window she watched, open-mouthed as three cars pulled up on the edge of the woods at the bottom of the meadow, with stick people getting out and rushing around. Within minutes another vehicle arrived with more people and finally a black van. Although the view was uninterrupted, it was some distance and Rosie couldn't make out any details or recognise the figures.

Instinctively she knew the commotion was somehow

connected to Frank Stokes – it had to be – and by association, to her. Once again the man had brought mayhem to her ordered, peaceful life and very soon the police would be back at her door with more of their prying questions.

Noah, who'd slept during the walk home, was now awake and demanding food, so Rosie put his bottle in to warm and began to mix a tiny portion of baby food in a plastic bowl, rice and apple, his favourite. She wouldn't ring Mike again. He'd been disturbed enough today and there was nothing she could tell him for sure, just a feeling, an unwelcome foreboding. It would wait until the police came which they most certainly would. Spooning tiny portions of the sloppy mixture into her son's mouth, a strange sensation of resignation came over her. Trouble seemed to follow her around. How, Rosie wondered, would this latest dilemma end?

With Noah fed and settled in his cot Rosie dared to look out of the window again, inexplicably drawn to the scene. The circus was still in progress; yellow tape fluttered in the breeze cordoning off the woods from the path and more cars were in attendance. The familiar view was tarnished somehow, leached of all colour except the flapping yellow tape which screamed 'crime scene'. How long would it take them to come up the hill to knock on her door?

Making a coffee and a sandwich she didn't want, Rosie took them into the lounge. It was only then that she noticed the open window. Rosie was sure it was closed when she'd gone out in the morning yet now the curtains were blowing gently, silently and for the first time ever Rosie was afraid to be in her own home. It was no longer her place of safety, her sanctuary, and that awful feeling of losing control washed over her. Had someone been in the cottage while she was out? Almost falling onto the sofa and with her head swimming she gave way to the hot tears which had been ever present since the awful letter from Frank Stokes.

There was still a police presence on the edge of the woodland when Mike came home from work six hours later.

'What's going on?' he asked, a frown etched on his sweat streaked brow. 'There's one of those police mobile incident rooms in the village. Whatever it is must be serious.'

'I don't know. I wondered if it was anything to do with Stokes but the police haven't been again.' Rosie looked at her husband expectantly. He appeared to know even less than her.

'It might not be connected.'

'Mike, the man's been missing since he came here and now something serious is going on close to our home. It has to be Stokes. Look at the tape and the police guard. Do you think Stokes is dead?' The words came out as a whisper as if saying them quietly would make them less real.

'We'll soon find out, look!' Mike's eyes fixed on the window and as Rosie followed his line of sight, she saw the car climbing the track to their cottage.

CHAPTER SEVENTEEN

These visitors were not uniformed officers, but detectives. They stood on the doorstep, warrant cards in hands and solemn expressions fixed on their faces. The man introduced himself as DI Tom Harris and his colleague as DS Emma Russell.

'May we come in?' Harris asked.

'Of course.' Mike stood aside to allow them to enter and led them into the lounge where Rosie waited, chewing on her fingernails. The DI was a tall thin man with a long face and a mass of grey wiry hair clipped short at the sides and too long on top. A grey jacket which had seen better days hung off his spare frame, the sleeves too short for his long arms. His sergeant was impossibly young and very pretty, petite with dark hair tied neatly into a ponytail and huge brown eyes in an oval face. She offered a quick, tight smile. The DI maintained a poker face, his pale blue eyes taking in his surroundings.

'What's happened?' Mike asked. Rosie thought he spoke too quickly although they both wanted confirmation of what had occurred.

'A man's body has been found in the woods. We believe it to

be Frank Stokes, a gentleman who visited you on Wednesday?' The DI raised one eyebrow, clearly expecting an answer.

Rosie gasped. In her heart she'd known it must be Stokes yet hearing the words still shocked her.

Mike replied. 'Yes. We spoke to two of your colleagues this morning which I'm sure you already know.'

Is it true that the police only ever ask questions to which they knew the answers, or was it a myth?

The inspector simply nodded.

'How did he die?' Mike asked.

'I can't give out any details except to say we're treating it as murder.'

Rosie's eyes widened. She'd assumed perhaps he'd suffered a heart attack or something – he didn't look the picture of health – but murder. Who would want to kill him?

'Mrs Cantrell, can you tell me about your relationship with Mr Stokes?'

'There is no relationship!' She was suddenly irritated. Why wouldn't they leave her alone? 'I told your officers this morning that we saw Stokes on Wednesday and he left before lunchtime. We haven't seen him since.'

'And can you tell me the purpose of his visit?' DI Harris asked.

Rosie clasped her hands together to stop them shaking. 'He was planning to write a book or an article about certain events which happened in the past and wanted me to give him an interview. I told him I wasn't interested and asked him to leave and not to contact me again.'

'And what time was that?'

'Around eleven or eleven thirty, I'm not entirely sure.' Her eyes flicked from one officer to the other, convinced they didn't believe her although they didn't pursue the matter.

'Thank you, Mrs Cantrell. If you think of anything else

which might be helpful, please ring me.' He offered a card and Rosie absently thought that maybe she could start a collection as she took it and put it on the mantelpiece next to the one from that morning.

The detective continued. 'As you appear to be the last people to have seen Mr Stokes alive, we may need to speak to you again, perhaps tomorrow?'

Mike jumped into the conversation. 'But why? I don't see what else we can tell you.'

'New information comes to light all the time in a murder investigation. It's a matter of asking questions and collating information as we receive it. You're not the only ones we'll be speaking to; officers are conducting house-to-house enquiries in the village as we speak.' His words stung Rosie who felt churlish at her reluctance to help. Stokes was dead and although she didn't like the man, she wouldn't wish a violent death on anyone. The question as to whether he was married or had any children suddenly popped into her mind.

'It must be terrible for his family. How are they taking it?' she asked.

'I believe he was divorced and estranged from his daughter,' Harris told Rosie.

'Still, it must be a shock for them. If we can help, I'll be here all day tomorrow and Mike will be at work – the market garden at the other end of the village?' Rosie glanced at Mike who appeared annoyed at her co-operation.

'Thank you. We'll leave you in peace now.' DI Harris gave a perfunctory smile and the officers left.

———

Rosie was grateful to have Noah to focus on as she bathed him, after which Mike gave him his bottle while she cooked pasta.

Nothing was said of the visit and the grotesque reason for it, their baby may have been only four months old but neither wished to discuss a murdered man in front of him. When Noah was asleep in his cot and the meal's debris cleared, Mike poured two glasses of wine and they sat by the open window.

'I thought perhaps Stokes might have suffered a heart attack. He didn't look the healthiest of souls, did he?' Rosie remarked.

'No but then who around here would want to murder him?'

Her eyes filled with tears, 'I think that's going to be our problem. I'm the only person with a motive.'

Mike drew her towards him and kissed her gently. 'Darling, no one's going to believe you killed him over a stupid book or whatever it was he was planning. You've nothing to worry about.'

Mike's words didn't quite reassure her and no matter from which angle they looked at the events, Rosie wasn't comforted. It had been a long and stressful day. She'd had enough of it.

'I think I'm ready for bed now,' she said, 'though goodness knows if I'll sleep.'

Surprisingly, Rosie did manage to sleep and only woke on hearing Noah at about 6am. Her first thought was that it was another glorious morning but as consciousness dawned, the shocking events of the previous day flooded her mind and the day was spoiled. Mike was in the bathroom so Rosie climbed wearily from bed and went to lift her son, taking him downstairs to warm his bottle.

Although it was Sunday it would be another working day for Mike. When her husband came downstairs, showered and ready for work, Rosie remembered to tell him about the open window the day before. It had gone completely out of her head.

'You probably left it open, love. You've had a lot on your mind of late, don't worry about it.' And with those words he kissed her and Noah, grabbed a slice of toast and headed off to work.

Rosie could concentrate on nothing other than Frank Stokes and the visit from the police. It was difficult to believe that the man who'd stood in her home so recently was now gone, murdered, and for what reason?

In his line of work, Stokes was bound to have made enemies but to be murdered seemed extreme. And why here, in Thursdale? Perhaps, Rosie reasoned, she should have been more open with the police – explained her past more fully and why Stokes had suddenly sought her out. It was hardly relevant, yet it would probably be better to tell them herself before they found out from somewhere else and assumed she had something to hide. Rosie decided to ring DI Harris but not until after nine, he'd been working late last night and she was unsure what time he'd be available, especially as it was Sunday. But before the chance to do so presented itself her phone rang.

'Rosie? It's Lisa.' She sounded breathless. 'Mike asked me to let you know the police have been here and taken him back to the station to question him. What the hell's going on? Is it about the man who was murdered yesterday?'

Lisa's call completely threw Rosie. She realised everyone in the village would know about Stokes but why would the police want to take Mike away for questioning? 'When did they come?' she asked in a daze.

'A few minutes ago, they've only just left. He didn't have chance to ring you.'

'Do you know where they've taken him?'

'Bedale, I think. Did you know the dead man?' Lisa was bound to have questions; everyone would have questions but Rosie didn't want to answer them.

'A long time ago, yes. Did the police say what they wanted with Mike?'

'Just to ask a few more questions. They stressed it was voluntary and said he wasn't under arrest.'

Thoughts crowded in on Rosie – why did they want to speak to her husband and not her – should she get a solicitor, or go to Bedale to see what was going on?

'Lisa, what shall I do?' She was panicking, unsure of her next move. 'Do you think I should go to Bedale?' There was a moment or two of silence before her friend replied.

'If they only want to ask Mike questions he probably won't be very long and I'm sure he'll ring you as soon as he gets the chance. You can hardly go chasing after him with a baby in tow, can you? Unless you want me to come and mind Noah?'

'No, you're right, Mike will probably be back soon,' Rosie mumbled. Even level-headed Lisa sounded uncertain. 'Thanks for letting me know.' Rosie ended the call and paced the kitchen anxiously. Why would they want to speak to Mike? He'd only met Stokes for the first time on Wednesday. With no chance of settling to anything constructive she decided to go ahead with her plan to ring DI Harris. Perhaps he would enlighten her as to why they needed to speak to Mike.

Tapping in the number from the DI's card, Rosie's fingers trembled. Why did that awful little man, Stokes, have to seek her out, to throw her back into a life of worry and confusion when things were going so well?

'DI Harris.' The voice was clipped, hurried.

'Hello, it's Rosie Cantrell here. I believe you have Mike with you. Can you tell me why?' She suddenly doubted the wisdom of ringing, fearful of antagonising the police.

'Yes, Mrs Cantrell, I'm just about to go into the interview room to speak with him now. We have some routine questions, nothing to worry about at this stage.'

Rosie wondered what *at this stage* meant. Should they worry further down the line?

'We told you everything yesterday.' She sounded pathetic, even to herself.

'There's a couple of discrepancies we need to clear up. I'm sure your husband will tell you when he gets home.' The man was clearly trying to end the call but Rosie continued, wanting to be more open with him.

'Right, okay. I was going to ring you this morning to clear up a few things. When I heard the news of Stokes's death last night I was shocked and perhaps didn't fully explain the history I have with him. I'm sure it has nothing to do with his murder but I can tell you more about why he came to see me if you think it'll help?'

'Yes, that would be helpful, thank you. Perhaps I can call to see you this afternoon?'

'Fine, I'll be here.' Rosie rang off, allowing the detective to get on with his job and wondering if she'd made things better or perhaps worse, yet she had nothing to hide and desperately wanted the police to know it.

CHAPTER EIGHTEEN

Two hours passed before Mike rang from work by which time Rosie was on to her fourth cup of coffee, her nerves jangling from the effects of too much caffeine, and imagining all kinds of scenarios as to why the police took him to the station rather than simply asked their questions at the market garden.

'I'm back, nothing to worry about.' His breezy manner triggered Rosie's anger. Did he not realise she'd been doing nothing but worry all morning?

'What do you mean?' she snapped. 'Don't you think being taken to the police station for questioning is something to worry about? I've been frantic not knowing what was going on.'

'Look, I'll explain later. There are things which need doing here so I'll have to go.'

'You need to tell me now! DI Harris is coming to see me this afternoon so I need to know why he spoke to you this morning and what you told him.'

'What? Oh sod it, Rosie, why's he coming to see you? When did he ring?'

'He didn't ring. I rang him. I thought it would be better to tell him why Stokes visited us and explain my history with him rather than wait until he found out from someone else. It won't be relevant to the murder and I've nothing to hide.'

'Don't talk to him alone, Rosie. Tell me when he's coming and I'll come home.'

Rosie detected a note of panic in Mike's voice. 'I don't know what time, he didn't say. Look, don't come home; as you said you've work to do and we can't keep putting on Lisa. Now, are you going to tell me why they wanted to speak to you or should I ask DI Harris?' This was not the sort of conversation she usually had with Mike; they were both tetchy and he seemed unusually evasive.

'It was nothing and it's all cleared up now.' Rosie could hear Mike moving about, going into the brick shed probably out of Lisa's hearing. 'It's just that someone in the village told the police they'd seen me in the pub with Stokes on Wednesday lunchtime, that's all.'

'Why would they say such a thing?'

'Because it's true, I did go to see him to make sure he was going to leave you alone. On my way to work after Stokes's visit, I noticed his car in the pub car park and on impulse I went in. It wasn't planned and nothing untoward happened, it was all very amicable. I even bought the man a drink. I simply wanted to reiterate what we'd already told him.'

Rosie could hardly believe Mike would do such a thing – and then to lie about it wasn't like him at all. 'Then why didn't you tell the police about it? Why say you didn't see him after he left our cottage? You must have known they'd find out.'

'It wasn't me who said we didn't see him again, it was you, remember. You spoke for us both and I just didn't correct you.'

Rosie was losing patience. 'Don't split hairs with me, Mike! Surely you know how bad this must look to the police and why the hell didn't you tell me you'd seen Stokes again?'

'Because nothing happened – I simply told him not to call again, ever.'

Rosie could picture Mike running his fingers through his hair as he always did when he was exasperated, which he seemed to be. Anger with him for not telling her was bubbling up inside but having this conversation over the phone was frustrating.

Mike eventually spoke. 'Okay it's happened. And I can't change it. The police know so let them make of it what they will. I've told them all I can.' His words were emphatic and she knew the conversation was over for now but would hang between them until they discussed it fully later.

After the call, Rosie sat in silence for a few moments considering Mike's revelation. Why would he seek the man out again when they'd sent him away from their home? Strange dark images nudged themselves into her mind, unwelcome thoughts which were completely insane – Mike was a gentle soul, wasn't he? She'd never known him to be violent in any way. Surely his anger was righteous indignation on her behalf... he would never act on it... would he? Mike's words from Wednesday echoed in her mind, *leave Frank Stokes to me*.

Rosie shook her head to erase the unpalatable images and thoughts which crowded in on her and turned her attention to Noah. He was such a good little baby, happily amusing himself in his crib, catching his toes in his little fists and chuckling away as if life was perfect, which it had been until Frank Stokes had appeared.

DI Harris and DS Russell arrived at 1.30pm, impeccable timing as Noah was settling down for his afternoon sleep. Rosie offered coffee and was surprised when they accepted. The DI's demeanour was more relaxed than on his previous visit, resulting in a less tense atmosphere. When they were seated, mugs in hands, Rosie decided to first clear up the misunderstanding with Mike and the last time they'd seen Stokes.

'I think perhaps I inadvertently misled you when I said Mr Stokes left on Wednesday before lunch and we didn't see him again. At the time I didn't know Mike had popped into the pub when he saw his car so I assumed I was speaking for both of us when it should have been only for myself.'

DS Russell raised an eyebrow. 'So, your husband didn't tell you he'd seen Mr Stokes again that day?'

Oh hell, Rosie thought. Had she made the incident seem even more suspicious?

'We'd hardly seen each other. My husband works such long hours and it must have slipped his mind. I'm sorry, it wasn't deliberate.'

'We understand, Mrs Cantrell, although you must see how it looks to us? In a murder enquiry, we have to ask so many questions and collate all the answers. When they don't match up, we need to investigate further. With your husband's previous conviction for assault and the fact that he didn't mention meeting Stokes in the pub, naturally we needed to probe a little deeper.'

'Mike's previous conviction...' Rosie felt the blood drain from her face – this was news to her – yet perhaps she shouldn't let the police know.

'Yes. We run basic profiles on everyone connected to a case.' DS Russell continued, thankfully unaware of the hesitation.

Rosie nodded as if cognisant of what they were talking about. Here was something else to discuss with Mike. It appeared she wasn't the only one with past secrets. The woman then looked at her expectantly which Rosie took as her cue to begin her story.

Taking a deep breath, she tried to put this latest shock from her mind. 'Yes, I see. That was one of the reasons I wanted to tell you more about my connection with Frank Stokes. Almost ten years ago my twin sister was murdered, a terrible time which was made worse by the intrusion of the press, Frank Stokes among them.'

She was interrupted by DI Harris. 'Mrs Cantrell, we know all about your sister and Gary Drake. Our colleagues in Liverpool have been to Mr Stokes's flat and found the notes he was working on for his upcoming book. They're very detailed and erm, quite revealing. Your old and new names are clearly set out, together with this location. I haven't yet had a chance to read these notes, although I've been made aware of what happened to you and I'm sorry for all you went through.' DI Harris's blue eyes held a degree of compassion.

Rosie was stunned – how quick was that? Thank goodness she was offering the information now otherwise they may have thought she had something to hide and was being deliberately evasive. The detective's empathy might also explain his more relaxed mood. It was a relief for Rosie not to have to talk about Alison and relate the details of that dreadful time.

'I'm sorry I wasn't more open yesterday it's just – well Stokes's visit and now his murder has thrown me, it's been an unsettling experience which brought back some pretty horrific memories.' Rosie's voice was cracking. Things really were getting to her. 'And I still don't see how my past or what happened to Alison has any bearing on Stokes's murder. Surely you don't think I would kill him simply to stop him writing a book?'

'To be blunt, we look at all lines of enquiry and as Mr Stokes was working freelance naturally we have to consider his current projects and your story seems to have occupied most of his time over recent months. We will of course be looking into other articles he's written, particularly from his past when he worked as an investigative journalist – there'll be many other leads to follow. With the kind of work he did, Mr Stokes made more than a few enemies.' DI Harris smiled and Rosie found his words reassuring. The perpetrator must be someone from the journalist's past, she was only surprised and annoyed that whoever it was had chosen to follow him to her home to murder him. The detective's ensuing words, however, unsettled her again.

'I do need to tell you that our colleagues in Liverpool found several detailed notes on the proposed book which have raised issues they'd like to discuss with you. As I say, I haven't had the chance to read Stokes's notes in any detail myself, yet it appears they've presented the Merseyside police with a few concerns about your sister's death. Perhaps you could be available to see them tomorrow?'

Rosie's heart was beating rapidly and she could hardly breathe – what was happening here? 'But why drag it all up again? Alison's death has nothing to do with Frank Stokes except that he reported it at the time. Surely it's not relevant?'

'I'm sorry, Mrs Cantrell. As I said we have to look at all possible leads.' DI Harris drained his cup.

At least the detectives had the good grace to look as if they were sorry as they thanked her for the coffee before leaving.

CHAPTER NINETEEN

Part of Rosie wanted to ring Mike as soon as DI Harris and DS Russell left, yet she was still annoyed with him for not telling her about meeting Stokes in the pub. And now there was this past conviction of which she knew nothing. What the hell was that all about? Having thought she knew everything there was to know about her husband, it now appeared she didn't. It also looked as if she would be having another visit from the Merseyside police, and the details of Ali's awful death would be dragged up and chewed over again. Could things possibly get any worse?

Mike was late home and as soon as he walked through the door, the tension between them became palpable, an unwelcome atmosphere which Rosie was determined to end, but only after everything was out in the open. Noah was already in bed so Mike went upstairs to change and look in on his sleeping son. When he returned to the kitchen they sat down to eat, neither wishing to be the first to open the dialogue.

After pushing her food around the plate for a couple of minutes Rosie was the first to cave in. 'We need to talk, Mike. I want to know why you went into the pub to see Stokes – and it also appears you have a conviction for assault, something else you failed to mention. Why didn't you tell me? It's not the sort of information I appreciate the police knowing when I don't.'

For a moment Mike looked shamefaced until he suddenly slammed down his knife and fork. 'Look, as far as Stokes is concerned there's nothing else to tell! As I told you on the phone, I saw his car and decided to have another attempt at persuading him to leave you alone – that's all there is to it. He was fine when I left him – still breathing, okay?'

Rosie looked down to the food going cold on her plate and ignored the sarcasm; after all she'd entertained such awful thoughts earlier. 'And what did he say? How long were you with him?' The police would have asked these same questions and she had a right to know the answers too.

'I told him not to bother calling again as you weren't going to change your mind. He listened, allowed me to buy him a drink and then the smug bastard just smiled and wouldn't commit to anything. I was furious but kept calm and left after five minutes, no more than that, I swear. Whoever told the police I'd been with him would probably also tell them that I left alone, and Stokes was still there, alive and kicking at the time.'

'Was Lisa at the garden when you got to work?'

'No, she'd already left on the delivery rounds, why?'

'So you have no one to confirm this?'

Mike glared at his wife, who said nothing more. 'What? Do you actually think I lay in wait for him, followed him from the pub and murdered him? Do you really think I need an alibi?' He was shouting and Rosie felt shame at having even considered he was capable of such an atrocious crime.

'No, of course not. I just don't know why you didn't tell me at the time, or the police for that matter. And today, to find out about your past conviction from them was rather embarrassing, yet it certainly explains why they took you to the station for questioning. So, what was it all about?'

'It wasn't anything of consequence, Rosie, I swear. I was a kid at the time, just turned eighteen – it was a scuffle in a pub. I was stupid and macho and ended up lashing out at a comment I took exception to – someone called the police and I ended up being charged with common assault. It was a first offence and I was given a fine. Had I been a couple of months younger it would have been a simple caution and no record. It wasn't a big deal and hardly the sort of thing I would talk about on a first date. I always meant to tell you, yet somehow as our relationship progressed the time just never seemed right. But it wasn't some huge secret I was deliberately trying to hide.'

'So, it appears we both have past secrets which we didn't share?' Rosie almost laughed at the irony. She could hardly criticise Mike for not telling her about a minor assault when she'd kept her whole past life a secret. 'I still don't understand why you didn't tell me about Stokes.' She worried the subject as if picking at a scab with the same effect of making matters worse.

'Perhaps because I knew you'd have a go at me?' Mike sighed and took up his knife and fork. Rosie said nothing more, he apparently wasn't in the mood to have a reasonable conversation. They ate in silence for a few minutes.

Finally, Mike asked, 'So, what happened with the police this afternoon?'

'DI Harris knew all about my past. The Merseyside police have already searched Stokes's home and found his notes on the proposed book and they want to speak to me about it tomorrow.' Rosie's eyes filled with tears and Mike's mood instantly softened.

'Oh, love, I'm sorry. Do you want me to stay at home tomorrow?'

'No, you can't afford to let things slip at work. I'll be fine. There's nothing new I can tell them – I don't know what they're hoping to achieve by raking over the past.'

Suddenly Mike's arms were around her and he held her as she sobbed, stroking her hair and telling her it would be fine, a promise she knew he could hardly make, yet words Rosie desperately wanted to believe.

———

'Mike,' she said to him much later, 'let's not argue about this anymore. I feel bad enough for having brought it all into our lives. I don't want to fall out with you over it.'

'We won't fall out, Rosie. We'll fight it together. Once the police realise we had nothing to do with the murder they'll leave us alone and hopefully find the real killer – and the sooner the better.'

CHAPTER TWENTY

After a restless night Rosie awoke the following morning feeling exhausted. Completely drained, with a throbbing head and gritty eyes she could barely concentrate on simple mundane tasks. Even Noah picked up on her mood and refused to take his bottle, flailing his little fists when she tried to persuade him. The forthcoming visit from the police was all she could think about and Mike, sensing her dread, offered to stay with her.

Although longing to say yes, Rosie knew he needed to get to work. Lisa was always willing to step in but she was young, still learning the ropes and required supervision. Kissing her husband goodbye, Rosie insisted she'd be fine, forcing a brave smile before scooping up her son to give him her undivided attention and hopefully take her mind off whatever the day might hold.

DI Theresa Lloyd and DS Peter Naismith arrived at 10.30am and entered Hilltop Cottage, their expressions inscrutable. Rosie offered coffee which they declined so she settled Noah in his crib and sat in the lounge with her visitors.

The detective sergeant took out a notebook and pen while his boss opened the dialogue.

'Mrs Cantrell, while assisting our colleagues from Bedale in their enquiries into the murder of Frank Stokes we searched his home in Liverpool and came across copious notes on a book he appeared to be writing. As you seem to be the main subject of the book, we hoped you could tell us why you were assisting him in writing it, and how much is factual?' The woman's manner was brusque, officious and Rosie felt they'd reached their conclusions before entering the house.

Shocked, she answered, 'But I wasn't helping him! You've got it all wrong. Frank Stokes wrote to me a little over a week ago, which was the first time I'd heard from him since my sister's death. He mentioned doing a feature about her – us – for the tenth anniversary and the possibility of a book – and that he'd be coming to see me. It was a complete surprise. I changed my name when I moved here so goodness knows how he traced me. Until then I hadn't heard about the book and certainly didn't want any part of it.'

'About your change of name, Mrs Cantrell. Wasn't it a bit extreme? Why did you decide to run away and come to Yorkshire under a new name?' DI Lloyd made it sound suspicious as if her actions were devious, nefarious even.

Rosie sighed; it wasn't going to be easy making these people understand. 'I was nineteen. My parents and grandmother were dead and my sister recently murdered. There was no one for me to turn to and the press, Frank Stokes among them, was hounding me. It wasn't a matter of running away. I needed to carve out a new life to regain some kind of sanity and Liverpool wasn't my home town anyway. Being completely alone with no ties to the city I decided to leave, to start afresh somewhere else.' It shouldn't be necessary to explain her reasons and Rosie was frustrated and annoyed in equal measures. The questions were intrusive, dredging up those old painful memories she'd worked so hard to suppress.

The DI moved on. Her voice betraying nothing, not even an iota of compassion. 'The inquest into your sister's death returned an open verdict. Do you understand what that means, Mrs Cantrell?'

'Yes. Ali's death was suspicious but because Gary Drake died before he came to trial, he couldn't be convicted.' She swallowed hard, wondering where this was going. It was an effort to keep calm, to breathe evenly and Rosie wished she'd asked Mike to stay.

'That's not strictly correct. Yes, your sister's death was recorded as suspicious and with Drake's subsequent death a trial obviously couldn't proceed; it doesn't mean he was presumed guilty. As there wasn't a conviction, the open verdict still stands and at the time the police weren't looking for anyone else in connection with your sister's death. However, the case was not closed. Now that we have Mr Stokes's notes, we think there may be grounds to review your sister's death.' Both detectives scrutinised Rosie intently, watching for a reaction.

'I don't understand. What could a journalist have written to make you doubt that it was Gary Drake who killed Ali?' This whole interview was surreal and Rosie felt like an observer, as if she was outside the room, peering in. 'Can I see these notes?' she asked.

'I'm afraid not. They're now evidence in a murder case; I'm sure you can see?'

Rosie understood that much although nothing else. 'So how can you investigate something which happened so long ago and why?'

'We'll start by looking again at all the old and any new evidence. We've already spoken to the man who was with you when you found your sister in Grainger Street. It might be a cold case, Mrs Cantrell, but we have ways of investigating, and as Ms Ashby's next of kin, one of the reasons we're here is to officially inform you that we're looking again at the case.'

'But what new evidence can you possibly have? Ali said it was Gary who pushed her down the stairs. You have a statement from the man who helped me as well as mine to attest to that. He heard her too.' Rosie couldn't believe her ears. Surely this was a nightmare – couldn't they see it was Drake who killed Ali?

'Your sister said only one word, "Gary". She may simply have been asking for him in her time of need, after all he was her partner and they were living together at the time.'

'What utter rubbish – Ali was telling me he'd done it! Your colleagues knew it then and Gary admitted he'd beaten her before. He was a bully and a violent one too.' Rosie was angry and felt intimidated by the presence of these two police officers in her home. A knot was forming in her chest, making breathing difficult as she listened to the DI's monotonous voice.

'Other things have recently come to light which weren't disclosed at the time. One in particular is the issue of your trust fund. Why did you not tell us at the time there'd been arguments over the money, Mrs Cantrell?' The DI leaned forward on the edge of her seat. Rosie was stunned at the insinuation.

'We didn't argue over the money! Ali and I agreed to keep the trust fund until after university, for our futures. It was never an issue and I didn't know the money was missing until after Alison died.' How did they know about the trust fund, Rosie wondered? Then it dawned on her; she'd reported it as having been stolen after seeing the solicitor and Stokes had somehow found out. They must have read it in his notes. 'Go and see the solicitor in Stroud if you don't believe me, William Jenkinson, he'll tell you!' Did she sound desperate, Rosie wondered? She certainly felt it.

The DI was calm and composed, quite the opposite of how Rosie was feeling. Lloyd continued. 'We have officers visiting Mr Jenkinson today, Mrs Cantrell. Our main purpose for coming here today is to inform you we're reviewing your sister's case. I suggest you think seriously about what we've discussed and we'll talk later. You might even wish to consider legal representation. And if there's anything you'd like to tell us, perhaps something you've neglected to mention before, please get in touch at any time.' The implication was clear, leaving Rosie stunned.

When the officers left, Rosie flopped onto the sofa, drained. The room was silent of voices yet the noise crowded in on her; the ticking clock, the hum of the fridge in the kitchen and the rush of blood throbbing in her ears. What was happening here? And what could Stokes have written to make them look again at Ali's murder? Was the detective hinting that they thought Rosie had something to do with her sister's death? It certainly appeared so.

As questions flooded her mind Rosie felt quite nauseous. Once again she was being sucked into a nightmare of suspicion and death, only this time she couldn't change her name and disappear. This time she needed to stand her ground and fight for the life she cherished.

Rosie lost all track of time until Noah's cries disturbed her reverie. Attending to his needs helped bring some semblance of normality but the visit from the police couldn't be readily dismissed from her mind, or the unthinkable implications of it.

Relating the morning's events to Mike later still didn't ease her mind. 'They're reopening the investigation into Ali's death,' she told her husband solemnly.

'Surely they can't do that without new evidence?' Mike's brow furrowed as he gave his wife his full attention.

'Apparently they've found the notes Frank Stokes made and are factoring the missing trust fund money into the equation, even though I didn't know about it until much later. They hinted that I had something to do with it, that we quarrelled over the money – but it isn't true, Mike. We didn't argue!' Rosie's tears flowed freely – tears she'd bottled up all day not wanting Noah to sense her mood.

'Your solicitor will vouch for you, won't he? He can confirm you didn't know the money was missing.'

'Yes, they had someone visiting him today. Maybe I'll ring tomorrow to speak to him.' William Jenkinson could be their one spark of hope in this frightening situation – he'd surely back her up. 'And we need to know what's in Stokes's notes but they said I couldn't see them.'

'Perhaps you could ask Mr Jenkinson where you stand legally. I think at some point the police have to disclose anything they want to use as evidence but we need proper advice.' Mike ran his fingers through his hair, the usual sparkle in his eyes dimmed.

'We can't afford legal advice, Mike. We'll have to deal with it ourselves but maybe William can advise us.'

'Let's not worry for now; you need to rest. Ring him tomorrow and at least find out what the police wanted with him.'

CHAPTER TWENTY-ONE

Mike had been somewhat relieved when Rosie refused his offer to stay at home the previous morning, although his reasons were valid – there was always so much to do at work. Watering alone took up so much time in the summer, much of it done by hand as only two of the greenhouses were fitted with drip irrigation systems.

His words of comfort to Rosie were easier to say than to practice and although he tried not to show it, Mike was every bit as worried as his wife. He'd not known her all those years ago; not known Alison or the dynamics between the sisters, so he was trying to reassure Rosie when he felt anything but convinced himself.

This Frank Stokes business couldn't have come at a worse time. Mike hadn't taken a day off for over a week, not since the Saturday Rosie had stunned him with the story of her past, and now he felt guilty for not being able to spend more time with his wife when she needed him the most. He also hated putting on Lisa. She was great and didn't complain but they couldn't afford to lose her by overworking her.

'Hi, Mike. How are things?' Lisa appeared in the doorway.

'Fine thanks. Do you know where the order sheets are?' His distracted rummaging was adding to the usual mess on the desk. Lisa reached over his head to the pigeonhole above and pulled out a wad of papers.

'Oh, thanks, I should have known.'

'Your mind doesn't seem to be on the job at the moment. Is everything all right at home?'

'Why?' he snapped, wondering what she'd heard.

'Hey, don't bite my head off. It's just that there's a lot of talk in the village – you know – about the murdered man. They're saying he was a friend of yours. Is it true?'

It wasn't a surprise that people were talking about them, nothing went unnoticed in such a small community and murder was far from being an everyday occurrence.

Mike let the order sheets drop onto the desk, swung the chair around to face Lisa and gave her his full attention. 'Okay, so what are they saying?'

'Only that the police have visited you more than once and it's not because you found the body, Florence Smith found him – quite near your place too. They're saying he was an old friend of Rosie's?'

With a sigh, Mike looked at Lisa and decided to confide in her, after all they may need her help with Noah and it was hardly fair to expect it without being open with her.

'The man was a journalist, certainly not a friend although yes he did visit Rosie before he died. It's rather complicated and I can't go into all the details but I've recently found out that my wife has a past of which I was unaware. Her twin sister was murdered nine years ago and this journalist, who'd hounded her for a story at the time, was planning to write a book about the case which he expected Rosie to sanction and even help with.

Naturally, losing her sister was traumatic and she didn't want anything to do with his book so we told him to leave. That's about it in a nutshell.' It was a sketchy account yet perhaps all Lisa needed to know.

'Wow! A murder in the village is unheard of but for Rosie's sister to have been murdered too is something else. And you knew nothing about this until recently?'

'Nothing at all. She only told me when Stokes contacted her and it seemed inevitable I'd find out through him.'

'That's hardly fair on you, Mike! Why didn't she tell you before?' Lisa's reaction and the sharpness in her voice surprised him.

'It was a harrowing time, which understandably she wanted to forget. We didn't get together until five years later. She'd changed her name by then and moved to Bedale – the woman I met and married was Rosie not Samantha.'

Lisa's tone softened. 'Poor Rosie, it must have been awful. She's lucky you're standing by her, many men wouldn't – the police don't suspect she's involved in the murder, do they?'

'I don't know what the police think. I neglected to tell them that I'd met the journalist in the pub last Wednesday, which is why they hauled me in for questioning yesterday. They suspect everyone and it appears they're far from finished yet. Police from Merseyside are reviewing Rosie's sister's death now, and asking more questions.'

Lisa squeezed Mike's arm. 'How awful. Look, if I can help just shout – babysitting or anything.'

'Thanks, Lisa. There may be times we'll need to take you up on it, I haven't a clue what will happen next although this seems far from over. But I hate to put on you, at your age you should be out having a good time. Isn't there a boyfriend in your life – won't he mind you working all hours?'

'There's no boyfriend, Mike, so no worries there!' She smiled. 'I love working here with you, it's so rewarding. You know I'm always up for extra hours and I'm not bothered about overtime pay. I know the business is struggling and I'm okay financially, I've actually got a bit put aside, a family legacy which enabled me to buy my little cottage, so I'm good.'

'You *own* Lilac Cottage? I always assumed you rented it.' It was a lovely cottage, smaller but in much better repair than their own.

'Yes, I know how lucky I am. My great aunt had no family of her own and as yours truly was her favourite niece she left a substantial sum to me; not millions, sadly, or I might be off travelling the world but I'm comfortable. Actually...' Lisa was perched on the corner of the table they used as a desk and wrinkled her nose thoughtfully.

Mike picked up on her hesitancy. 'Go on.'

'Perhaps this isn't the best time to mention it but I've wondered how you'd feel about allowing me to invest in the business? We work well together and I know it's been a struggle to make ends meet recently so maybe a partnership would be the way forward?'

'That's quite a proposition. I've not thought much further ahead than the next week or so.' Lisa was great to work with yet did he and Rosie want to take on a partner? It was true they'd struggled since Noah came along and Rosie stopped working, but the only partnership they'd considered was with each other – maybe it was time to rethink their business plan. 'I'd need to think about it and discuss it with Rosie, naturally.'

'Cool! I'd be happy to put in some capital. Maybe then we could expand a bit, take on extra help and give you and Rosie a bit more time together. We'd be able to improve the irrigation system too which would save time and manpower, and maybe even cultivate the back two acres?'

'You've really thought about this, haven't you?'

Lisa smiled. 'Yup, I'd love to be a partner! I believe in what you're doing, Mike – it's my dream too – the organic methods you use and your concept of more sustainable gardening – but perhaps I shouldn't have brought it up now. You've got a lot on your plate at the moment with Rosie and the police. There's no hurry for a decision, I only thought it might ease things to know you have options. Now, until we have a better irrigation system I'd better get on with the watering. It's going to be a scorcher again today.'

Mike returned to the order sheets yet found his concentration lacking. Lisa's idea was undoubtedly a surprise but could certainly take the edge off some of the pressure they were under and bring the possibility of expansion closer. He'd talk to Rosie about it later.

Rosie, however, was full of her conversation with the solicitor. 'William told the police everything he could remember and was almost apologetic about it. I think he still feels guilty, but he did nothing wrong, it was Ali who deceived him – under Gary Drake's influence. I don't know why the police think I had anything to do with the missing money – I reported the theft myself when we discovered it.'

'Did you ask William if he could advise us?'

'Yes, he said he'd help where he could although criminal law isn't his forte. He suggested a friend who might take our case on but his fees are eye-watering. We'll just have to hope it doesn't come to that. I can't bear the thought of getting into debt.'

It was much later in the evening after Noah was sleeping that Mike told his wife about Lisa's offer and, as expected, she was as surprised as he'd been.

'It's certainly generous but do we want to take on another partner? The dream was always to own the business outright.' Rosie looked tired and Mike wondered if he'd been wise to introduce the subject at all.

'I know, but we didn't factor in having a family so soon, did we? I wouldn't be without Noah for the world, yet his arrival did alter our plans and stopped you from working full time with me. Maybe it's time for a rethink?'

'Yes, but is it the right time with everything else going on in our lives?'

'You're right but Lisa's not pressing for an answer. She just thought it might help to know we have options with things as they are at the moment.' Mike was ready to change the subject.

'Exactly how much did you tell her?'

Mike paused before he answered. 'I, er, outlined the situation. Lisa offered to help and I felt she had a right to know.'

'How much of an outline?' Rosie frowned. 'Did you tell her about my past?'

Mike didn't need to answer, his face told her all she needed to know.

'Oh, Mike, why? You know I value my privacy. It'll be all over the village now and I don't think I can bear it!' Her eyes filled with tears.

'Lisa won't say anything. She's simply concerned and wants to help. I think everything will come out in the open soon anyway. Now the police are involved the press will become interested and who knows where it'll all end?' Instead of his words placating his wife she stood and ran from the room. Mike heard her footsteps on the stairs and their bedroom door slam and for a moment he wondered if he'd made a mistake in confiding in Lisa, yet they were carrying such a heavy burden and one which looked as if it would become worse before it was better. They needed help and Lisa was probably the best person to offer it.

CHAPTER TWENTY-TWO

A trip to Bedale was not something Rosie had anticipated but a late evening phone call from DS Peter Naismith took her by surprise. The sergeant asked, rather than instructed if she could make herself available at 2pm the following day at Bedale police station. Her question as to why received a vague non-committal answer – a voluntary attendance to help with their inquiries. At least she wasn't being asked to travel to Liverpool for the interview.

'What about Noah? You can hardly take him with you. Shall I take the afternoon off?' Mike's tone told Rosie this wasn't what he wanted to do.

'No. I'll ring Bella to see if she's free to have him for an hour or two. She's only seen him a couple of times since he was born, we're well overdue a visit.'

A quick phone call later and the arrangement was finalised – Bella would be delighted to see them and made Rosie promise to get there early so they could spend time together catching up. Bella's company would go a long way to improving Rosie's mood and hopefully take some of the sting out of the reason for her visit.

Rosie set off soon after Mike left for work the following morning. The appointment wasn't until the afternoon but a morning with Bella was precisely what she needed; her friend's down-to-earth common sense would undoubtedly help in putting everything into perspective. It would also give Noah the chance to become reacquainted with her before he was left in her care.

Bella Brookbanks was perhaps the closest person Rosie had to family other than Mike and his parents. Proprietor of Bella's Pantry, she'd offered a job and a home when Rosie most needed it. Perhaps the woman would never know how much her kindness meant to the broken young woman who turned up on her doorstep, alone and desperate.

Five years later it was a wrench for both women when Rosie moved on to a new life with Mike, promising to keep in touch and generally managing to do so even though they both led busy lives. Rosie didn't share her history with Bella, who didn't pry, accepting her as family and growing to love her as the daughter she'd always longed for but sadly never had. Driving to Bedale now seemed to Rosie in many ways like coming home.

The day was hot as Rosie parked in the shade of a side street near Bella's Pantry and walked around the corner in time to see Bella winding out the canopy to provide much-needed shade for those customers who were already filling up the outside seats.

Bella looked up. 'Sweetheart!' She threw her arms wide to enfold her friend. A hug from Bella was like being wrapped in a warm duvet and Rosie sank gratefully into her embrace, surprised at the sudden relief washing over her.

Bella bent down to peer into Noah's car seat and tickled his chin. 'And who's this handsome young man? Gosh he's grown so much!' The baby smiled and kicked his legs in response, his mood good after sleeping throughout the journey. 'Come inside out of this heat so I can see you both properly.'

Bella was a tall well-built woman of about sixty, her round face wreathed in smiles at the sight of her visitors and her silver-grey hair tied back, with damp strands escaping from their clips. She led the way into the café and paused, watching Rosie's face for a reaction.

'Wow, you've refurbed. I love it!' Rosie glanced around taking in the changes – a fresh new colour scheme, new tables and chairs and a re-modelled counter in front of the kitchen all met with her approval. 'When did you do this?'

'Before the season began. You were busy having this little man so I didn't get round to telling you. Just goes to show how long it is since you visited – shame on you making me do all the running at my age!' Bella laughed. She was as strong and active as a woman half her age and knew it.

'I'm sorry, things have been rather hectic.'

'I'm teasing, sweetheart. Now come upstairs. Olive's in charge today so I've all day to devote to you two.' Rosie gave Olive a little wave and a smile of thanks before trotting behind Bella to her rooms upstairs. The premises occupied three floors, the café on the ground floor with kitchen and storage, Bella's four spacious rooms above and the little flat Rosie once occupied on the third floor.

Nothing upstairs had changed and the familiarity was comforting in a way Rosie hadn't realised she needed. Lifting Noah from his seat she laid him on a blanket to play with the toys she'd brought with them.

'Goodness me, he's beautiful. He'll be a heartbreaker all right when he's older!' Bella, eyes dancing with delight, shook a toy rabbit above Noah's head prompting chuckles and much waving of arms and legs. She then turned her attention to his mother, looking intently into her face as she asked, 'Now, what's this mysterious appointment all about?'

Perhaps it was Bella's gentle tone of voice or the comforting feeling of coming home but tears filled Rosie's eyes.

'Oh, Bella, everything's going wrong. It's not an appointment – it's an interview with the police. It's a long story which perhaps I need to tell you before I expect you to help.' She searched her friend's face for signs of shock and saw only empathy.

'Is it connected to your past?' Bella's voice was low, almost a whisper.

'Yes, but what do you know of my past – I didn't tell you...'

'You didn't need to tell me, sweetheart. When you turned up here looking for work – gosh, it must be nearly ten years ago now – I thought you looked familiar. You know me, once I see a face I never forget it. Your face was indeed familiar and a pretty young girl wouldn't want to hide away here unless she was running away from something, so I did a little checking and lo and behold you were in the papers. Your story didn't only hit the headlines in Liverpool, Rosie, we heard about it here too and a very sorry affair it was. I figured you'd tell me all about it if you wanted to but it was clear you needed a home and a job and I was happy to provide it. And I have to say you've been nothing but a blessing to me since the day you first walked into the shop. I needed help too; what's it called, a symbiotic relationship?'

'I'm sorry for not confiding in you. I was in a mess and needed to forget those awful events, to begin again...'

Bella raised her hand, palm outwards. 'Sweetheart, you don't have to explain. You've been as good for me as I hope I've been for you. I'm here for you now if you still need me – and not just to look after Noah. You know you've become the daughter I never had, don't you?' Bella's words touched Rosie deeply and she again struggled to hold back the tears. But she needed to explain how much worse the situation was and hoped Bella wouldn't regret her promise.

'One of those reporters from Liverpool visited me recently, a man called Frank Stokes who wanted to turn my "story" into a book. We sent him packing. I wanted nothing to do with it or him, but his body was found near our home a few days later. He'd been stabbed.'

Bella gasped. Rosie continued to update her friend, explain the sudden visit to Bedale and why the police wanted to see her.

'As we were apparently the last people to see the man alive the police have been asking us questions although we know nothing which can help them. Today I'm seeing officers from the Merseyside force who're reopening the case into Ali's death. I'm scared, Bella, and haven't a clue what to expect.'

When Rosie finished her tale, Bella again wrapped her arms around her and held her while she sobbed – a cathartic release which even Mike had been unable to provide. When the tears dried, Rosie, outlining the tensions between her and Mike, explained how the police were interested in him because he met with Stokes in the pub, and then there was his past record. Bella listened patiently without comment until Rosie fell silent.

'It sounds to me as if you're both going through the wringer. I'm not a great one for giving advice but if you tell the truth, which I know you already have, it'll work out eventually. One day you'll look back on all of this as history. And you will get through it. I promise.'

CHAPTER TWENTY-THREE

After eating a light lunch with Bella and watching her friend happily giving Noah his bottle, Rosie set off alone. In her five years of living in Bedale she'd never had cause to enter the police station, a relatively new building not far from Bella's Pantry.

Walking along Market Place memories flooded Rosie's mind, all of them good ones. They were years of healing, of taking stock and recovering sufficiently to move on with a new life, much of which Bella facilitated by providing a home, employment and unquestioning support. The tiny flat on the top floor above Bella's own became Rosie's safe haven and held nothing other than good memories for which she would be forever grateful.

Mike first visited Bella's Pantry as a customer. Employed nearby at a large garden centre, his enthusiasm for working the land and ambitious plans for an organic market garden of his own impressed Rosie. Becoming a regular customer (and not just for the scones, Bella teased), Mike eventually asked the quiet young waitress out.

Rosie enjoyed listening to the tall skinny young man with

the wiry red hair, whose nut-brown skin glowed from being outside and who smelled of fresh air and wild meadows, and she surprised herself by accepting. With more than a little encouragement from Bella the romance blossomed and Rosie gradually relearned what happiness was. The young Mike tried his best to be romantic, to sweep his love off her feet and his efforts were rewarded as she returned his love and eventually agreed to be his wife.

A left turn into The Wynd took her past the Methodist Church where Rosie and Mike were married – more treasured memories of her recovery, eased by life in this small market town. It had been a bittersweet day, a watershed moment as Rosie travelled from her past life into her new; a time of great emotion when she desperately, yet secretly, missed her family.

Past the church a left turn took her into Wycar Street, the road to the Bedale police station. Her steps slowed and her heart rate increased. How this interview would unfold was impossible to guess as she was still unsure exactly why the police needed to speak to her again, but Rosie couldn't help anticipating what horrors might occur next. As much as she loathed revisiting Alison's death, those awful events filled her mind.

What could Stokes have written to persuade the police to look again at the crime? Why couldn't they simply accept that Gary Drake was responsible? Rosie was all for police investigations into miscarriages of justice but this wasn't the case in Ali's murder. Drake beat her to death. Period.

As the station's red tiles came into view it was an effort not to turn and sprint back to the safety and comfort of Bella's Pantry. But Bella's words resonated in her ears – tell the truth – it was all she could do.

Rosie recited her name to the officer behind the desk, an overweight man who lounged lazily on his chair shielded from the world by a plexiglass screen. He blinked slowly, reminding Rosie of a lizard, and asked her to wait in the lobby. Usually Rosie enjoyed people watching, inventing back-stories for strangers and imagining where they lived, their families, occupations – yet now each approaching figure caused her to jump. Breathing deeply and willing herself to calm down won her a degree of composure so by the time DS Peter Naismith appeared she felt as ready and prepared as possible.

The detective sergeant led her through swing doors and down a narrow airless corridor, his rubber soles squeaking on the linoleum. They entered a small room where DI Theresa Lloyd waited, the only natural lighting came from a high frosted window and an electric fan whirred on a corner table, a welcome breeze grazing Rosie's hot skin. DS Naismith motioned to a seat opposite the inspector which she took while he sat beside his boss. Two against one; the interview appeared weighted against Rosie before the first word was spoken.

'Thank you for coming in today, Mrs Cantrell.' The DI smiled briefly, a tight false smile. 'I'd like to tape our interview if it's okay with you?'

'Isn't that rather formal? Am I under arrest for something?' Rosie frowned, suddenly unsure of her rights. Should she have had a solicitor with her?

'No, you're not under arrest. This is an informal interview and entirely voluntary. You're free to leave at any time you wish. The recording is for our reference and also yours. Are you happy to continue?' The woman's hand hovered over the machine. Rosie nodded her assent, refusing would seem churlish and probably set the interview off on a wrong footing. With the machine switched on, the DI opened a file in front of her and shuffled her papers.

'We spoke about Mr Stokes notes when we visited you in your home. Have you had any more thoughts regarding his book?' The woman's hooded eyes held Rosie's, unblinking as she spoke.

'No. As I explained then, I didn't know about the book until he visited me the day before he died so I can tell you nothing whatsoever about it.'

'For the tape, I'm showing Mrs Cantrell a selection of notes from Frank Stokes's workbook.' DI Lloyd sounded anything but informal as she spun a sheet of paper around for Rosie to read. A few moments of silence followed as she tried to concentrate. The notes were not in any order and the handwriting was difficult to decipher. Scribbled jottings, crossing outs and doodles in the margins made them almost illegible, as if a spider had crawled across the page. Rosie skimmed over the words she could make out.

Early childhood squabbles.

Daddy's drinking – possible violence at home? Samantha's POV here – misery memoir always sells!

Parents' accident – had he been drinking?

Relationship with Drake – dates twins swapped him – ask Samantha.

Did they fight over him?

Did they double date or pretend to be each other.

Samantha's POV here – she could write this chapter!

The DI turned the page away before a horrified Rosie could read any more. Stokes was surely making it up. Nothing she'd read reflected the reality of what happened.

'These notes suggest you were collaborating with Mr Stokes on this book.' DI Lloyd's words both shocked and angered Rosie.

'No, that's not how I read them and it certainly isn't true!' How dare they presume such a thing and to put their slant on the journalist's notes just because it suited their purpose. 'It sounds to me as if he was planning a work of fiction, digging for dirt – but there wasn't any! My father wasn't a drinker, nor was he ever violent. And as for the suggestion that Ali and I fought over Gary Drake – well it's just ludicrous!'

Rosie suddenly remembered the letter Stokes sent her which she'd had the forethought to bring and rummaged in her bag to find it. Then, with a flourish she slammed it on the table between herself and the detectives.

'Here! Read this. This is the letter Frank Stokes sent me – the first I'd heard from him in over nine years. It's clear from what he says that I hadn't been *collaborating* with him as you suggest. Those notes are pure fiction – what he wanted to write and nothing resembling the truth at all.'

Silence filled the room while the detectives read the letter. Rosie was aware of her rapid heartbeat, convinced it could be heard by the others too.

DI Lloyd finally spoke. 'We'll have to examine this in greater detail to ascertain that Mr Stokes did write it.'

'The handwriting looks pretty similar to me and you're bound to find his fingerprints on it as well as mine and Mike's.' Rosie was furious. Did they think she'd gone to the trouble of forging the letter just to exonerate herself – and of what she still had little idea. Were they interviewing her about reopening her sister's case, or about Stokes's murder? It was unclear, as if they were fishing for something to pin on her.

'And if you look at the date you'll see it's recent. This was the first I'd heard from Mr Stokes since I left Liverpool. You can tell by what he writes that it's an initial contact, he still calls me Samantha.'

A look passed between the detectives which Rosie couldn't interpret and DS Naismith took over the questioning.

'Let's leave the letter and the notes for now, shall we? We'd like to keep this for verification if it's okay with you, Rosie? We'll give you a receipt for it, naturally.' His tone was more reasonable, friendlier than his colleague and he was using her Christian name, *good cop bad cop*, she thought.

The sergeant continued. 'We'd like to ask you a few questions about your trust fund. Firstly, can you tell us how much it was worth?'

Momentarily taken aback at the change in subject and tone, Rosie took a deep breath and answered. 'It would have been in the region of two million pounds, maybe more with interest. Didn't Mr Jenkinson tell you all this?'

'He was most accommodating, yes. And when did you visit Mr Jenkinson concerning the money?' DS Naismith's face was unreadable. Rosie wasn't sure where he was going with his questions yet remembering Bella's advice to tell the truth she thought it best to be open.

'It was a few weeks after Ali's death when I'd decided to leave Liverpool and make a fresh start. I can't remember the exact date, sometime in July probably. William will have a note of it, I'm sure.'

'Did you not also visit your solicitor in May?' DI Lloyd took over again. *Bad cop.*

'No.' Rosie answered, puzzled they should ask.

'Our problem here, Mrs Cantrell, is that William Jenkinson can confirm the dates when the trust fund was closed which was May 29th and May 30th yet he can't say with any certainty whether it was Alison or yourself who visited on those dates. It appears he was duped and is unsure which sister it was who signed the documents to close the trust fund. It seems the only way to confirm your story that it was Alison is if we have an alibi for your movements on those two days to confirm you were not in Stroud.'

'But it was over nine years ago. I can't possibly remember what I was doing then!' Rosie was horrified. Did the police think she'd been the one to close the trust fund, posing as Alison?

The rest of the interview passed in a haze. Rosie's concentration was all over the place and many of the questions were impossible to answer as so much time had elapsed with dates and locations a distant memory. She'd spent years actively trying to forget the events they were asking her to recall.

The detectives quizzed her about her relationship with her twin and any animosity she might have felt from losing Gary Drake to her sister. They'd got it all so very wrong and Rosie's frustration threatened to overwhelm her. How could she explain the love between herself and Ali; their unique bond and the fact that she would never hurt her? Try as she might it seemed as if the detectives had already made up their minds and this interview was not to be the end of the matter, only the beginning.

Eventually Rosie left the police station to walk back to Bella's Pantry. Much of what occurred was already a blur but Rosie rang Mike as promised, knowing how anxious he'd be. Still bewildered she tried to relate the interview although much of the detail was already forgotten. They would talk later. Right now she needed to breathe in the fresh clean air, to rid her lungs of the heat and tension of the police station and to hurry back to her son. Rosie desperately needed to hold Noah in her arms, to feel his sturdy little body, his baby breath on her face, and remind herself that he was her future. She would fight to clear her name for Noah's sake as much as her own.

CHAPTER TWENTY-FOUR

Mike put the phone down and sighed.

'Is everything okay?' Lisa stood in the doorway of the brick shed, their makeshift office.

'Not really. Rosie sounds dreadful. The police appear to have given her a rough time although she didn't go into detail. We'll talk tonight but they asked where she was on particular dates as far back as nine years ago – it's as if they suspect her of something.'

'That's awful. Poor thing must be devastated. Do you want me to finish off here so you can get home early?'

'Thanks, but it's okay. Rosie's still in Bedale so I might as well carry on a while longer.'

Lisa seemed in no hurry to leave and was keen to talk. 'I wonder what they think she's done. I thought they knew who killed her sister?'

'Trouble is the bastard who did it was killed himself before there was a trial so it was never conclusive and the coroner recorded an open verdict. Today they showed Rosie notes from that journalist, Stokes, which they seem to be taking as gospel and which raise all kinds of questions. Then there's the trust fund. As the money was never recovered the police appear to suspect her of taking that too.' Mike ran his fingers through his hair, tugging at it in frustration.

'What trust fund?' Lisa asked and he suddenly realised he'd not mentioned it before.

'Rosie had a trust fund set up by her parents. After Alison died she discovered the money was missing and it was never found.' He explained briefly making a mental note to remember what he'd said to whom in future.

'How strange. It must be so difficult for you, Mike – I mean, you didn't know Rosie back then or her sister so you don't actually know what happened do you? I wonder why she's been so secretive about it? Did she never talk about her past?'

'I suppose I never pushed for details. She was young when her parents died and struggled to cope, she told me that much. But no, Rosie didn't even tell me she had a twin sister or the circumstances surrounding her death.'

'I have to say I'm surprised she didn't trust you enough to confide in you.'

Mike was momentarily taken aback and felt suddenly defensive of his wife. 'She's had a traumatic time in the past. It's hardly surprising she wanted to put it all behind her.'

'Yes of course. I didn't mean anything by it, it's only that I find you so easy to talk to, so I'm surprised Rosie doesn't as well.' Lisa smiled and put her hand on his arm. 'You know you must look after yourself as well as Rosie, this is hard on you too. It's brought you under suspicion at a time when you could do without extra pressure.' Lisa smiled a gentle, sad smile. 'You do know I'm here for you if there's anything I can do, anything at all?'

'Thanks. That's good to know. And while we're talking –

about the offer you made the other day? I mentioned it to Rosie and we both feel it's not the right time to be making any big decisions. Let's get through this nightmare first and when things settle down we'll talk seriously about it then, eh?'

'Fine, no pressure. The offer's there should you want to take it and you're right, lousy timing! Okay, now I've been reading up on wireworm and might have found a solution, an organic product. Look...' Lisa was back in work mode and tapped on her iPad searching for a site selling organic pest controls. 'I thought this might be worth a try before we lose the whole carrot crop?'

Mike was happy to switch to discussing work rather than personal issues. Lisa was great and a good friend to them both yet there was nothing anyone could do to help in this situation no matter how willing they were.

Mike, late home again, was greeted with a sigh from Rosie who'd already put Noah to bed. They ate a dried-out meal in silence, pushing the unappetising food around their plates, each waiting for the other to open the discussion. Eventually, dishes cleared and seated in the lounge with a glass of wine each, Mike took the lead.

'Tell me all about it. Was it as rough as you'd expected?' He took her hand gently in his and with her eyes glistening, Rosie began to relate her experience at Bedale police station, the frustration and fear evident in her words.

'They're accepting Stokes's notes as factual even though they're just ramblings and make no sense at all. I only saw one page on which he appears to have outlined some chapters to be written from my perspective, which the detectives took as confirmation I've been colluding with him.'

'Did you show them Stokes's letter?'

'Yes, that at least seemed to surprise them. To us the letter implies a first contact but if they read it with the same preconceived ideas with which they've read Stokes's notes I'm still in trouble. They've kept it to test for authenticity, another indication that they don't trust me. I find it incredible that the police presume everything I'm telling them is a lie and Stokes's ramblings are true. I suppose the job makes them suspicious.'

'You've nothing to worry about if you tell the truth, Rosie.' Mike smiled and squeezed her hand. His wife was suffering and he was powerless to take away her pain.

'That's pretty much what Bella said too and what I've been trying to do since this whole fiasco started. I do feel it might be time to consider getting legal help. I know we can't afford it, yet I felt so out of my depth today that I'm beginning to wonder if we can't afford not to? Do you think your parents might be able to help?' Rosie ran her finger around the rim of her glass while Mike considered this.

His parents lived in Hastings and were not well off. His dad, a long-distance driver and his mum a school dinner supervisor, managed comfortably yet were not wealthy people by any stretch of the imagination. The Cantrells had accepted Rosie into their family with open arms, even insisting on paying for their wedding which Mike knew was a sacrifice.

'I can ask. It's probably about time we let them know what's going on, do you think?'

'I hate the thought of worrying them but you're probably right. It would be terrible if the press took an interest and they learned about our problems from there. Ring them tonight. Maybe your dad will offer to help financially so we won't have to ask?'

'Or we could always consider Lisa's offer of help. If she's prepared to invest in the garden maybe we could re-mortgage the cottage to raise some money?'

'It's a generous offer but we'd be tying ourselves into a partnership we don't really want. We'd also be indebted to Lisa. I think it's too soon to decide, especially with everything else that's going on.'

'Yes, you're right. I'll ring Dad and see how he reacts.' Mike kissed her on the forehead and took his phone into the garden to make what he knew would be a difficult call.

Mike spoke to his parents for over forty minutes giving a brief account of his wife's past life and present troubles. His mother, listening on speaker, was tearful.

'Poor Rosie – give her our love and tell her we'll do whatever we can to help.'

'Thanks, Mum. It's getting to the point where we think we may need to employ a solicitor but the cost would be astronomical.'

'Never mind the cost, we'll help out, won't we, Mary?'

'Yes, of course – do whatever you need to, son. Dad and I are behind you all the way.'

When Mike probed further about whether his parents could afford to help, Jim waved his enquiries away. 'We can always do one of those equity release things which are popular these days. Some of our friends have recently done it and they say it's marvellous.'

'I'd hate for you to have to do something so drastic...' Mike protested.

'Nonsense. If you need our help, you've got it. Now go and tell Rosie that we'll do anything we can, just say the word.'

'Thank you both, but don't do anything yet, with a bit of luck things might not get that bad. We'll let you know what happens.' The call ended with promises of keeping in touch and even talk of a visit if the Cantrell seniors could arrange time off work.

Mike related the conversation to Rosie who was clearly horrified at the suggestion of raising equity on their home.

'These things aren't safe, Mike! You hear such awful tales about them. I couldn't live with myself if they went into debt on my account.'

'Don't worry, they're not going to do anything yet. Dad's too rational to act without thinking it through first.'

CHAPTER TWENTY-FIVE

Rosie was unsure when they would next hear from either the Merseyside or Bedale police. It wasn't as if they were going to keep her in the loop, so they were entirely in the dark about how either investigation was going. When Mike left for work the following morning, she decided to take Noah for a long walk; they would call into the village mini-market for a few items she needed and perhaps even stop for a latte in the bakery coffee shop. It was too easy and possibly cowardly to avoid the village. Rosie dreaded meeting people whom she would usually seek out, but why shouldn't she get out and about – she'd done nothing wrong, nothing to be ashamed of.

On leaving the cottage Rosie's eyes drifted to the woodland at the bottom of the hill. The crime scene tape was gone and the familiar much-loved view was restored. If only her peaceful life could be returned as readily, she thought steering the buggy in the direction of the village. Lifting her face to the sun, Rosie allowed its warmth to permeate her body and breathed in the pleasant scented air. Although still warm there was a subtle change in the atmosphere. It was the beginning of September and the meadow was dry, parched from the glorious summer weather and thirsty for rain. Was it the approaching autumnal feel she sensed or simply the change in her mood? A dose of fresh air and exercise would do them both good and as she pushed her son down the path towards Thursdale, Noah played his favourite game of waving his legs in the air, trying to catch his toes and making his mother smile.

Passing the village school, Rosie paused to watch the children play in the yard, their happy laughter a delight to hear. Two girls turned a skipping rope while another jumped over it and Rosie was transported back to her childhood when she and Ali spent hours skipping together, one end of the rope tied to a tree while they took turns turning the rope and skipping. Today's chants and rhymes were almost the same ... *there's somebody under the bed, there's somebody under the bed* ... she could picture herself and Ali at six, gap-toothed and smiling, their long fair plaits bouncing down their backs as they skipped.

Would Noah still attend this school, Rosie wondered, or had recent events changed their future? She certainly hoped he would become a pupil here, together with a little brother or sister perhaps? A small family school was precisely the place she wanted for Noah. It was one of the reasons they'd chosen Thursdale to settle in.

Rosie dragged the buggy backwards into the mini-market, picked up a basket and carefully manoeuvred her way around the narrow aisles, collecting nappies, milk and eggs. At the counter Helen Parker smiled as she rang the purchases through the till.

'How are you, Rosie?' The older woman's smile was warm and genuine.

'Fine thanks, and you?'

'Can't complain. Noah's looking well.'

'He is and getting bigger by the day.' Rosie paid for her purchases and turned to leave. 'Bye, Helen!'

There, Rosie thought as they left the shop. *That wasn't too much of an ordeal.* Helen would know of the police interest in her and Mike; she was the first to hear all the village gossip but had been civil, pleasant even. Hopefully everyone else would react in the same way, she wasn't going to hide away as if she'd done something wrong. Next stop the café.

Chrissie Walker owned and ran the bakery, with the café, a recent addition, already proving popular with the locals and the few tourists who passed through. She was about Rosie's age and the women had become friends during the five years the Cantrells lived in the village. Una, Chrissie's mother, helped out in the café and smiled as Rosie pulled the buggy inside.

'Hello, strangers, good to see you!' Una made a beeline for Noah, never able to resist a baby. It was no secret that Una longed for her daughter to make her a grandmother and she was famous for dropping undisguised hints.

'Sit down, love. Chrissie's in the kitchen I'll tell her you're here.'

'Don't disturb her if she's busy. I'll just have a quick latte and maybe one of her delicious macaroons?'

Una smiled and went off to fill the order.

So far, the only other customers were Florence Smith and Ginny Yarrow, women Rosie knew only to pass the time of day with. She nodded and smiled at the pair. Florence returned the smile with a cheery good morning while Ginny avoided eye contact and turned away to whisper to her companion. It was a small space in which the woman's low voice could be heard. A few words carried to Rosie's table, the gist of which was clearly about her – *bringing the wrong sort to the village – there must be something she's hiding – the police suspect her of involvement in that man's death.*

Poor Florence looked mortified at her friend's gossip. Her cheeks flushed as she attempted to change the subject. Rosie was suddenly incensed. Standing and moving over to the women's table she asked, 'Have the police told you something they've neglected to tell me, Mrs Yarrow?' Rosie stared at the woman, waiting for an answer.

'Well, no, but...'

'But what?'

'You know what they say; there's no smoke without fire.' Ginny looked smug at having thought of such an original retort.

'Rosie dear, we're sorry for your troubles and don't think you're involved at all, do we, Ginny?' Florence looked sternly at her friend who shrugged in reply.

'Thank you, Mrs Smith.' Rosie turned again to Ginny Yarrow. 'If you have anything you wish to say or ask, please do so to my face in future. At least you'll get an accurate account rather than hearsay or gossip.' She returned to her seat just as Chrissie came from the kitchen with two lattes and a plate of her homemade macaroons to sit with her friend.

'Good for you!' Chrissie grinned, having caught most of the conversation. 'The old bat needed putting in her place.'

'Is this what people are saying about me? That there's no smoke without fire?' Rosie was shaking at the confrontation, her bravery deserting her.

'No, definitely not. This is the first negative comment I've heard and to be perfectly honest no one takes Ginny Yarrow seriously – she's a gossip so take no notice. Now, how are you holding up and can I do anything to help?'

'Oh, Chrissie, I wish you could!'

The other two customers stood to leave, Ginny with her nose in the air whilst Florence squeezed Rosie's shoulder as she passed and winked at her. Rosie returned the smile, understanding Florence's divided loyalties.

'See, I told you! Ginny bloody Yarrow's in the minority. Thursdale's not one of those gossipy villages, Rosie, we're your friends. We know you wouldn't be involved in something as horrendous as murder and want to help.'

Encouraged by Chrissie's words a relieved Rosie confided something of her past and the connection to the murdered man. Now Mike had told Lisa, Rosie's story would soon become public knowledge and she wanted a truthful version to be out there not a Chinese whispered version.

Leaving for home an hour later, Rosie was pleased she'd gone to the village. If Thursdale was to continue to be her home, which she certainly hoped, they needed to feel comfortable with their neighbours. The morning proved that this was still possible with perhaps the odd exception, but then there would be gossips like Ginny Yarrow wherever you lived.

CHAPTER TWENTY-SIX

Other than the visit to the village and subsequent confrontation with Ginny Yarrow, Rosie had nothing to report to Mike that evening which in a way was refreshing yet in another, worrying. She'd hoped there would be news of her 'interview' with the Merseyside police, confident that once they confirmed Stokes letter as genuine, they'd drop the case and remove at least one of the couple's present worries.

The more Rosie reflected on her visit to Bedale the more convinced she became that the police had no evidence to suspect her of any wrongdoing. If she had been the one to steal the trust fund from Ali, what did the police think she'd done with the money? Would her family be living hand to mouth, struggling to set up a business and occupying a house which needed so much attention? Surely the police applied common sense in their investigations in addition to looking for concrete evidence, and if so, was it reasonable to suspect her of hiding the money for nearly ten years without spending any?

An inherent trust and belief in the justice system gave Rosie hope that truth would prevail, yet at times despair wormed its ugly head in and allowed her thoughts to wander to the very worst possible scenarios. Maybe past life experiences had shaken her core belief of good overcoming evil but she stoically refused to let Mike witness these low points. If only they knew if the police were any closer to finding Frank Stokes's murderer, perhaps then they could regain their peace of mind.

Noah was sleepy. With his evening bath over and a bottle given by his daddy, he was settled for the night. Rosie and Mike watched some mindless television in a futile attempt to relax and eventually resorted to a glass of wine before deciding on an early night themselves. An unwelcome tension had stolen into their relationship, creeping in between the pair and driving a wedge between them which neither openly acknowledged yet were both painfully aware of. At times they shared their thoughts but more often didn't, not wanting the investigations to dominate their lives. Constant deliberations over their plight seemed as pointless as Ben chasing his tail and would probably leave them just as dizzy.

Rosie was permanently tired yet couldn't sleep and Mike was growing increasingly snappy, impatient with his wife when he knew she craved and needed quite the opposite. The physical side of their marriage suffered too. Rosie was either too tired or upset to make love which frustrated Mike, exacerbating his lack of patience. They both longed for their ordeal to come to a conclusion yet neither knew when such a time would come.

Rosie tossed and turned in bed. It was 5.45am and the sun was rising above the meadow – there would be no more sleep for her. Attempting to leave the bed without disturbing Mike she became aware of blue throbbing lights dimmed by the bedroom curtains and knew precisely what they were. The knowledge filled her heart with dread.

'Mike, wake up! I think the police are here.'

As her words seeped into her husband's consciousness, a loud hammering on the door confirmed Rosie's suspicions. Downstairs Ben barked, his paws skidding on the tiled floors adding to the commotion as he spun round and round, excited at the thought of early visitors. Noah woke suddenly, shrieking at the abrupt, loud noises. Mike dashed downstairs two at a time to open the door while Rosie lifted Noah, holding him close to comfort them both.

'Police! Open the door!' Shouting accompanied the loud banging as Mike fumbled with the lock and bolts.

'What?' Still half asleep he stood aside, alarmed at the sight of three police cars. DI Tom Harris, DS Emma Russell and several uniformed officers swarmed into his home almost knocking him over in the process. DS Russell waved a piece of paper under Mike's nose.

'In accordance with Section 8 of the Police and Criminal Evidence Act, we have a warrant to search these premises.' She moved forward into the lounge as she spoke, almost pushing Mike in front of her. 'Where is your wife, sir?'

'I'm here. What's going on?' A pale trembling Rosie stood in the doorway, Noah still crying in her arms.

'We have a warrant to search your home, Mrs Cantrell. Would you and your husband remain in here with this officer, please?' It was an order rather than a request; they had no choice other than to comply. A young PC was already standing to attention beside the lounge door, ready to spring into action if they had the nerve or the energy to attempt an escape.

'But why? What are you looking for?' Mike appeared nonplussed. Wearing only pyjama bottoms and with his hair tousled he looked half asleep.

'Shall we sit down, Mr Cantrell, and we can talk?' DI Harris took over as his colleague left the room to supervise the search,

Ben trotting close on her heels, tail wagging and wondering what the new game was.

Rosie was perhaps a little more together than her husband and faced the detective. 'Don't you need a good reason to search a property? Can I see the warrant, please?' She took the paper the DS had left with her boss and scanned the words, most of which she couldn't take in.

'It's perfectly legal, Mrs Cantrell. We feel there are sufficient grounds to proceed with a search for evidence.'

'What evidence?' Mike sounded furious.

'We'll know when we find it, sir.'

'What grounds do you have to do this?' Rosie asked, stroking Noah's soft downy hair to try to soothe him.

'You were the last people Mr Stokes visited and then you, Mr Cantrell, spoke to him in the pub afterwards and neglected to tell us of that meeting. It appears you also forgot to tell your wife. We now know death occurred later the same day, a time for which you have no alibi. Mr Stokes's body was found within a mile of your home and his car was in the car park of the pub where he was last sighted with you, Mr Cantrell.' DI Harris was all business now.

'So are you looking at Mike as a suspect or me?' Rosie asked, sounding braver than she felt. The detective's eyebrows raised slightly and she realised he suspected them both. Did they think she'd actually helped her husband murder another human being over some stupid book?

Noah continued to grizzle.

'He needs his bottle,' Rosie stated. Surely they would let her go into the kitchen for that. DI Harris nodded to the PC at the doorway.

'Would you like to come through to the kitchen?' he asked and she glared at him; he'd spoken as if this was his home not hers. Then, passing Noah to Mike she followed the officer into her kitchen which swarmed with police, like ants on syrup. They were in every cupboard and drawer and Rosie stood open-mouthed watching a female officer going through the contents of her fridge. What could she possibly hope to find in there to assist them in a murder inquiry?

'Could I get a bottle out for my son?' Rosie asked curtly, upset and annoyed at how her home was being taken over in this way. This was her safe space, her nest, and strangers were all over it.

'Yes, sorry.' The woman had the good grace to apologise as Rosie took the bottle from the fridge door and turned to switch on the kettle for water to warm it.

DS Russell stood beside the cutlery drawer she'd opened and to Rosie's horror took photographs of the contents.

'What are you doing?' Rosie snapped.

'This set of knives; there are five here, is that right?' The detective's gloved hands lifted out one of the knives and dropped it in a plastic evidence bag.

'No, there are six...' As she spoke the words Rosie realised she'd probably just incriminated herself yet she remained intent on telling the truth whatever happened. Looking into the drawer, sure enough a medium-sized knife was missing. 'There was six last time I used them although I can't be certain when that was.' The words stuttered from her mouth as DS Russell nodded curtly and bagged the rest of the set.

With the bottle in a jug of hot water Rosie returned to the lounge. Her whole body was trembling – where was the other knife? Surely it must be a coincidence that one was missing. Unable to tell Mike what was happening she tried to concentrate on the animated conversation between her husband and DI Harris.

'They were washed on Wednesday night – you can take them by all means although they won't help you because I didn't kill Stokes.' Mike turned to Rosie and explained. 'They want to take the clothes I was wearing last Wednesday for forensic examination and even my bloody work boots!' As the words left his lips Mike realised what he'd said – it was blood on his clothing the police were looking for.

'But I've washed them since then.' Rosie was shocked. This was surreal, the police were seriously considering them as murderers.

'What else are you going to take?' Mike asked.

'I'm afraid we'll need your mobile phones and laptops. And when we're finished here I'd like you to accompany us to your place of work to search there too.' At least the DI looked as if this was as unpleasant for him as it was for them.

Rosie pulled her dressing gown tighter around her middle and dropped her head to concentrate on feeding Noah, who guzzled greedily on the bottle, unaware of the nightmare his parents were experiencing.

DS Russell poked her head into the room, an excited expression on her face 'Boss, can you take a look at this?' The DI followed his sergeant, leaving the couple guarded by the PC at the door.

Rosie whispered to Mike, 'There's a knife missing from the drawer.'

'What! Which knife?'

'One of the set. There's only five in there – the sergeant's taken a photograph and bagged them to take away!'

'It must be somewhere else; you'll have put it in another drawer...' Mike faltered over his words.

What felt like an inordinate number of their possessions were being taken away; swallowed up inside plastic evidence bags to be examined forensically by strangers. It didn't take a degree in criminology to know it wasn't looking good for them.

The police remained at the Cantrells' home for over two

hours. Rosie tried to concentrate on her son, feeding and changing him but Noah was fractious, picking up on his mother's tension and the unusual activity in their home. Almost as soon as the police were out of the door, taking her husband with them, Rosie broke down in tears, fearing she couldn't take much more of this suspicion hanging over them.

CHAPTER TWENTY-SEVEN

With quiet restored to Hilltop Cottage, Noah finally slept while his mother pulled herself together resolving not to indulge in a pity party. The situation was what it was. Self-pity would be counterproductive.

Rosie inspected every room and grew increasingly saddened by what she saw. Although attempts had been made to replace things where they were found, the house was inevitably a mess. The police officers had searched every drawer and cupboard with contents hurriedly pushed back inside so the drawers wouldn't close properly in many cases.

In her bedroom, she shuddered as she discovered her underwear riffled through. Her favourite bra was discarded on the floor, a black lacy one she'd bought with Mike in mind, and her face warmed as she picked it up. The thought of strangers touching such personal items was loathsome, and tears again stung her eyes. Even in Noah's room his clothes had been disturbed – what could they possibly hope to find among his Babygros and nappies?

In a fit of temper Rosie gathered all her son's clothes

together with her and Mike's things and took them downstairs to wash. The day wasn't as hot as of late but a strong wind was blowing – she'd wash everything before putting it away again – unable to bear the thought of strangers having handled their clothing.

When the clothesline was full of the first load of washing the phone rang. It was Mike. The police had searched the market garden as thoroughly as they had Hilltop Cottage and taken away his work's computer. What they expected to find neither could imagine. They simply hoped their possessions were brought back soon so life could return to normal. Rosie was thankful they still had a landline at the cottage. They'd kept it on as the signal for mobiles was at times patchy and today validated their decision. She wouldn't like to be alone without a phone when the atmosphere was filled with suspicion and murder was in the air.

'What did Lisa say about the search?' Rosie asked, unsure if she really wanted to know.

'There wasn't much she could say. We arrived as she was opening up and it was a shock, naturally. DI Harris took her aside to ask a few questions but I haven't had the chance to talk to her yet; she's out with the deliveries. They took very little else other than the computer, only a couple of old jackets and a pair of wellingtons. I'm trying to be optimistic about this, love. At least when they find nothing among the items they took they'll leave us alone and look for the real killer.'

'I keep thinking about the knife, Mike. Where can it be? I've tidied around in the kitchen and can't find it anywhere.'

'Don't worry about it. They haven't said if they've found the knife which killed Stokes yet, have they?'

'Not to me although they don't share much.' Rosie sighed. He was right; worrying wasn't going to solve anything. Noah began to whine. 'I'll have to go now, Noah's awake. We'll talk later, okay?' She ended the call and ran upstairs.

As she lifted Noah and changed his nappy, Rosie wondered what the village residents would make of the morning's events. If it was too early for anyone to notice the police arriving at their home, someone would undoubtedly have seen the convoy as it left, and with Mike in the car too. Ginny Yarrow would feel justified now, her speculation fuelled by the search. Rosie could almost hear her high-pitched grating voice – *See, I told you there was no smoke without fire!*

Rosie settled Noah in a sling which she tied around her front, the close contact being exactly what they both needed, and carried him around the house while restoring order, then she took him outside in the fresh air to hang out more washing. Noah smiled and kicked his legs, enjoying the game. As she was thinking about making lunch, the telephone rang again. This time it was Bella, her voice as welcome as spring sunshine.

'Hi, sweetheart. Just wondered how things are going?'

Rosie's resolve to be strong was weakening at the sympathetic tone of her friend and she launched straight into an account of her troubles. 'Oh, Bella! The police have searched the house this morning and taken away all sorts of things!'

'What! Did they have a warrant?' Bella sounded indignant on her friend's behalf.

'Yes, we checked it over and it appeared legitimate but the whole experience was unsettling. I feel violated, Bella, and the house isn't the same, it feels dirty somehow.' Rosie sounded whiny, even to herself but Bella brought out the little girl in her and she needed to grumble, to be listened to.

'Rosie, my love, I think it's time you found yourself a solicitor.'

'We've talked about it, although surely when the police find nothing they'll leave us alone? We want to avoid the expense of a solicitor if we can.'

'Tell me what the police took, sweetheart.'

'Our mobiles and laptops, some of Mike's work clothes and boots, a couple of jackets – and a set of kitchen knives.'

'Hell, Rosie, this is serious! They're looking at one of you for murder; you must get a solicitor!' A short silence ensued as Rosie sighed at the impossible situation, then Bella spoke again. 'I know just the man – he's a regular in the Pantry – he loves my cherry pie so it'll be mates' rates, I'm sure. I'm going to ring him now – and I'm paying the bill.'

'No, Bella, we couldn't let you do that! Maybe we can take out another mortgage, or there's someone interested in investing in the garden...' She knew she sounded desperate, pathetic even.

'Don't argue with me. You know I always win. I refuse to stand by and see you suffer like this when I have the power and the means to do something about it. And anyway, what am I going to spend my money on at my age? I'll be blowed if I'm saving it all for care home fees!' Bella was typically insistent and although Rosie continued to protest, relief was already flooding her anxious mind.

'This solicitor's called Stuart Iveson – he's a teddy bear – yet on the ball with his job. I'm going to ring him straight away and give him your number so expect a call soon. Now, before I go, tell me how that lovely little boy of yours is.'

Rosie looked down at Noah, who was contentedly sucking his fist, his eyes gazing into her face. 'He's so lovely and such a good baby, Bella. He keeps us going through this nightmare. If it wasn't for him...' She was overcome with emotion which at least now wasn't all negative, there was a dollop of relief somewhere in the mix. Thanks to Bella they would be able to receive the professional help they so badly needed.

'Shh, don't upset yourself. Stuart's the best and he'll be in touch soon, I promise. Now I'll get off and give him a ring. Keep in touch, Rosie. I'm here for you anytime you need me.'

'I know, and I'm so grateful. Thank you doesn't cover it.' The call ended and for the first time that day Rosie could breathe easily. She would ring Mike to tell him the good news. Heaven knew they could do with some.

CHAPTER TWENTY-EIGHT

At six thirty on Saturday evening, Rosie threw open the door to welcome Bella Brookbanks and Stuart Iveson. The women hugged and the men shook hands after which Mike offered wine or beer and they settled down to talk. Stuart was about the same age as Bella, tall, medium build with thick silver-grey hair and a round pleasant face. He wore wire-rimmed glasses which gave the impression of an intellectual and his manner and bearing instilled immediate confidence into the younger couple. From his frequent glances and smiles in Bella's direction Rosie quickly surmised it wasn't only her cherry pie he liked – she would quiz her friend about their relationship later.

'Tell me exactly what the police took and what they said to you.' Stuart appeared keen to get down to business so Mike and Rosie related the harrowing experience of having their home searched and showed him the receipt the police gave them detailing the items taken.

Stuart listened intently and nodded. 'You do realise the police are suspecting one or both of you of murder?' His expression was serious yet his cornflower blue eyes held compassion. 'Their interest in the knife and your clothes are most concerning. Did you know there was a knife missing?'

'No, I use them all the time but never count them, why would I? It's a medium-sized one that's missing although I have no idea when I last saw it.' Rosie felt a complete fool.

'And do you know if the police have recovered a murder weapon?'

'They've not said as much to us but they don't, do they?' Mike said. 'They keep us in the dark. Will they have to tell you what they're doing now that you're our solicitor?'

'If they charge you with a crime then yes, full disclosure will come at some point but it's not unusual for them to hold things back until the last minute. Is there anything in particular you're worried about?'

'Everything, if I'm honest,' Mike answered. 'I can see how it looks from the police's point of view. We're Stokes's only connection to the area and the last people to have seen him alive. They seem to be concentrating all their efforts on us, but let's face it, our motive's very flimsy. Why would we kill him just because he threatened to write a book about Rosie?'

'I can assure you the police will be exploring other avenues too. They need hard evidence before even making an arrest these days. If they contact you again to ask further questions, which is a strong possibility, I want you to insist I'm with you before saying anything. It's your legal right and you both need to exercise it.' Stuart spoke firmly and Rosie found his voice and manner reassuring.

'So, you think we'll be getting another visit?' she asked.

'That depends on what they find. If they have the murder weapon and it turns out to be your missing knife it will be more than another visit, I'm afraid it will probably be an arrest.'

'If it is our knife we certainly didn't use it – do they think we'd be so stupid?' Mike chewed on a fingernail and Rosie thought he looked like a little boy in trouble.

'That will be the time to take your fingerprints and a DNA sample – probably from both of you. Look, I know this is all very scary but it's best to stick to the truth and allow the police to do their job. They'll find the real killer eventually.'

'And our lives are ruined in the process?' Mike snapped. Rosie gently touched his arm and he sighed. 'I'm sorry, Stuart. I know you're only trying to help and we're so grateful to you both but the strain is taking its toll. We're at the end of our tether. Rosie was snubbed in the village yesterday and there's been talk about us!'

'It was nothing, Mike, we can live with a bit of gossip and at least now we have Stuart fighting our corner.' Turning back to Stuart, Rosie continued. 'There is something I thought of which might be relevant. Last week I think someone was in the cottage when we were out – the window was open when I returned home and I'm sure I'd locked it. Perhaps someone broke in and stole the knife? It was last Saturday, the day they found Stokes's body...' Rosie paused and thought about her own words. 'But the only trouble with my little theory is that Stokes had been dead since Wednesday. Sorry, I'm just rambling here, trying to make sense of it all.' She shook her head as if trying to clear her mind.

'No, it's good to work these things through and I'd suggest you write down any other thoughts as they come to you, for clarification and also so we can discuss events and be clear in what we present to the police. In fact, keep a diary of everything which happens from now on.'

'Thank you. It makes such a difference having your help, and you too, Bella. Words aren't enough to express how I feel!' Rosie sniffed back her tears. Recent events had robbed her of all usual resilience and lack of sleep heightened her emotions.

'No thanks are needed, sweetheart; we're family!' Bella

gushed, her eyes sparkling. 'And I want you to ring me any time, day or night if you need help. I'm always willing to look after Noah, you know, or anything else. Call me, promise?'

Rosie nodded gratefully. As their visitors stood to leave Stuart gently placed his hand in the small of Bella's back, guiding her towards the car. For a moment Rosie forgot her own troubles and silently wished her friend happiness with this lovely man. Bella had been married once, in her early twenties but her husband had died in an accident at work a few months after their wedding. Rosie occasionally wondered if their tragic pasts gave her and Bella a connection, an instinctive understanding of each other which drew them together.

The Cantrells waved goodbye before spending the rest of the evening talking over what had transpired. They agreed Stuart was a good man, capable and understanding, and they were fortunate to have him representing them. And as for Bella, well she was amazing, a true godsend and a wonderful friend. By the time the couple retired to bed they'd exhausted every angle of their dilemma and with her mind so full, Rosie again doubted sleep would come.

CHAPTER TWENTY-NINE

Rosie tossed and turned in bed. The night was hot, the room airless even with the window open, and her head ached with the heavy atmosphere, a portend of a storm perhaps? Mike snored beside her, irritatingly oblivious to his wife's restlessness. At 1am she crept downstairs to make a milky drink and swallow a couple of paracetamols, returning after half an hour feeling barely any better. Her mind stubbornly refused to switch off; the events of recent days running through her head on a continuous loop.

As exhaustion finally overcame her, Rosie drifted into a dream, a nightmare. Frank Stokes stood before her, his hands outstretched as if begging for help, his lips moving without sound in a pale deathly mask. Suddenly his face altered in a bizarre melting fashion and the man transformed into Gary Drake, throwing back his head and laughing at her, stepping closer – too close.

His eyes penetrated Rosie's very soul, intent on doing her harm and she recoiled, nauseous in his presence. Behind his shoulder she caught a glimpse of Ali, and shocked, Rosie gasped for air. Poor sobbing Ali with her bruised face and broken limbs. Rosie wanted to run, to get away from Drake, to seize her sister and escape but her body refused to obey, obdurately immobile. She wanted to hold her twin, comfort her and wipe away her tears, yet reaching out to Ali was futile. The more she tried the more the distance between them increased and Rosie was powerless to help in her sister's time of need.

Gary stepped even closer, a leering expression daubed on his face. Suddenly he raised his arm. A knife glinted in the light – her missing kitchen knife! Rosie opened her mouth to scream yet no sound came; she was incapable of helping herself or Ali, at the mercy of Gary Drake...

Then at last she found her voice and heard her piercing scream.

'Rosie, wake up. It's okay, you're dreaming!' Mike was shaking her arm.

'There's a dead mouse in the bed!' She jumped up as if scalded and threw the covers back. 'And the knife – he has the knife!'

'Stop it, love, you're dreaming – there is no mouse, no knife, I promise!'

Gradual awareness of her surroundings brought clarity but not comfort. It was their room, their home, and the pale morning light was seeping through the curtains. Rosie flopped down onto the bed drenched in sweat, her breathing shallow and rapid.

'Hey, it's fine, you're okay now.' Mike gently rubbed her shoulders, trying to calm her down. 'You've been dreaming. Lie back down and go to sleep, it's still early.' He pulled her closer but she remained agitated, irrational thoughts tumbling through her brain, vivid images which seemed so real and refused to be shaken off.

'Mike, listen!' Rosie's voice was urgent, demanding when her husband clearly wanted to go back to sleep. 'I dreamed about Gary Drake – and I think maybe he's the one who killed Stokes!'

Mike switched on the lamp and peered at his wife. 'Honey, you're half asleep. Gary Drake's dead, you know he is. Lie down and try to get some rest before Noah wakes.'

'No, listen, please! What if he's not dead? What if it was someone else who died in prison and Gary's still alive? He beat Ali so badly I could hardly recognise her. Maybe he did the same to another prisoner and then stole his identity? He could have paid a guard to help him fix it, couldn't he? With my money! And now he's out and he's found me. Gary's been watching me I know he has, just as he did before Ali died. It all makes sense, Mike, don't you see?' Rosie's breathing was rapid, her eyes wide with terror. Her hands were working, the fingernails scratching at her palms.

'No, I don't see. I think you've had a nightmare and you're confused. Go to sleep. You'll feel better in the morning.'

Sleep was impossible. Rosie lay down and remained still until Mike's even breaths told her he was asleep. She left their bedroom and crept silently along the landing pausing by Noah's open bedroom door, overcome with a desire to check on her son. Inside his room she stood next to his cot listening to his breathing. It was steady, peaceful, his rosebud lips parted with a tiny damp patch blooming on the sheet. Reassured, Rosie resisted the urge to pick him up, to hold him close and feel the warmth and comfort of his tiny body. Instead, she went silently downstairs and after pacing restlessly around the rooms of their home to expend the nervous energy within her body, she sat in the lounge.

The hot dry spell of weather had finally broken and rain was lashing against the windows. In the stillness and half-light of early morning the rattling windowpanes sounded eerie and the pounding rain unnerving. Slate grey clouds seemed to fill the room as well as the sky – heavy and foreboding. Rosie imagined Gary Drake outside watching the cottage, laughing at the trouble he'd brought to her door, laughter which carried inside on the draughts whistling around her feet, mocking, almost clawing at her body. Shivering, she pulled her dressing gown tighter. Was it really such a stretch to believe Drake was still alive? The idea was terrifying, but also sadly plausible.

'Rosie, wake up.' Mike's voice was in her ear, his hand shaking her shoulder. She must have fallen asleep on the sofa and sunlight streamed through the window; the storm dispersed. Noah was in her husband's arms and she reached out to take him, the innocent smile on their baby's face melting her heart.

'You should have come back to bed.' Mike went towards the kitchen and she heard him fill the kettle to make coffee. Was he mad at her? She followed him and stood close.

'I'm sorry. I couldn't sleep. The dream was so vivid.'

Mike didn't look at her; his mood unreadable. Remembering the nightmare and the things she'd said about Gary Drake, it all seemed so foolish in the light of day. Mike warmed a bottle for Noah and made coffee for them both. While Rosie fed their son, he looked directly at her.

'I'm getting worried about you. You're becoming obsessed with Gary Drake when he's dead and there's nothing he can do to hurt you anymore. We've got enough to worry about without you fantasising that the man's haunting you or whatever. You've got to pull yourself together, Rosie, to be reasonable.'

'I've said I'm sorry. It was a bad dream that's all. Please, let's not argue about it.' She reached her free hand out to touch Mike's and his face softened, the furrows on his brow disappearing into his smile.

'Okay, and as it's Sunday and it's been raining there's no watering to do so I only need to go into work for a couple of hours. We'll try to have a normal family day when I'm back, shall we?'

'Sounds good to me.' Rosie returned his smile and determined not to think of Gary Drake, Frank Stokes or the police for the rest of the day.

CHAPTER THIRTY

Only partly successful in blocking out her troubles on Sunday, Rosie's all-consuming problems hovered in the dark dusty recesses of her mind, ready to jump to the fore as soon as her guard dropped. In the cold light of day she reluctantly accepted the likelihood of Drake still being alive was next to impossible and although she couldn't dismiss the notion entirely, Rosie decided not to mention such thoughts to Mike again.

Rosie and Mike turned their attention to Noah, willing him to stay awake and offer a focus other than the one they were consciously avoiding. The baby enjoyed their undivided attention and helped them maintain their resolve not to overthink their situation or dwell on negativity.

When Mike returned from work, they ate a cold lunch and then took Ben for a walk in the meadow. They stayed in their home for the rest of the day, enjoying being together and trying to pretend everything was normal.

Sheer exhaustion guaranteed sleep that night, a welcome dreamless sleep for Rosie who woke refreshed on hearing Mike climb out of bed and patter to the shower. It was Monday; she turned over in the warmth of their bed and in the early morning silence wondered what the day might hold.

Questions flooded her mind. How long would it take the police to process the items they'd removed during the search? Would they have worked over the weekend to do so, and when would they hear from them again? So many questions with so few answers but at least they now had the certainty of help from Stuart Iveson. She would never be able to thank Bella enough for her generosity yet suspected her friend would derive pleasure from being able to help, as would Rosie if their roles were reversed.

Climbing out of bed, Rosie went downstairs to make coffee and start breakfast before Noah woke. The house, tidy after the intrusion of Saturday's police search was beginning to feel like home again and she wondered how to fill her day, how to keep her mind as well as her body active and unwelcome thoughts at bay. The problem was resolved for her by the sound of a car climbing the path to their door. A flashback to Saturday's early morning visit prompted immediate panic as for an instant Rosie sat as if glued to the chair, anticipating flashing blue lights. None came.

The vehicle pulled quietly to a stop and as she plucked up the courage to go to the window, a gasp escaped her lips as she saw Jim and Mary, Mike's parents, exiting their car. Rosie ran to open the door calling Mike simultaneously, a huge smile on her face as her in-laws walked towards her, Mary's arms open wide. Rosie almost fell into them, tears in her eyes at the delight she felt at seeing this lovely lady. Ben, determined not to be left out, pushed his way in between the women, whining until Mary made a fuss of him too.

'Sorry to arrive unannounced. We didn't want to give you the chance to put us off coming!' Mary was half laughing, her voice betraying a nervousness. Did she really think they wouldn't be welcome? Jim, exaggeratedly stretching his legs, joined in the hug as Mike came through the front door his mouth open in surprise.

'What are you doing here? You must have driven all night.' He too hugged his parents before leading the way inside.

'Got it in one – we left at midnight – the roads are so much quieter through the night and we managed it in a little under five hours.' Jim was clearly proud of his driving skills, a typical lorry driver.

'You must be exhausted. Sit down, I was about to make coffee.' Rosie busied herself with drinks while Mike's parents flopped down at the kitchen table.

'Dad's tired but I've slept most of the way. Is that Noah I can hear?' A huge grin split Mary's face at the sound of her grandson's cries.

'I'll get him.' Mike ran upstairs to return a moment later with Noah snuggled into his chest.

'Oh, my word, haven't you grown!' Mary was out of her seat and stroking her grandson's cheek while Noah shyly clung to his daddy.

Rosie chuckled. 'He'll come round soon enough and you'll wish he hadn't!'

'Never, he's a sweetheart and so like his daddy was at that age.'

Jim chipped in. 'It's the hair.' They smiled. Noah's red hair was undoubtedly from Mike's side of the family. Rosie's father-in-law, short stocky with a perfectly round head, was losing his once-red hair and Mary, a tiny bird-like woman had also once been a redhead but was now a lighter honey blonde, with a bit of help from a good hairdresser. If it hadn't been for their colouring, Rosie would have found it hard to accept these two were Mike's parents. Her husband was tall and had filled out during their marriage, years of manual work adding muscles to his once-skinny frame.

'So why are you here?' Mike looked at his mother with affection and a twinkle in his eye. 'Were you missing me?'

'We want to help and it's a little difficult from three hundred miles away.'

'Thanks, Mum.' He bent to kiss her, then gave his father an awkward man-hug.

'Yes, thanks!' Rosie added. 'You'll never know how good it is to see you. But what about work? Hasn't school just re-opened, Mary?'

'It has but I've taken a week off. The head was very understanding and didn't pry and let's face it, they're not going to miss a dinner lady, are they? Jim's due some holiday too and we told them our family needed us, so here we are! I thought maybe you could do with some help with this little fellow, and Jim's itching to get stuck in at the market garden.'

Rosie let out an audible sigh, feeling such relief. Simply having these lovely people around would be support in itself. They were so willing – she hadn't known how much she needed their presence.

Mike's eyes were brimming with tears. 'Thank you, both of you. You don't know what this means to us. Yet you must be tired. Sleep first, eh?'

Mary made a dismissive motion with her hand. 'I'm fine though I dare say your dad will welcome getting his head down for a few hours?' Jim nodded and Mary offered to make up the spare bed while Rosie fed Noah.

'I'll have to get to work. Come down later, Dad, when you've had a sleep?' Mike grabbed some toast and a coffee his wife had put in his to-go mug, kissed her and Noah and dashed off, still beaming.

Within an hour Jim and Mary were settled in, Jim sound asleep in the spare bedroom and his wife delighting in bouncing her only grandson on her knee.

'Tell me about your family, Rosie,' Mary asked suddenly. 'I don't mean all those awful things which happened to your sister. Mike's probably told us as much as we need to know about that. I wondered what kind of people they were, what they were like? I'd like to know if it's not too painful to talk about them.'

Rosie, surprised by the request, sat down next to Mary and Noah and paused for a moment. Strangely, she welcomed Mary's questions, yet was so accustomed to purposely not thinking about her family she was unsure where to begin.

'Well, we lived in Stroud in a house which my father designed – he was an architect – quite a brilliant one who was in great demand. My mother stayed at home with us but had many interests and was always busy working voluntarily for some charity or other. We were blessed with a happy childhood and, as twins, Ali and I were very close. I've got some photographs somewhere if you'd like to see?' Rosie had almost forgotten about them; they were stored in an old box at the bottom of the wardrobe which she hadn't opened since they'd moved to the cottage.

'I'd love to see them if you don't mind?' Mary's face lit up and Rosie ran upstairs to find the box.

CHAPTER THIRTY-ONE

Rummaging in the back of the wardrobe prompted bittersweet emotions and a pang of something Rosie couldn't identify. Having kept very little by way of her family's belongings, everything she possessed was in this one large wooden box, a small trunk really, which she struggled to lift. Heaving it onto the bed, she gingerly lifted the lid to be greeted by the distinctive scent of many years' worth of memories.

Rosie sat down to compose herself as the items hidden away for so long, elicited childhood recollections of her parents, her grandmother and Alison. Staring into the box she lifted out a gold chain with a beautifully embossed locket, an item which contained their parents' photograph – a piece of jewellery Ali had worn every day.

Tears stung Rosie's eyes as she held it in her fingers. She remembered hiding it away after Ali died, finding it too painful to look at never mind wear it herself. Gently opening the locket, the grainy images smiled up at her bringing not the pain she anticipated but a warm swell of affection. Carefully Rosie unfastened the clasp and hung the gold chain around her neck.

It felt good, as if her parents were somehow with her as it nestled comfortingly on her chest.

The paw of a soft toy caught Rosie's eye next. Tugging it from its resting place provoked another rush of emotion on recognising Silky, Alison's favourite toy rabbit. There was a picture somewhere too, Rosie recalled, and rummaged deeper in the box to find it, drawing out a silver-framed image that took her breath away.

Her father had snapped the picture in their garden as their mother held the rabbit aloft and the five-year-old twins jumped up and down, trying to grab at it, like playful puppies. Dressed in identical yellow summer dresses, Rosie could almost feel the soft cotton fabric between her fingers – Granny had made those dresses and embroidered white daisies on the bodices – how Rosie loved that dress.

Five minutes passed before she suddenly remembered why she'd come upstairs. Grabbing a pile of photographs from inside the box, Rosie hurried back to the lounge to show her mother-in-law.

Sitting side by side the women studied the images. Rosie sniffed, pulling out a handful of older pictures. 'This is my parents on their wedding day.'

'What a handsome couple, and is this your grandmother?'

'Yes, Dad's mum. They were always very close and I can't remember Granny not being with us for every major event. Here's Ali and me as babies.' Again the images didn't bring the pain Rosie anticipated just the evocative memories of a happy childhood and a swell of pride filled her chest.

'Oh, how cute! Goodness you were so alike; how did your mother tell you apart?' Mary poured over the handful of baby photos and the later images of the two girls, dressed the same, identical in every way.

'Mum and Dad always knew, it was Granny who struggled.

We were very mean and played tricks on her. When she looked after us Granny always put ribbons in our hair to tell us apart, blue for me and red for Ali yet as soon as we could we'd swap them over to fool her! Poor Granny but she laughed and joined in the fun.'

'Wow, you certainly grew into beautiful girls!' Mary commented on the later images. 'And what a lovely home you had. Your father must have been very talented.'

'Thank you, he was and we adored him. I suppose we were lucky to have such a perfect childhood. We were sixteen when they died, and it seemed like the end of the world. Perhaps I should focus on being grateful for the years we did have them.'

'Tell me about Alison. I know what she looked like but was she like you in other ways?' Mary's questions didn't seem at all intrusive, nor, surprisingly, did they upset Rosie.

'Alison was beautiful inside and out. She was cleverer than me – I used to grumble that she'd been given all the brains and didn't need to study as hard as I did. She was kind and loving too. Ali wanted to do medical research to find cures for diseases, save the world you know, and she'd have been brilliant at it too.

'She always thought of other people, putting them first and looking for the good in everyone, overlooking any faults. I think that's what got her killed in the end – she was too trusting. Ali believed everyone was inherently good; it wouldn't occur to her that Gary Drake was using her to get at her money. She simply assumed he was genuine.' A silent tear trickled down Rosie's cheek. Mary put her hand on her daughter-in-law's arm.

'Thank you for showing these to me. You should cherish your memories, Rosie. In the end they are all any of us have left.' Mary patted Rosie's arm affectionately.

Rosie took her photographs back upstairs. Strangely, dragging out the usually taboo box of memories had soothed her. Over the last two weeks, since that dreadful letter from Frank

Stokes arrived, it felt as if the protective veneer she'd hidden behind – the skin of Rosie Cantrell – had been peeled back leaving her vulnerable and exposed.

Having spent so many years trying to block out those early memories and denying her past life, Rosie now wondered if she'd been wrong to do so. It was as if she'd dug a moat around her past to keep others and even herself from revisiting it. In doing so, had she been deprived of the comfort those memories could bring, assuming it was the only way to cope?

Suddenly horrified at the notion that her strategy had been wrong, guilt washed over her. The way she'd cut herself off from her past was so unfair, not only to her but to Mike and Noah. Her son had a right to know his heritage and learn what wonderful people his grandparents and aunt were. Hurrying downstairs to Mary again, Rosie felt the need to explain.

'Mary, I'm sorry for not telling you about my past before. You must think I'm terrible not to have trusted you or Mike. I thought it was the best way – the only way I could cope, yet now I'm not sure. Perhaps I was wrong?'

'Rosie, love, we all do what we think is best at the time. It was your way of coping and was what you needed then. We don't think any worse of you for not telling us but I'm grateful for seeing those pictures and hearing about your lovely family. Don't fret over pointless regrets. There's time enough for Mike to learn about your family and to teach Noah where he comes from.' Mary's gentle smile eased Rosie's mind. 'And now, I think this little man is getting tired. Shall I put him in his cot for you?'

'Yes, thank you. I'll prepare something for dinner, shall I?'

Rosie's heart swelled with love. Her own family may no longer be with her but Mary and Jim were here and more than willing to help. She hadn't realised they were precisely what she needed.

CHAPTER THIRTY-TWO

Waking on Tuesday morning, Rosie felt somewhat lighter than of late, and attributed the sensation to having Mike's parents staying with them. Mary in particular generated comfort and eased some of the fear which was Rosie's constant companion, yet in her heart she knew this nightmare was far from over. Each waking moment brought with it the anticipation and dread of another knock on the door – another twist to the narrative in which they were inexplicably caught up and Rosie jumped at the slightest sound.

They'd heard nothing from the police since the early Saturday morning visit; whether this was a good thing or bad it was impossible to say. Presumably examination of the items they'd removed would take time, yet until the police accepted that she and Mike had nothing to do with Stokes's death, Rosie's nerves were on edge.

Downstairs, Rosie found Mary pottering in the kitchen, making herself at home with the kettle singing and the smell of bacon under the grill.

'Hope you don't mind, love, but Jim likes a good breakfast and we had all this stuff in the fridge at home so I brought it with us. It needs using up.' She smiled at Rosie who impulsively hugged her mother-in-law.

'I think I could eat some of that myself and Mike's in the shower; it'll do him good to have a proper breakfast instead of eating on the run.' As if on cue Mike appeared with a sleepy Noah in his arms.

'Hmm, something smells good! Here, take your son while I let Ben out.' The little dog's ears pricked up and he ran to the kitchen door excited to explore the garden.

'Any sign of your dad?' Mary shouted after him.

'I think he's in the bathroom,' Mike called back over his shoulder. 'He's keen to spend a full day at the market garden after only a couple of hours yesterday, which is fine by me.'

'So what shall we do, Rosie?' Mary turned to her daughter-in-law. 'I thought a trip to Bedale might be nice. Perhaps we could go to Bella's Pantry for lunch, my treat. I'd like to see Bella again. Is that okay with you?'

'Yes, I'd enjoy it, thanks.' Anything to take her mind off things, Rosie thought.

After breakfast the men went off to work while the women cleared away before setting off for Bedale. Rosie considered ringing Bella to let her know they were coming, then decided against it; they would surprise her at work.

The morning was crisp, cooler than of late with a distinctly autumnal feel. Rosie filled her lungs with the fresh cool air, almost tasting the change and breathing in the scents of the meadow. It was a time of year she loved when the colours were changing on the trees, the hues of reds gold and orange brightened each day and the sun's warmth was still enough for long walks to pick the blackberries in abundance in the hedgerows. Perhaps she and Mary would go walking tomorrow with Noah; they could take a picnic and go down to the river, although well away from the spot where Stokes's body was found. Rosie even avoided looking in that direction from the cottage window.

During the drive Mary chattered to Noah who was entranced with his grandma and loving the attention. They sang nursery rhymes and Rosie relaxed into the kind of welcome normality she'd not experienced for days.

The journey was short and arriving early they had no trouble finding a parking spot. Noah, sleepy by then, snuggled down in his buggy, his eyelashes fluttering on his pink cheeks as he drifted into a contented sleep. A leisurely wander around the shops was in order. Mary loved the small independent traders in Bedale and couldn't resist looking in a babywear shop, intent on spoiling her grandson.

'There's nothing he needs, Mary.' Rosie smiled knowing her mother-in-law wouldn't be dissuaded.

'But he's growing so quickly. I'll just get something in the next size for him, something a bit warmer now the weather's turning cooler.' Mary picked out a pale blue woollen knitted suit which Rosie had to agree was perfect.

Over an hour later and with a clutch of carrier bags, the women made their way to Bella's Pantry anticipating the delight on Bella's face. As they turned the corner Rosie came to a sudden halt, shocked to see DI Theresa Lloyd and DS Peter Naismith coming out of the café. Tempted to turn and race off in the opposite direction, the police officers saw Rosie before she had the chance to do so and approached her.

'Hello, Mrs Cantrell.' DI Lloyd attempted a smile. The woman's eyes bored into Rosie's with unnerving intensity and Rosie found herself wondering if she practised her *fierce look* in front of the mirror each morning.

'Good morning.'

'We've just been talking to Mrs Brookbanks as part of our enquiries and your friend has been most helpful. Enjoy the rest of your day.' The detective turned abruptly to cross the road with Sergeant Naismith hurrying behind. Rosie was unsure if she'd wanted more from the woman – an update perhaps?

Mary caught hold of her arm. 'Was that...'

'Yes. The police from Merseyside. They're looking again into Ali's death. I suppose Mike told you?' Rosie felt the colour drain from her cheeks as Mary nodded, steering her into the café where the startled proprietor greeted them enthusiastically.

'What a lovely surprise!' Bella hugged them both. 'It seems I'm well blessed with visitors this morning.'

'Yes, we saw the police. What did they want?' Rosie was tense, her previously relaxed mood had vanished; it appeared she couldn't escape from the menacing events of recent days.

'Look, come upstairs where we can talk in private. Olive will bring us coffee, I'm sure.' Bella lifted a still-sleeping Noah from the buggy and led the way up to her flat. 'It's lovely to see you again, Mary. I didn't know you were coming.'

'It was a spur-of-the-moment decision. At times the distance between us is intolerable.' Mary sighed.

Their coffee arrived and once Olive returned downstairs Bella spoke more freely.

'Now, Rosie, the police being here is no big deal – I'd anticipated their visit, although they didn't have the courtesy to make an appointment. Stuart said they'd be looking into your life since you left Liverpool and as a large part of it was spent here with me I was half expecting them.' Bella gently rocked a sleeping Noah as she spoke.

'So what did they ask?' Once again the cloud of the investigation threatened to plunge Rosie into despair.

'Nothing I couldn't handle, sweetheart, don't you worry.

They were interested in what you spent your money on – did you buy designer clothes, go on extravagant holidays abroad – that kind of thing. Naturally I told them you'd never owned a pair of Christian Louboutins or Manolo Blahniks in your life. And as for holidays? Well, I needed to bully you into taking a day off when you worked for me and I told them you spent your free time in your little flat upstairs. All in all, I simply told the truth. Here have one of those cherry scones, Mary, they're delicious.'

'Oh, Bella, do you think they believed you?' Rosie frowned.

'Just to make sure they did, I took them upstairs to see the flat where you lived for nigh on five years. I've not touched it since you left and it most certainly doesn't look like the home of someone with money, which is why they were asking. I asked that DI woman if she would live there if she had pots of money stashed away and she couldn't bring herself to answer.' Bella was clearly indignant on Rosie's behalf; the police would have left with a flea in their ear for sure.

'Stuart warned me they'd be looking into your finances. They always follow the money apparently and will have been in touch with your bank too, to find out how much you have in savings and if you have any unusual expenses.' Bella continued. 'It's horrible for you, I know, but when they find nothing they'll leave you alone.'

Rosie wished she shared her friend's confidence. 'They certainly won't find anything. Do they really think we'd be living hand to mouth if I had access to my trust fund? They've seen the cottage – I love it though it's not exactly The Ritz, is it?' Turning to Mary she began to apologise. 'I'm sorry, Mary, this isn't the pleasant trip out we intended.'

'Don't apologise. At least you know now that Bella's put the police straight on a few points. I can't possibly see how they think you could have stolen your own money – it's a ridiculous notion!'

Rosie sighed. 'Try telling them. Common sense doesn't appear to come into play with police investigations; it's all about facts and evidence.' Their lovely day out was marred by meeting the detectives yet perhaps it wasn't all lost and she did want to ask Bella about a different, more cheerful, subject.

'Now you've mentioned Stuart, tell me about him. He seemed to be more than just a friend when you came to Thursdale on Saturday?' Rosie smiled as Bella actually blushed.

'Oh, don't be silly! He's just a good friend whose company I enjoy occasionally.'

'And exactly how occasionally is that?' She raised an eyebrow, not allowing Bella off the hook quite so easily.

'We've been out for a few meals together, and as you know, he's a regular customer. But I'm sure he doesn't think of me as anything other than a friend.'

'That's not the impression he gave from the way he looked at you. He seems fairly smitten. Tell me about him?'

'You always were a nosy one! How do you put up with her, Mary?' Bella was clearly enjoying the teasing and delighted to talk about Stuart. 'As you know, he's a solicitor and a very good one too. Stuart's a widower. His wife Angela died four years ago. I didn't know her and only met him at the beginning of the year when he started coming in for coffee. His practice is in Bedale, just off Market Street so it's quite handy for him.'

'Very handy!'

'Do you really think he likes me in that way – you know...' Bella sounded like a schoolgirl rather than the confident woman she was.

'I do, Bella, I most certainly do!'

CHAPTER THIRTY-THREE

Mike and Jim had always derived pleasure from spending time together working outdoors and today was no different. The weather was almost perfect, and they arrived home hungry and full of talk about the market garden and future plans, plans which Rosie thought somewhat premature considering their current circumstances. It was Jim who had instilled a love of gardening in Mike from when he kept a small allotment near their home and spent as much time there as his work commitments or his wife allowed. As a child, Mike accompanied him, trailing behind pulling up weeds and learning skills which would benefit him later in life.

Over their evening meal the adults shared the events of their day and Jim was shocked to hear that the Merseyside police were still investigating Rosie.

'Why would they think you stole your own trust fund? Surely you can't steal something that belongs to you?' His question was reasonable.

Rosie tried to explain. 'Technically half the money belonged to Alison. The police appear to be investigating the possibility that I stole the money by posing as her when the reality was that it was the other way around.' The memories inevitably brought sadness. 'Ali and I never fought over money but they can't seem to get past this being a motive, so apparently I'm now a suspect in my sister's death.'

Jim was clearly horrified. 'No! That's ridiculous! Oh, Rosie, how terrible for you!'

'I'm sure they'll realise their error soon – Bella certainly seems to have put them right on a few things. When they find there is no money, they'll look elsewhere.' Mary, forever the voice of reason, changed the subject and turning to Mike asked, 'So, what are your plans for tomorrow?'

'Dad's going to help me with some of the heavy digging. It's been great having him around. I can't wait for you both to retire and visit more often!'

Jim looked up from his plate. 'Cheeky sod! We're a long way off retirement yet but it's times like these that I wish we lived a bit closer.' Jim's concentration shifted back to the lasagne on his plate. A day in the fresh air had clearly given him an appetite.

Mary insisted on clearing up after dinner and shooed Mike and Rosie out for a walk with Ben. Noah was sound asleep so they took the opportunity of precious time together before returning for an early night.

The Cantrells' respite was short-lived as Wednesday morning commenced with another unwelcome intrusion into their home by the police, yet this time it wasn't for questions or searches.

Mary, first up again, was starting breakfast in the kitchen when her eye was drawn to the window where she saw three cars climbing slowly up the track to Hilltop Cottage. Staring wide-eyed Mary blinked to ensure she wasn't mistaken but as the first car drew closer, the reality was confirmed.

'Mike, Rosie, the police are here!' she shouted upstairs, her voice thick with panic. The two thundered downstairs followed by Jim, where they watched with an awful sense of déjà vu as several officers exited the cars. Rosie's breathing was rapid as she watched Mike open the door to allow them in, silently speculating as to what the police wanted this time. It seemed to take an age for Tom Harris to enter the cottage, his DS close behind him. He nodded grimly and stepped aside to allow Sergeant Russell to approach Rosie.

'Rosie Cantrell, I'm arresting you for the murder of Frank Stokes. You do not have to say anything. But it may harm your defence if you do not mention when questioned something which you later rely on in court. Anything you do say may be given in evidence.' A police constable took a pair of handcuffs from his belt and snapped them on Rosie's wrists. She gasped in disbelief, her legs suddenly weak, her voice lost.

This can't be happening; it's all a dreadful mistake!

DS Russell then turned to Mike who held his wife's arm, loudly protesting her innocence.

'Mike Cantrell, I'm arresting you for conspiracy to murder Frank Stokes ...' As she continued with the same caution, Mike pulled away, resisting the handcuffs.

'This is ludicrous. We had nothing to do with the man's death!' A second constable held Mike still while his colleague put on the cuffs. Mary and Jim were remonstrating too yet their words went unheard.

'My baby!' Rosie found her voice and sobbed as the sound of Noah's cries came from upstairs, woken by the commotion playing out below. *What will happen to Noah if I go to prison?*

'We have a social worker with us to take your child into care, Mrs Cantrell. He'll be well looked after.' The inspector's voice held a degree of concern, perhaps, Rosie thought, even a little regret.

A harassed-looking woman stepped forward and attempted a smile.

'No!' Rosie shouted, her eyes darting to Mary.

'There's no need to take him anywhere! We're his grandparents. We'll look after him.' Mary's words were brave yet a tremor shook her voice. The inspector looked to the social worker who nodded her assent. Harris turned to leave the cottage.

Mike was halfway out of the door looking back over his shoulder, his voice urgent. 'Dad, ring Stuart Iveson, his card's on the windowsill – tell him what's happened!'

Jim nodded and turned back to look for it.

Rosie felt somewhat removed from the whole situation, a strange out-of-body experience as if watching a TV film playing out with her as a character, the villain of the show. The officer leading her to the car put his hand on her head as she climbed inside. Numb with shock and fear, she turned to see Mike being bundled into the next vehicle.

He looked pale, shaken, and as their eyes briefly met, Rosie felt the weight of responsibility heavily on her shoulders. This whole fiasco was of her making – her fault. And now her family's future was in danger. They were being torn apart and Rosie was powerless to prevent it from happening.

Suddenly Mary and Jim were alone in the kitchen watching incredulously as the cars took away their son and his wife. Noah's cries jolted Mary from her trance and she ran upstairs to comfort him while Jim found Iveson's card and dialled the number.

CHAPTER THIRTY-FOUR

Stuart Iveson was more than a little surprised to receive a call from Jim Cantrell, not that an arrest wasn't imminent but he didn't expect it to be Rosie. On learning of Mike's neglect to tell the police about his second encounter with Stokes, together with his previous arrest for assault, Stuart assumed Mike would be their chief suspect, not his wife. His priority now was to discover what evidence the police had uncovered to switch their attention to Rosie.

The solicitor immediately sprang into action and rang his colleague, Ian Preston, asking him to attend the police station to represent Mike whilst he supported Rosie. The two men moved swiftly and arrived at Bedale's Wycar Street station a couple of minutes before their clients. Stuart was horrified to see the young couple brought in in handcuffs, both clearly dazed and Rosie unnaturally pale, her face tear-streaked.

Recognising DI Harris, Stuart stepped forward to announce that he represented Mrs Cantrell and his colleague, Mr Cantrell. Harris nodded at the solicitor who then asked if they could speak to their clients in confidence. The inspector had no problem with this and after Stuart briefly introduced Ian to Mike, they were shown into separate rooms and left to talk.

Rosie's anguish showed in her face as she turned to Stuart. 'Why can't I see Mike?'

'They won't risk you colluding, getting your stories straight as it were. Please don't worry about Mike. Ian Preston's an experienced solicitor, he'll guide him through the process.'

'Process is the right word. It feels like I'm on a conveyor belt, no longer in control.'

'Now listen, Rosie, we don't have much time and I need you to focus so you'll know what to expect in the coming hours. Tell me exactly what the police said before reading you your rights.' Stuart's voice was firm but kind and Rosie was so glad of his presence.

'They said they were arresting me for Frank Stokes's murder, then the sergeant read my rights and a constable put handcuffs on me.' She absently rubbed her wrists where the metal had grazed the skin. 'They were going to take Noah – there was a social worker with them. If Mike's parents hadn't been there, they'd have taken him away!' Her voice rose in panic. 'They won't take him off me, will they? Will they let me go home after they question me?' Rosie was anxious to be with her son even though she knew Mary would care for him well.

'It's highly unlikely that anyone will take Noah. If his grandparents are able to look after him social services will be satisfied, so please don't worry about your baby – and I'm hopeful of getting you released on bail. Now please listen carefully, Rosie. Concentrate on what I'm saying. The inspector will ask you questions and I want you to answer only, *no comment*. It won't be easy, the questions might shock you and you'll want to answer but until we know exactly what they have by way of evidence you must say only *no comment*. Ian will advise Mike to do the same. Do you understand?'

'But won't it be better to tell them what they want to know so I can get out of here quickly? I've nothing to hide, Stuart, you know that.' Tears welled in her eyes as she looked at him for help.

'Perhaps the time will come when we can answer their questions but not today. Trust me on this one, Rosie. It won't be pleasant and your natural instincts will be to speak up for yourself but don't; try to remain strong and silent. When they eventually give up asking, I'll be able to arrange bail, which will take time and you'll be kept in a holding cell until the formalities are complete. Again, you'll need to stay strong and we will get through this. I know from experience that DI Harris is a fair man. He wants the truth as much as we do.'

'Then why have they arrested me – and Mike – neither of us had anything to do with Stokes's death!'

'I know, yet they must have found something to point them in your direction and I intend to find out exactly what it is. So, remember, *no comment.*'

Rosie nodded. Stuart handed her a large white handkerchief and told her to keep it. She thanked him, sure she'd need it before the day was out.

A knock on the door signified their time was up. DS Russell entered the room and asked them to accompany her to the interview room, the same one the detectives from Merseyside had used to interview Rosie. Her heart was hammering as she took her seat, glad of Stuart's presence beside her fighting her corner. DS Russell switched on the tape recorder, stated the names of those present and commenced the questioning.

'Mrs Cantrell, you're here to answer questions regarding

your arrest for the murder of Frank Stokes. Do you understand this?'

Rosie hadn't noticed how pale the woman's eyes were before, an ice-blue, cold and unsympathetic. Her mind whirred; should she reply no comment to this question? She glanced at Stuart who smiled and nodded, so turning back to the sergeant she replied simply, 'Yes.'

Stuart interrupted. 'My client is at a disadvantage here and I would like to know what grounds you have to charge her? What evidence has led you to this erroneous conclusion that Mrs Cantrell committed this crime, of which I can categorically state she is innocent?'

The sergeant sighed. 'Of course, let's begin with the evidence shall we.' She pulled a large clear plastic bag from beside her chair and dropped it on the table in front of Rosie.

'Do you recognise this jacket, Mrs Cantrell?' *Those eyes, so cold.*

The answer was yes, although Rosie didn't say so – it was hers, the police must have taken it when they searched the cottage. Rosie averted her eyes from the jacket. 'No comment.'

'We removed this item from your house on Saturday 7 September 2019 during a lawful search of the property.' The sergeant paused. Rosie remained silent.

'A forensic examination of the jacket has found traces of blood which match Frank Stokes's. We believe this jacket to be yours, Mrs Cantrell, and that you were wearing it when you stabbed Mr Stokes. Am I correct?'

Rosie took a sharp intake of breath. 'No comment.' Her voice cracked, shocked by the bitter accusatory words. How could Stokes's blood have got on her jacket; she hadn't worn the thing for weeks. If Stuart was surprised he didn't show it and remained silent, allowing the detective to continue without interruption.

Emma Russell reached for another evidence bag and placed it on the table. 'Do you recognise this knife?'

'No comment.'

We both know it's my knife!

'We found this knife in the woods about a hundred yards from where Mr Stokes's body was discovered. Again, forensic examination revealed traces of his blood. The knife was partially buried in the undergrowth.' DS Russell opened a file next and lifted a photograph from the top of a pile of papers, swivelling it around to show Rosie.

'This is a photograph of the knives in your cutlery drawer, taken during the search. At the time you told me there were six knives when there were only five in the drawer. Is that correct, Mrs Cantrell?'

'No comment.' Rosie's mind was spinning and her head throbbed. Surely this wasn't happening; it was a nightmare!

'When we first spoke to you, you stated that the last time you saw Mr Stokes was between 11 and 11.30am on Wednesday 28 August, is that correct?'

'No comment.'

Emma Russell again dipped into her file and placed a photograph of Frank Stokes in front of Rosie. He was dead. Barely recognisable with grey skin sunken into his skull, his jaw slack in death. A small gasp escaped Rosie's lips as she turned away from the photograph, feeling suddenly nauseous at the sight of the image.

DI Harris leaned forward, rested his elbows on the table and steepled his fingers as he took over the questioning. 'Mrs Cantrell – Rosie. I understand your solicitor will have advised you to answer "no comment" which I'm afraid doesn't allow us get to the truth. How can we help you if you won't talk to us?' Harris removed the image of the dead Stokes, Harris's long thin face too close to hers – she could smell cigarettes on his breath. 'Did you kill Frank Stokes?'

His directness startled Rosie who missed a beat before replying. 'No comment.'

'Okay. Well, let me tell you what we think happened on the morning of 28 August.' The DI sat back in his chair as if settling down for the long haul as he continued, 'Frank Stokes arrived at your home, not entirely unexpected as he'd written to inform you of his coming. He put to you his proposition – a book, a feature, whatever you like to call it – and you argued with him. Perhaps you wanted a more significant cut of the proceeds or more input into the content, I don't know, but Stokes left without reaching a satisfactory conclusion. He told you where he was staying and that he would first go to the pub in Thursdale if you changed your mind. I think you then discussed the matter with your husband and for some reason decided that Mr Stokes needed to disappear – permanently.'

Rosie's eyes widened. Blood raced rapidly through her veins, throbbing in her ears, her whole being longed to shout out, to deny these lies, yet she remembered Stuart's caution as the detective continued.

'Then, Mike went to the pub to speak to him, possibly telling him you'd changed your mind and wanted to help his pet project, and he asked Stokes to meet you near the woods. Your husband then went to work, making sure he was seen leaving the journalist in the pub. But his employee wasn't at the market garden to give him the alibi he'd expected. You then went to meet Mr Stokes and eradicated your problem permanently, using the knife from your kitchen drawer. He wasn't a big man and certainly not a healthy one so it was easy to catch him unawares, he wasn't expecting an attack. Unfortunately for you, your jacket absorbed some of his blood and we found the knife during a fingertip search of the woods.'

Rosie listened to DI Harris's words with absolute horror. This couldn't be happening, but the blood pounding in her ears and the knot in her gut told her it was real. When Harris ceased his vile lies, she slowly shook her head and was about to speak, to deny his appalling theory.

Stuart, reading the signs, put his hand on her arm and spoke for her. 'Inspector Harris, we've listened to your story and that's all it is – pure fiction. My client did not kill Frank Stokes and I think it's now time to end this interview. Mrs Cantrell does not intend to answer any more questions and may I remind you that she has a young baby at home who needs his mother. I wish to apply for bail and ask for this be accelerated due to Mrs Cantrell's family responsibilities.' Stuart held the detective's gaze as he finished his speech and waited.

DI Harris drew in a deep breath, nodded politely and switched off the tape. Gathering his papers, he stood to leave. DS Russell remained, not quite finished. She informed Rosie that they needed to take her fingerprints and a DNA sample, and asked her to stay in the interview room until someone came to do so. The sergeant then left the room but a uniformed officer who'd been standing by the door throughout the interview remained with Stuart and Rosie.

It wasn't long before someone came to take a mouth swab, scan her fingertips and take a photograph, the whole experience making Rosie feel dirty and decidedly like a criminal. She was then led away to the holding cells, a reassuring smile from Stuart the only comfort to take with her.

CHAPTER THIRTY-FIVE

The cell stank of disinfectant which caught in Rosie's throat, almost making her retch. A stainless steel toilet and a basin were in one corner with a bench across the back wall covered only with a thin plastic mattress. Rosie had nothing with her except the handkerchief Stuart had given her; no phone, no bag, no coat and although the weather was warm, she shivered with fear.

The only window was too high up to see out of, making the small space feel claustrophobic. Sitting on the mattress, Rosie wrapped her arms around her body and finally allowed hot tears to flow freely. It must have been late morning; two, maybe three hours since the police took her from her home and Rosie had no idea how long it would be until she was allowed to return to her son. Wiping her eyes with Stuart's handkerchief, his promise to secure bail was the only strand of hope on which to cling, but would he be successful? If he wasn't, perhaps Mike might be granted bail and at least one of them would be home for Noah.

With nothing to do, no window to gaze through and only her thoughts for company Rosie soon found her mind drifting, speculating on her future, on her past and finding nothing to bring comfort or hope.

The image of Stokes's body flashed persistently into her head – his grey face, drained of colour and life – a man who was so recently alive and animated now still forever. How could the police possibly think she'd killed him – that she had the stomach to plunge a knife into another human being's flesh no matter how much she disliked him?

Rosie was suddenly weary with her head too heavy to support anymore. She lay down on the mattress staring at the ceiling, exhausted and yet full of nervous energy. Rolling onto her side in the foetal position she nibbled at her finger-ends, gnawing the skin until it became raw and bleeding. If only she could sleep, escape into oblivion, yet it was impossible. Her mind refused to slow down. Perhaps she should count the seconds, willing them to turn into minutes, the minutes to hours until finally she'd be allowed home to hold her son, to know she wasn't going insane, for surely being locked in this cell would drive her mad.

After an hour, perhaps more, the door opened and a woman constable entered carrying a mug and a plate with a sandwich. Rosie jumped up, hopeful, but the young officer pushed the plate towards her.

'Best try to eat something. These things can take time.' She placed the coffee on the edge of the sink and turned to leave, locking the door behind her. Was it lunchtime, Rosie wondered? She didn't think she could possibly eat although reason told her to try. She'd had no breakfast and being faint with hunger wouldn't help her mood. Was Mike still here? Was he also eating a stale sandwich and drinking weak coffee?

Mike's experience at the Bedale, Wycar Street police station mirrored that of his wife's. His interview followed on from Rosie's which gave him extra time with Ian Preston, valuable time which the solicitor used to fully acquaint himself with the events of the last couple of weeks. For Mike, recalling recent goings-on was painful yet simultaneously a release and he discovered Preston to be a good listener and quick to grasp the facts.

When DI Harris and DS Russell were finally ready to interview him, Mike was well briefed and knew to answer 'no comment' to all the questions however angry or frustrated they made him feel. The suggestion that Rosie had recruited his help to lure Stokes to the woods for her to kill was particularly hard to stomach – were the detectives deliberately trying to provoke him? But he replied as instructed, attempting to let them know how he felt by the glares he directed their way.

The whole idea was preposterous, ludicrous, and he longed to tell them precisely what he thought of their speculation, yet even though the two men had only just met, Mike trusted this solicitor and accepted Ian's advice to do things by the book. Mike was confident of his and his wife's innocence and mentally held on to that knowledge, trusting that truth would prevail. One day they would look back on this experience as history, a bump in the road of their life together.

Mike's primary concern was how Rosie was holding up. Knowing the tragedies of her past, he feared this would be too much for her to bear. He'd asked Ian Preston if there was a chance he'd be allowed to see her and was unsurprised by the negative answer.

Seven hours after the couple were arrested, they were released. Their solicitors worked hard to arrange bail and after a day Rosie and Mike thought would never end, Stuart finally drove them home.

As the car pulled up outside Hilltop Cottage, Mary opened the door, her arms open wide to embrace her son and daughter-in-law.

'Noah?' Rosie could say no more.

'He's in the lounge, love, don't worry. He's been fine today but he'll be happy to see you both.'

Rosie ran straight to him and lifted her son from his bouncing chair, holding him close and breathing in his distinctive baby scent. Noah gurgled and smiled, delighted to see his mother and blissfully unaware of the horrendous day she'd endured. She clung to his warm little body trying not to let him see her tears and Mike joined them, stroking Noah's face and smiling at his son.

Mary had followed her into the house. 'I was just going to bathe him,' she said.

'I'll do it!' Rosie whisked her son upstairs to run his bath and change him into his pyjamas, driven by a need to be alone with him, to lose herself in a world where only she and Noah existed.

Stuart followed the couple into the house where Mary offered coffee which he accepted gratefully. It had been a long day for him too. Still wearing his professional hat, he wanted to talk briefly to his clients before leaving them for the night and was happy to wait until Rosie joined them again, understanding the effects of their ordeal.

When Noah was asleep in his cot and Rosie returned downstairs, Stuart attempted to prepare them for what would happen in the next stage of the investigation.

'It's going to be a waiting game, I'm afraid. There does appear to be solid evidence for the CPS to proceed with the charges – namely the knife and your jacket, Rosie. Now they have your fingerprints there's little doubt they'll be on the knife too, which we can explain but they will view as more evidence. The police are still investigating and I'm hopeful they'll discover the truth of what really happened to Mr Stokes. As part of your bail conditions, I've given an undertaking that you'll not leave the area and I need to take your passports back to the police station. Perhaps I can have them now?'

Mike jumped up and went to the dresser to find them. It was a small price to pay to allow them their freedom until this whole debacle was cleared up. He handed the passports to Stuart and after further reassurances and instructions, the solicitor left. The occupants of Hilltop Cottage breathed a collective sigh of relief.

It was 8pm. Mary passed on a message from Bella who'd rung to offer any support she could, a message which received only the briefest of nods from Rosie. Jim was full of questions about their day but she couldn't face further interrogation and with a few brief words of thanks, excused herself and went up to bed.

'Rosie?' Mike was startled by his wife's apparent rudeness.

Mary put her hand on Mike's arm to stop him from following her upstairs. 'Leave her, son. She's all washed out after such a gruelling day.'

Mike's face crumpled as he spoke. 'She's hardly spoken since they let us go – even in the car she wouldn't accept any comfort and pulled away from me when I tried to hold her.'

'We all have our ways of coping and maybe this is Rosie's. Give her time. She'll come round when she's ready. Now what about you? Would it help to talk, or would you rather not?'

Mike's reply was to go over every detail of the interview, the words tumbling quickly from his mouth as if he needed to be rid of them, to spit them out. His parents listened silently and kept their concerns to themselves. None of them could remember a bleaker day.

CHAPTER THIRTY-SIX

Rosie was already up, showered and dressed when Mary came down the following morning, with a full coffee pot waiting for the others. Rosie's body stiffened as Mary reached out to hug her. The older woman stepped away and smiled. 'Good morning. Can I help with breakfast?'

'Yes please. If you don't mind making something for yourselves and Mike, I'll see to Noah.' Rosie's voice was small, uncertain and she almost ran from the kitchen and up the stairs to wake Noah.

When the men came downstairs they ate quickly, planning an early start to what would be a full day. After he'd finished eating, Mike went upstairs to find Rosie and returned in a matter of minutes, rolling his eyes at his mother.

'She's barely speaking to me, as if it's my fault.'

'No, she doesn't think that, I'm sure. Just give her time. I'll try to talk to her today.' Mary gave Jim a huge parcel of sandwiches, far more than they could eat and said goodbye to them as they left the cottage. She then cleared the dishes and tidied around with still no sign of Rosie although she could hear Noah upstairs.

Eventually Rosie did appear with a hungry Noah demanding his breakfast.

'Would you like me to feed him or shall I leave you to it?' Mary asked gently.

Rosie's eyes filled with tears. 'Don't be nice to me, Mary. I don't deserve it!' A fat tear rolled down her cheek. 'I've brought this upon you all – Frank Stokes came looking for me – it's all my fault and I'm so sorry!'

'No one's to blame here – it is what it is, but one day it will pass, I promise you. For now you have to stay strong for this little man and for Mike. Let me feed Noah while you eat something – if you won't look after yourself, at least let me care for you.'

Rosie allowed Mary to take Noah and feed him while she nibbled at some cold toast left on the table by the men. They sat around the kitchen table mostly in silence, speaking only to Noah, encouraging him to take pureed fruit from a spoon before he happily sucked on his bottle.

As if sensing his mistress's mood, Ben crept under the table and rested his chin on Rosie's knee, a little whine earning him a tickle on his ears.

When Noah finished his bottle Mary asked, 'Would you like me to take Noah out while you have a rest, or a soak in the bath, perhaps?'

'Thanks, I'd like that, but only for an hour or so? I don't think I'll be able to sleep, though maybe a long bath will help.'

'Of course. Is there anything you'd like me to pick up in the village?'

'No, the freezer's full – there's plenty of food to last a month.' She kissed Noah on his head and returned upstairs.

After hearing Mary leave the cottage, Rosie ran the bath and eased her aching limbs into the scented water. Sleep had eluded her again, her mind working overtime reliving the day at the police station, going over and over the questions they'd asked and trying to make sense of the evidence the police had gathered. During the interview and subsequent hours in the cell, Rosie was tense; her body wound tightly, unable to relax. Now her shoulders ached and her head throbbed. She knew Mary was right and she must take care of herself yet part of her wanted only to curl up in a ball and disappear.

It was as if the nightmare of Alison's death was returning and even worse if possible – this time, Rosie was accused of being a murderer. Would they also charge her with Alison's death – it seemed a strong possibility.

Still unable to relax even in the warmth of the bath, Rosie's mind travelled to some very dark places; revisiting Ali's awful last day, Gary Drake's despicable actions and now Frank Stokes's murder.

It would be so easy to slip beneath the water, to let its warmth engulf me and sink into oblivion, to escape from this nightmare and find release! Can I do it? Is it even possible, or would my lungs demand oxygen, physical need trumping the desire to die?

Rosie's thoughts were interrupted by the phone ringing, the landline downstairs. Her eyes shot open and she was immediately horrified at the shadowy thoughts she'd entertained. Jumping out of the bath she grabbed her robe and hurried downstairs, seizing the phone with wet hands.

'Hello?' She sniffed, wiping her face with the back of her hand.

'Hi, sweetheart! How are you holding up?' Bella's voice sounded like honey. So welcome, so timely – how timely her friend would never know.

'Oh, Bella, it's you!' Rosie could say little more, she was so overcome with emotion.

'Is it a bad time? You sound rather funny. I can call back later?'

'No, it's fine. Perfect timing except that I've just got out of the bath.' She almost laughed, her heart was pounding and it felt as if something was bubbling up inside her chest; was she verging on hysteria?

'Are you dressed?'

'No, but don't go. It's lovely to hear your voice. Have you spoken to Stuart?'

'Yes and he's so wired, determined to get to the bottom of this. He said it was quite an ordeal yesterday. Have you recovered?'

'I'm getting there, thanks. Stuart was great and I really appreciate how hard he's working for us. Perhaps I didn't thank him properly last night. I was a bit out of it. Will you pass on my gratitude?'

'Sure will. It's become personal for him now. Be assured he'll work his socks off for you. And how's that lovely little boy of yours and Mike too?'

'They're fine. Mary and Jim are still with us. I hate to think what would have happened if they hadn't been here when the police came. They had a social worker with them and were going to take him away!'

'I know and if ever anything like that happens again, which hopefully it won't, you must ring me. I'll drop everything and come. Don't ever feel you can't call on me – I'm working fewer hours in The Pantry these days, there are plenty of others to cover – promise me you'll ring if you need me?'

'I will, and thanks, you don't know how much that means to me.'

The women chatted for a while longer and ended the call when Mary arrived home with Noah.

'We've had a lovely walk. The weather's holding well for

September and I think it's done us both good. Now, did you enjoy your soak?'

'Lovely thanks,' Rosie lied. 'That was Bella on the phone checking up on me. I do feel much better now.' She kissed a sleeping Noah and went upstairs to dress.

It was time to get her act together – to pull herself together for the sake of her family. She'd survived trauma before and would do so again. This time she had even more to fight for.

CHAPTER THIRTY-SEVEN

Rosie thought the ringing was in her dreams, yet the noise persisted, pulling her out of sleep, bringing awareness of Mike jumping from the bed and dashing downstairs to answer the phone. She switched on the lamp and checked the clock – 4am. Who could be ringing at this hour?

Making her way downstairs, Rosie heard Jim go into the bathroom, disturbed no doubt by the phone. Fortunately, Noah hadn't woken. Mike sounded unusually animated, almost shouting as she caught the tail end of his words, 'I'm on my way!'

'What's happened?'

'The market garden's on fire, look!' He was already at the window tugging back the curtains. An orange glow was visible in the distance and they heard sirens disturbing the silence of the night.

'No!' But Rosie could see for herself as red and orange flames leapt into the darkness framing the rooftops of the houses.

'That was your friend, Chrissie. She heard glass shattering and looked out of her window to see the fire. She called the fire service who're just arriving by the sound of it. I've got to get down there! How the hell it caught fire I have no idea, there's nothing flammable to ignite except a couple of cans of petrol, but they're locked away in the shed!'

Jim appeared at their side and gasped as he saw the flames. 'What the hell...'

'It's the garden, Dad! The bloody place is on fire!'

'I'll come with you.' Jim turned and rushed back upstairs to dress, his face grey, a reflection of his son's. Mike followed, passing Mary on her way down, woken by the commotion.

'Rosie, what is it?' she asked.

'The market garden's on fire, look!'

Mary joined Rosie at the window to see the flames leaping into the air, illuminating the whole village. Her hand flew to her mouth. 'No! How did that happen?'

'I don't know. The call was from Chrissie at the bakery; she called the fire service first, then us. Oh, Mary, what's happening? It's as if everything's conspiring against us. What have we done to deserve this?' Rosie was shocked and upset. A fire was the last thing they needed and she couldn't begin to imagine how it had happened – Mike was always so careful and kept only a small amount of petrol for the van and the generator he used to heat the greenhouses. As the generator wasn't in use at this time of year his petrol stock would be minimal and he always locked it away in a brick outhouse.

Dressed in record time, the two men dashed out the door with a shouted goodbye. Rosie called after her husband to ring when he had news yet her words went unheard, lost in the sound of the slamming door. He'd surely ring anyway when he had the chance.

It was a waiting game for the women while father and son drove wildly through the village, well-lit with lights in most houses and faces at windows straining to see what was happening. Three fire appliances were in attendance, sirens stilled, their engines and crew working hard to get the blaze under control.

'Stand back, please, sir!' A firefighter blocked Mike's way as he hurried to get as close as possible.

'I own the bloody place!'

'Right, but it's not safe to come any further. Stand over there, please, and let us do our job. The station officer will want to speak to you in a minute.' The man moved away and spoke to a colleague who came over to question him.

The man was sweating already, his face glowing in the light from the fire. 'What chemicals are on site, sir?'

'None! It's an organic garden. The only flammables are a couple of cans of petrol which are locked in the shed over there.' Mike pointed to the outhouse where they could see the padlock still in place even from where they stood. The station officer nodded and went back to his crew.

Jim shouted to make himself heard. 'There's a strong smell of petrol from somewhere, son.'

Lisa appeared beside the two men, clearly shocked by the sight which greeted her. 'Mike! What's going on? I heard glass breaking – oh, no – the greenhouses! They're destroyed!'

Nearly every pane of glass had blown out with the heat and beyond them they could see a shrivelled mass which had been two of the polytunnels. Unable to get through the gates they couldn't see the other tunnels yet presumed they'd suffered the same fate. The wooden tool shed and the lean-to were both burned to the ground, presumably the flames Mike saw from home were from them.

Lisa almost shouted into Mike's ear. 'How the hell did it happen?'

'I don't know, they haven't had time to talk to me yet but it must be deliberate. There's nothing here to start such a huge fire.' As he verbalised the words, they hit Mike hard. An electrical fire would almost certainly be contained in the shed they used as an office and as he'd told the station officer, there was little else on the premises to start such a significant blaze. It was heartbreaking to stand by helplessly and watch his dream literally go up in smoke.

'Oh, Mike! I'm so sorry!' Lisa clung to his arm, tears glistening on her cheeks.

It wasn't long before a small group of onlookers gathered, a few approaching them with expressions of sympathy and the odd offer of help; most simply gawping at the spectacle, then leaving to chew over the event and speculate as to how it had occurred.

From what they could see, the fire appeared to stretch over the vegetable plots. With nothing more solid than the crops themselves it was a sure indication that an accelerant had started the blaze. The flames were quickly extinguished, however, the firefighters used foam to bring the fire under control and Mike grimaced thinking of the effects on the soil. Moving to one side, he took out his phone to call Rosie and hurriedly explained what was happening, promising to fill in the details when he went home. Words failed him but he knew his wife and mother would still be awake later.

Mike surveyed the devastation – his neat vegetable beds were no more, swirls of smoke rising from the scorched earth in their place, foam and muddy puddles replacing the colourful rows of produce of which he'd been so proud.

A police car drew up as the fire was under control and two uniformed officers jumped out, heading straight for the station officer. The three men had a brief discussion before coming to talk to Mike.

'Was it deliberate?' he asked, already knowing the answer.

The station officer answered. 'No doubt about it. Can't you smell the petrol? Someone's gone to a lot of trouble to destroy your garden. Any ideas who?' All three men looked at Mike for an answer.

'No! I honestly haven't a clue.'

The constable yawned. 'We'll discuss it later, at a more reasonable time. Until they decide the fire's no longer a danger there's nothing much we can do here. Can I take a name and address, sir, and we'll call on you in a few hours' time?' The police seemed in a hurry to get off. Mike recited his name and address and the officer gave him a sheet of paper with an incident number on it.

'We'll call at about ten, okay?' He didn't wait for an answer and left Mike standing with the station officer.

'We'll be some time yet, I'm afraid.' The man spoke kindly. 'As soon as it's light, the fire and arson investigators will be here to examine the scene. There's little doubt it was arson although they'll need to find the seat of the fire, examine the physical attributes and gather any evidence. There's nothing you can do, sir, so I suggest you go home and get some rest.'

A bewildered Mike nodded. A devastating fire was bad enough but to discover someone started it deliberately was something else, something sinister. Anger, sadness and disappointment crowded in on him as he allowed Jim to lead him back to the car.

Lisa walked with them. 'Try to get some rest. Ring me after the police have been to let me know what's going on, will you? And you know if there's anything I can do, just let me know.' Her face held sympathy and Mike nodded wearily before setting off through the village in the direction of home.

CHAPTER THIRTY-EIGHT

J im and Mike returned home at around 7am, faces smeared and the lingering smell of fire on their clothes. After showering there was little chance of sleep and the four sat around the kitchen table drinking coffee and discussing the morning's shocking events.

'Can anything be salvaged?' Rosie asked her husband.

'It seems unlikely. The fire crew wouldn't let me in to have a good look around and even this morning their investigators have to go through the wreckage before I'm allowed anywhere near. It looked pretty horrific and if the flames were anything to go by there'll not be much left. Whoever the bastard was who did this certainly made a thorough job of it!' Mike growled.

Even though the men had showered and changed, the smell of smoke filled the kitchen and would likely be worse in the village. There'd already been two calls, one from Chrissie asking if there was anything she could do and the other from Helen Parker at the village store.

Rosie took the calls and spoke only briefly; the villagers probably knew as much about the event as they did and she had no new titbits of information for Helen to pass on to her customers. It was kind of them to express concern although Rosie couldn't help wonder how far their neighbours' sympathy would extend once they knew of her recent arrest for murder.

Rosie's attention turned to Noah. He was the one bright spot in their current darkness with his happy smiles, waving fists and legs. His mother almost envied his oblivion to the whole situation and silently prayed their lives would return to normal before Noah was much older.

As promised, the same two police officers called at 10am. When she showed the men inside, Rosie recognised one of them, PC David Wilson, who'd visited their home when Frank Stokes went missing. This time he was accompanied by PC Andrew Kirk. The officers brought in the smell of smoke on their uniforms and she wondered how long it would be before the odour faded. The offer of coffee was accepted and the policemen joined the family around the kitchen table.

PC Wilson took out his notebook. 'We've revisited the scene of the fire and the arson investigators are there already. There's little doubt it's arson, with petrol used as the accelerant. The padlock on the main gate was jemmied – we've bagged it up for forensics but whoever it was probably didn't touch it or wore gloves. Can you tell us how much petrol you stored there, Mr Cantrell?'

'Very little. A couple of cans at this time of year which were locked away in the outhouse and I could see the padlock still in place so whoever did this must have brought their own petrol.'

The constable nodded thoughtfully. 'Usually we'd consider this sort of attack to be vandalism, kids messing about, you know? Yet this one appears more targeted, planned even, and on a greater scale than we'd expect.' He paused, his eyes moving from Mike to Rosie and back again. 'And I'm sure it's crossed your mind too. Can you think of anyone who would do this?'

'No! Absolutely not!' Mike spluttered. Rosie shook her head

too, appalled at the notion and at a loss to imagine how anyone could hate them enough to do such a vile thing.

PC Kirk chipped in. 'What about a competitor? Is there anyone whose toes you've stepped on in opening the market garden in this locality? Or a disgruntled past employee, perhaps? Someone you sacked who's out for revenge?' The questions were reasonable enough but certainly didn't apply.

'No again.' Mike ran his fingers through his hair. 'We only have one employee and she's very happy with us. The garden's been up and running for nearly four years now with no competitors in the surrounding area, and most of our customers are local. We've built up our clientele slowly and I'm sure we've not been treading on anyone's toes.'

'And what about your customers, any complaints from that quarter recently?'

'No. As I said they're mostly local and any complaints we do get I go out of my way to resolve. I hardly think someone would go to such lengths simply because they'd been dissatisfied with a delivery of fruit and veg.'

'Is your market garden insured, Mr Cantrell?' PC Wilson again.

'Yes, it is.'

The officer wrote in his notebook. 'And do you keep any petrol here at the house?' Perhaps it was unfortunate that the constable asked the questions consecutively but Mike, already tense from the morning's events, lost his temper.

'If you're suggesting I set fire to the place myself as some sort of insurance scam, I take exception to that!' Rosie took hold of his hand and squeezed it under the table, hoping to calm him down.

'That's not why I was asking, sir. We have to cover everything. I'm sure you understand.'

'My husband was here in bed with me when the fire

started,' Rosie explained. 'And his parents were here too.' Jim and Mary both nodded.

Is giving an alibi becoming a way of life?

'There is another possibility.' PC Wilson hesitated for a moment. 'I wondered if the attack could in some way be connected to your other, er, more recent troubles? Perhaps news of your arrest regarding the murder has upset someone in the village and this is their way of letting you know.'

'I hardly think some kind of vendetta's likely and we haven't told anyone in the village about the arrests; it's not the kind of thing you advertise,' Mike snapped.

Mary interrupted, a bloom of red flushing from her neck to her face. 'Actually, it was mentioned on the local news. They didn't name anyone but they did say the police had arrested a local couple in connection with Mr Stokes's murder.'

Mike banged his fist on the table. 'What?'

Rosie's eyes filled with tears. Everyone would know it was them, so could the police be right? Was this a way of letting them know that someone in the village didn't want the likes of them living in Thursdale?

'Why didn't you tell us, Mum?' Mike glowered at his mother who looked away and sniffed.

'I thought you had enough to contend with.'

'We'll be doing house-to-house enquiries to see if anyone heard or saw anything, and in the meantime, if you think of something, please ring.' PC Wilson paused and handed them a sheet of paper. 'You've got the incident number and this is a crime reference number – this is the one you'll need for your insurance company.'

The police officers stood to leave and Rosie showed them out of the cottage before returning to the little huddle around the kitchen table where Mike was finally calming down.

'When do you think we'll be able to go in and take stock?' Rosie asked.

'I don't know. I thought I'd drive down after lunch. Surely the investigators will be finished by then.'

'I'll come too, if you'll watch Noah for me, Mary?'

'My pleasure, anytime.'

Mike sighed. 'If the office is still standing I could get the order book and ask Lisa to email our customers, although most of them will know about the fire and not expect their deliveries.'

'But what do we tell them about the longer term?' Rosie thought concentrating on getting the business up and running might help her husband's mood.

'I'm not sure there'll be a longer term. The ground's contaminated. Petrol will have seeped into the groundwater and killed off all the worms and organic matter which feed the soil. And that bloody foam they used to put the fire out will have done even more damage – we'll be looking at six months at least for the ground to recover, and then there'll be new polytunnels and greenhouses to erect. It's a huge task, maybe too much to take on.'

'Won't the insurance cover it?' Jim asked.

'Yes, to a point, although the policy doesn't cover loss of income while we tackle the damage and we'll lose our customers who'll probably find other suppliers and not come back.' Mike rested his head in his hands. 'And then we have these other bloody problems – our future's not at all certain – why the hell should we even bother?'

CHAPTER THIRTY-NINE

Mary prepared a light lunch and insisted they eat, but just as Mike was about to sit down the arson investigator rang to say he was almost finished and if they wanted to meet him at the garden he'd go over his findings with him. Mike grabbed a sandwich and his car keys and with Rosie following on they hurried out of the door.

The sight which greeted them resembled a scene from a science fiction film, a scorched landscape with the stench of smoke and petrol filling their nostrils. The couple gawped in horror at what had been their thriving garden; the place they worked so hard to build up – their little Eden, their dream.

Only the previous day the two acres were abundant with crops, ready or close to harvest after such a perfect summer. Green lush vegetation had soothed the eye: carrots, savoy cabbage, onions, spinach and French beans adorned the land, a colourful display set out in neat rows and beds. A sight to be proud of. Now there was nothing, the soil ruined by fire, a war zone, parched, black, unfriendly. It reminded Rosie of a graveyard although she didn't know why as even they have grass and order – perhaps it was the starkness, the death of their crops.

The only place untouched by the flames was the brick shed cum office and the small orchard at the far end of the garden. Sadly a crop of apples couldn't feed Mike's family and he doubted they'd be fit to eat, contaminated by the smoke and no doubt covered in soot. The wooden tool shed and lean-to were charred beyond repair.

The arson investigator was ready to leave. 'Nothing complicated about this one.' He sounded almost pleased, then his expression changed as he saw their faces. 'I mean, the cause is straightforward enough – petrol. Whoever did this must have come in a vehicle. They've used gallons of the stuff and wouldn't have been able to carry it, a fact which makes it premeditated too, I'm afraid. I think they doused the wooden sheds and then soaked everywhere else. Someone's got it in for you big time – it was systematic and thorough. I'll get straight on with my report and get a copy to the police, and no doubt I'll be hearing from your insurers too. Bloody shame for you both – the bastards want locking up and the key throwing away!' With that expression of sympathy the man turned, striding quickly back to his car, another job complete.

Rosie stood alone by one of the greenhouses, reduced to shards of glass blown out by the heat of the flames while Mike was in the office collecting the order books to take to Lisa. Rosie recalled the day they found this site after months of searching. Many of the plots they'd considered were either too small, too large or beyond their budget. Two to four acres was their brief, with access to mains services and good transport links. They wanted somewhere within a community, a place to settle and call home, where they could raise a family.

Thursdale was a village they were familiar with and loved, so when these four acres came on the market, they knew they'd found their own field of dreams and stretched themselves financially to secure it. Being close to Bedale and Bella was a bonus. The Cantrells were on the first step to a self-sufficient future, working hard but doing what they loved. Even after over four years they'd still only cultivated two of those acres – the extra acreage offered potential to expand in the future. Now Rosie was unsure if they had one.

For some unknown reason her old university friend, Yetta, popped into her mind. The tall strong girl from Romania had been an inspiration to Rosie during those dark days after Ali's death and now she remembered a conversation they'd had during that time. Rosie commented how Yetta was a glass-half-full person, an attribute she admired during a period when her own glass always seemed half empty. Yetta, in her typical matter-of-fact manner replied. *If you came from where I come from, you'd simply be grateful to have a glass at all.* Her words wedged themselves in Rosie's mind and now, standing in this charred ruin which had been their vision, she wondered what her glass was. The answer was clear. She had Noah, Mike, Mary, Jim, Bella and Stuart. Mike joined her and looked quizzically at the faint smile on her face but said nothing as she took his hand and they went back to the car.

Lilac Cottage was only a few minutes away from the market garden. They would drop the order book off and then get off home. Lisa wasn't expecting them but her Mini Cooper was parked outside so she wouldn't be far away. Mike rang the bell and Lisa answered almost immediately, insisting he went inside and waving to Rosie to join them.

Rosie had only been into her friend's cottage on a handful of occasions, Lisa generally visited them. The inside was as lovely as the exterior; smaller than Hilltop, the rooms cosy with the same character and style and beautifully furnished. Lisa certainly had good taste. Everything was neat and tidy; books stacked in order of size, an impressive collection of CDs and some fantastic prints on the walls. A huge flat-screen television was somewhat incongruous, dominating the chimney breast wall of an otherwise characterful immaculate room. Still, Lisa didn't have a small child with associated paraphernalia to clutter up her space, or even, according to Mike, a mortgage.

The open-plan ground floor allowed the visitors to see through to a modern stylish kitchen, probably a bespoke design and Rosie wondered if it had come with the cottage when Lisa bought it, or if she'd added it later. Although Rosie admired her friend's home, she wouldn't swap her lifestyle for Lisa's. Hilltop may not be pristine or modern but the views were unrivalled. It was perfect for their needs and Rosie loved it.

'Sorry to drop this on you but you did offer to help,' Mike explained. 'There are email addresses for most customers. I'd do it myself except the police still have my laptop and phone. I feel pretty lost without them and only getting by using Dad's.'

'No problem. I meant what I said about helping, you know. I was just making coffee. Would you like some?' Lisa appeared keen for them to stay so they sat while she fetched mugs of fresh coffee and biscuits.

Naturally curious, she asked, 'What did the police say?'

'Apart from hinting that I might have done it myself as an insurance fraud, not a lot. There's little doubt it was arson and whoever the bastard is, he did a damn good job of wiping everything out.' Mike's voice was unsurprisingly bitter.

'Why would they think you did it yourself? What would you gain?'

'The insurance money, I suppose, although that's not going to cover the full cost of the damage or the lost revenue.'

'What's the garden like?' Lisa asked, screwing up her face in anticipation of bad news.

'Not good – no, strike that, it's bloody ruined! The culprit was thorough and succeeded in wiping out nearly five years of hard work. Only the office has survived, I suppose because it's away from the greenhouses and built of brick but it's little consolation. I'm sorry, Lisa. I don't know where this leaves you regarding your job. Obviously there's work to do in clearing up the mess, yet I don't know if continuing is a viable option. I'll be getting in touch with the insurers this afternoon but I doubt they'll work quickly and an assessor will probably need to visit the site before they can make any decisions.' Mike sighed.

Rosie listened to the conversation and thought of all the work this act of wantonness would entail for her husband, and at a time when they were both already drained.

'Surely they'll cover the cost of the damage and you'll be able to set up again? And there's always the two acres at the back which you haven't cultivated yet, and I'm happy to help with the clearing up.' Lisa sounded hopeful, almost enthusiastic.

'Even if we could plan to get the garden back on its feet we have other problems. Didn't you hear on the news? Rosie and I have been charged with the murder of that journalist.'

Lisa's eyes widened. 'No! How the hell can they think you had anything to do with it?'

'It seems they have evidence – but I really don't want to talk about it now,' Mike replied.

'Of course not, sorry. But surely they'll find out you didn't do it; you're not murderers!'

Rosie interrupted to clarify. 'Thanks for the vote of confidence but actually it's me they've charged with murder, and Mike as an accessory.' She watched as Lisa's eyes opened even wider.

'So,' Mike took up the conversation again, 'you can see why we can't make plans. I know this leaves you in a difficult situation and I'm sorry. We'll keep you informed of any developments and will quite understand if you want to look for another job.'

Lisa smiled. 'No way. I love working with you both. And my offer of a partnership still stands. The garden still has a future and I've every confidence you'll be found innocent. Let's see what the insurers say first and then we can discuss it when we know all the facts.'

'You'd really consider entering into a partnership with us after all this?' Mike asked.

'Yes! Nothing's changed for me – still keen as mustard. If you like, I'll get some papers drawn up by my solicitor – no commitment, just to have them ready for when you decide.'

'Oh wow, that's brilliant,' Mike enthused, but Rosie voiced her reservations.

'I'm still not sure it's the right time. Can we see what the insurers say and get back to you, Lisa?'

'Sure. As I say, no pressure, and if it helps to know you'll have financial help, then the offer stands. I think the garden has a great future – we can move into the back acres, clear the fire-damaged earth and leave it to recover.'

After finishing their coffee the couple left to go home with much on their minds.

Once in the car and away from Lilac Cottage, Mike turned to Rosie and snapped, 'You certainly put a damper on that, didn't you? Lisa wants to help and you sounded really ungrateful!'

'And I thought we were going to make all major decisions together. We can hardly talk about it openly when Lisa's there.'

'Honestly, Rosie. What is it with you? So much negative stuff is going on in our lives and when help's offered you sound all churlish, it's as if you don't want Lisa's help.'

'I simply think it's a decision we need to consider carefully, and together. We've got enough going on without entering into partnerships – you shouldn't encourage her, Mike, the timing's all wrong.'

Mike pressed his mouth into a tight line and Rosie knew he'd say no more on the subject for now. She hated these heated discussions and was convinced a partnership was premature, yet it appeared it would be an uphill struggle to persuade her husband to act with caution.

CHAPTER FORTY

A welcome aroma of homemade soup greeted Rosie and Mike as they entered their home and soon they were seated in the kitchen, grateful for Mary's thoughtfulness. While they ate, with Noah on his grandma's knee, chewing happily on a teething ring, Mike described the damage to his parents who were naturally horrified.

Rosie listened to her husband's commentary in silence. He seemed less angry than earlier when he'd talked of giving up, and she noted his altered mood as he mentioned working the two acres which had always been their 'future' project, almost parroting Lisa's words. While pleased his darker defeatist mood of earlier had lifted, Rosie hoped it wasn't a sign that he'd decided to accept the offer of a partnership. But there would be time to talk later; it was unlikely Lisa would come up with a contract in the next few weeks and anything could happen in that time, as they well knew.

It was perhaps prudent to keep silent on the matter rather than fight with Mike over something which may never come to fruition. Lisa's solicitor may also advise caution when he knew the circumstances of her plans and she may even change her mind. Everything seemed to be up in the air at present, predicting the next hour was impossible, let alone the next few weeks.

After they'd eaten and Noah went down for his nap, Mike took his dad's mobile phone upstairs to ring the insurance company while Rosie intended to ring Bella but first she rang DI Tom Harris.

The man sounded unexpectedly understanding when Rosie gave her name and she wondered if perhaps he'd heard the news of the fire which was one of the reasons she was ringing. He did, however, seem surprised to hear of the incident.

'I know it seems unlikely but it crossed my mind that it might somehow be connected to Mr Stokes's murder.' As Rosie spoke, she realised how improbable the idea sounded.

The inspector bounced the ball back in her court. 'How do you mean, Mrs Cantrell?'

'I'm not entirely sure – it's just – well I know you've decided I'm guilty yet I know I'm not and this is another extraordinary event in such a short space of time.' Was she rambling? Rosie was beginning to wish she'd never made the call.

'Tell me a bit more about this fire,' Harris asked. So she launched into the details, the time, the method and the extent of the damage; the sheer bloody thoroughness of it all – nothing like random vandalism. Rosie visualised the man on the other end of the phone, imagining him sighing, tapping his finger as he waited for this madwoman to finish her ramblings.

'I just wanted you to know – I think someone's out to get us, well, me anyway, and now they've targeted our livelihood as well.'

There was a moment's silence before the DI spoke again. 'Thank you for letting me know, Mrs Cantrell. I'll certainly look at the incident on the system and consider your comments. Was there another reason for your call, or are we finished?' His voice was even, the tone inscrutable.

Rosie felt somewhat foolish but there was another reason for her call. 'Yes, there is something else. Our laptops and phones, when can we have them back? With the fire, Mike needs access to his computer to liaise with the insurers and his clients. It isn't easy to manage everything that needs doing and we'd be grateful if you could return them.'

'Yes of course. I understand your difficulties. I'll chase up the technical team this afternoon to see if the process can be speeded up a bit. Is that all, Mrs Cantrell?' DI Harris sounded reasonable, agreeable even, taking Rosie by surprise. Perhaps there was something in being innocent until proven guilty after all.

'No that's all and thank you, Inspector. I'm grateful for your help.' The call ended and Rosie felt quite pleased with the outcome – unless of course, the man was simply humouring her, a thought she chose not to entertain.

Bella's voice was more than welcome as Rosie took the phone into the tiny porch at the back of the house and sat in the sunshine.

'Oh, sweetheart, how awful! Tell me all about it.' Bella sounded distressed to hear the latest in the catalogue of unwelcome events in her friend's life, and Rosie found herself pouring out the details again; the horrors of the fire, the shock, the smell which still lingered at the back of her throat. Her words tumbled out and Bella listened, making sympathetic noises. When she ran out of words, Bella took over.

'It's hard, I know, but you must stay strong. You've so much to fight for, especially that lovely little boy of yours.' Bella offered to come to Hilltop Cottage but Rosie declined. Mike's parents were with them until Sunday. Perhaps she'd need her friend's support later when they left.

'How's Mike holding up?' Bella asked and Rosie found herself sharing their conversation with Lisa and the offer Mike seemed so taken with, expressing her own reservations.

'Goodness, it's hardly the right time to be entering into any legal partnerships. I'd have to agree with you on that one. Maybe Mike simply needs something to hang on to, a lifebelt for a drowning man? He'll see sense soon, I'm sure, and before you make any decisions, you could always ask Stuart to cast his eye over any contracts?'

'Oh, Bella, we couldn't put on Stuart for anything else! You've both been more than generous towards us, you'll never know how much it means.'

'Ah, hush! We're family and if the boot was on the other foot...'

Rosie swallowed hard. 'I know and I love you for it. What would we do without you?'

'You'll never know because I intend to stick around for quite some time yet. Actually, I have a bit of news of my own.' Bella sounded rather coy and Rosie correctly guessed it had something to do with Stuart. 'Stuart's asked me to marry him!' Bella blurted out.

'Oh, wow, that's sudden!' Rosie had expected Bella to say they were going on a proper date – getting married was something else. 'And what have you said?'

'Nothing yet. I need time to think about this, as you say it's all very sudden. We've been friends for a while and we get on well together, but marriage is such a big commitment. Maybe I've been on my own for too long to change my ways now?'

'It's a big decision, Bella, and one only you can make, but you're assuming he'll expect you to change, and why should he? He must love you as you are. I know I do.'

'I'm dithering with this one when usually I know my own mind so well. And I don't want to keep him waiting too long, he deserves an answer. Anyway, you've got enough on your plate without me asking for your advice.'

'What, you're asking me for advice? Gosh, I'm not sure I'm qualified to give it – except maybe to say go with your heart. You and I both know life can be cruel, so grab any chance of happiness you can get. And if you want an opinion of Stuart, I think he's a lovely man and a very lucky one if you decide to say yes. I'm so happy for you, Bella!'

Rosie ended her call and searched for Mike who she found stomping about in the kitchen with Mary trying to calm him down.

Mike banged a mug down somewhat too hard with lukewarm coffee spilling over the table. 'The insurance company kept me on hold for twenty bloody minutes! Then they put me through to the wrong department and when I eventually spoke to someone they said it would be next Wednesday before they can come out to assess the damage. What are we supposed to do until then? Don't they understand this is our livelihood? I need to get moving and organise the clean-up operation.'

'They have their procedures, son, don't fret about it. Perhaps there's no one local to come and assess the claim?' Mary squeezed Mike's shoulder and he sighed.

'I'm sorry, Mum. It's just so frustrating when I want to get on.'

Noah's cries claimed their attention and Rosie ran upstairs to bring him down to join them, his innocent smiles captivating them all, reminding them that not everything was looking bleak.

CHAPTER FORTY-ONE

Rosie was finding Mike's mercurial moods challenging; one minute he was hopeful and planning for their future, the next sullen and withdrawn. Mary and Jim did their best to reason with their son who appeared to take more notice of them than his wife. Rosie thought he spent an excessive amount of time on the phone with Lisa, generally upstairs where he claimed the reception was better on his dad's mobile but Rosie felt excluded – why did he not use the landline? She bit her tongue, not wishing to argue with him yet convinced that Mike was rushing into decisions he may later regret. It was one thing to plan the cultivation of the two unused acres yet a step too far to discuss a partnership, the wisdom of which Rosie was still unsure about.

Late on Saturday morning, Mary suggested a walk into the village. 'It'll be good to get out for some fresh air and I'd like to see the garden for myself. We could call into the village store for some milk too.'

Rosie frowned, hesitant to venture out now that it was common knowledge they'd been arrested for Stokes's murder.

'You can't hide away forever if you want to go on living here. Come on, love, we'll leave the men to their own devices and Noah will enjoy the walk.'

The weather was cooler than of late and they wrapped Noah up warmly in his buggy. Mary offered to push him, making the most of every minute with her grandson before they left the following day for home.

They passed only a couple of villagers – an older man whose name Rosie didn't know who touched his hat in greeting while walking his dog and a middle-aged woman, Sarah Brown, who would usually stop to chat yet today crossed the road in an apparent hurry to get away.

'Oh dear! Do you think we're going to get the cold shoulder?' Rosie remarked to her mother-in-law.

'If they have a problem so be it. You've done nothing wrong and I'm sure the police will learn that soon enough. Hold your head up; this is your home as much as theirs.'

Rosie smiled at Mary's logic and support. She would miss this lovely caring lady when she left to go home.

When they arrived at the market garden, Mary gasped, horrified at the damage. When she'd last seen it, it had been a vibrant colourful space, neatly planted with fresh healthy-looking produce. Not expecting this much devastation Mary was visibly saddened. 'Oh, Rosie, love! All your hard work ruined – who could be so cruel, so unfeeling?'

Rosie didn't want to speculate. Her mind was constantly full of unanswered questions as it was. 'Let's not hang around, Mary; it's depressing. I need some eggs and milk at the village store and then we'll get back to see what the men are up to, shall we?'

Ginny Yarrow came into view, heading towards them as they turned to go, shopping bag in hand and a tight-lipped expression on her face. Rosie wondered if she would cross the street too, however, the woman approached them obviously with something on her mind and intent on speaking it.

'Is it true you've been charged with murder, Rosie Cantrell?'

Rosie answered politely. 'It is, Ginny. For once your information is correct.'

'Shame on you! We don't want the likes of you living around here – it's no wonder someone burned this place to the ground. Perhaps you should take the hint and leave the village.' The woman's face contorted into a scowl and Rosie fully expected her to fold her arms over her bosom with an emphatic nod.

'Do you know something about the fire, Mrs erm...' Mary asked.

'It's Mrs Yarrow and no, I don't know anything. It just seems a fitting happenstance, that's all I've got to say.'

'And do you know for a fact that Rosie killed that poor journalist?' Mary didn't bat an eyelid while Ginny Yarrow turned bright red. This was a woman who wasn't used to being challenged.

'She must have done if the police arrested her!'

'So you don't believe in the justice system either? In this country I'm fairly sure a person is still innocent until proven guilty – or do you think we should do away with courts and people like yourself should decide who is guilty? Tell me, Mrs Yarrow, do you still have a ducking stool in your backward little village?' Mary said her piece politely with only the hint of a smile, while Rosie covered her face with her hand to hide her amusement.

'Well, really. There's no need for sarcasm!' Ginny Yarrow marched away without another word.

'Oh, Mary! I didn't think you had it in you.' Rosie laughed.

'That bit about the ducking stool was a bit much – I have to live in this village, you know!'

'Then I'm sorry for you having to live with ignorant people like her. But don't worry, when this is all over she'll be the one to be embarrassed, not you – the crazy woman will have to eat her words. And talking of words, did she really say *happenstance*? I thought that went out with the dark ages and ducking stools.'

It was good that they could chuckle over the encounter and their walk back through the village and into Helen Parker's shop thankfully proved less eventful. Helen was her usual cheerful self and enquired after Rosie's health with genuine concern, expressing regret for the fire and repeating her offer of help. There was nothing much anyone could do although Rosie appreciated the sentiment and said as much.

By the time they returned to Hilltop Cottage, Noah was fast asleep and Rosie was looking forward to relating their meeting with Ginny Yarrow. Yet as they reached the door, a police car pulled up behind them and her heart sank.

What now? Am I to be whisked off again for further questioning?

However, it was good news. An unfamiliar police constable exited the vehicle and produced two laptops and mobile phones from the boot.

'With DI Harris's compliments.' He smiled. 'And his apologies for keeping them so long.'

'Thank you, that's great.' Rosie could say little more – this would cheer Mike up no end and Jim could have his phone back.

Mary insisted on cooking lunch and for a while the atmosphere was lighter than it had been since the fire, yet they were all too aware that Jim and Mary would be leaving the following morning and the parting would not be easy.

Sunday dawned, a cool, fresh morning and the Cantrells were up early making the most of their last couple of hours together. With breakfast over, Mike helped Jim pack the car and the time for goodbyes arrived.

Mary held Rosie tightly and whispered words of encouragement, urging her to stay strong for her little family. Expressing gratitude, Rosie clung to her mother-in-law wishing she could stay longer but knowing Mary had her own life to lead and a job she loved to which she must return. Mary then hugged her son and grandson while Jim held Rosie, his strong arms and meaningful look saying more than the words which failed him. Within minutes their car bounced down the track and they were out of sight.

It appeared as if someone flicked a switch in Mike and almost as soon as his parents left he retreated into his own little world, straight back upstairs and on the phone again at a time when Rosie would have appreciated his company. Her husband's preoccupation was solely with plans for the garden and now his laptop was returned to connect him to the information needed to further his objectives, there was no stopping him.

Rosie poured her attention on Noah, tickling his tummy to hear the delightful throaty chuckle she so loved. Mike's voice carried downstairs, his hushed tones making the words indistinguishable and Rosie sighed. If Frank Stokes's murder had brought unexpected problems into their lives, the fire seemed to have exacerbated them, driving a wedge between the couple, and Rosie didn't know how to bridge the gap.

It was an hour before Mike ambled back downstairs, with no explanation of who he'd been talking to, leaving Rosie to draw her own conclusions. Eventually she could stand it no more and assuming he'd been talking to Lisa, attempted to open a discussion.

'Mike, don't you think it's a little unfair on Lisa to encourage her plans for this partnership when we haven't yet decided to go ahead with it?' She attempted to keep her voice light but her husband turned on her, an angry look in his eyes.

'Lisa's our only option to keep the market garden running! Do you think we should simply give it all up when she's prepared to finance us?'

'No, that's not what I mean. Things are just so up in the air at the moment and we don't know what's going to happen in the future. I'm thinking of Lisa as much as us – it's wrong to give her false hope.'

'So what are you saying? Do you think one or both of us are going to prison – because I know I'm innocent, Rosie? How about you?' His accusing look annoyed her.

'Oh for goodness' sake, that's not what I'm saying! Of course I know we're both innocent, it just feels like the wrong time to be making such a huge commitment.'

'It's our only option for getting the garden up and running again, can't you see?'

'No, quite honestly I can't. I think we need to slow down and take stock. We've built the business up from scratch on our own before and we can do it again. The back two acres aren't going anywhere and the insurance money will give us a good start when we're ready. We don't need Lisa's money; it's too tying to take on another partner.' Her voice sounded more whiney than she intended.

Mike was seething. 'Do you know what I think? I think you're envious of Lisa! You don't want me working close to her because you're jealous!'

Rosie couldn't believe this was happening – they never argued like this and where had all this jealousy stuff come from?

'And should I be?' She heard her words with the barely veiled accusation and regretted them instantly.

Mike stood and walked out of the room leaving her question hanging in the air, unanswered, and unwelcome thoughts festering at the back of her mind.

CHAPTER FORTY-TWO

For the rest of the day Rosie saw a surprisingly different side to her husband. He purposely kept out of her way and refused to initiate conversation, speaking only when necessary. Inwardly debating whether to confront the issue and continue discussing this partnership, she decided against doing so. Maybe he needed time to consider her point of view now that he knew how unhappy she was with the situation, and in all honesty, further confrontation was the last thing either of them needed. Rosie left Mike to his brooding and busied herself with stripping the spare beds and sorting out washing.

Lunch proved to be a silent repast with Mike speaking only to his son, leaving Rosie saddened that they'd come to this. By bedtime, exhausted, she flopped into bed, immediately falling into a sound dreamless sleep.

On Monday morning Mike was again glued to his laptop before Rosie was out of bed – research, he explained – his mood only slightly improved from the previous day.

Rosie was beginning to think the week would drag until an early phone call from Bella cheered her up. Her friend's voice had rarely been so welcome. 'I thought you might like a visitor?'

'That would be wonderful and precisely what I need just now!'

Bella entered Hilltop Cottage within the hour, a huge smile on her face and a warm embrace for both of her friends.

'I'll take this upstairs and leave you girls to your chatter.' Mike made a swift exit with his laptop, and Rosie shook her head.

'Sorry about Mike, Bella. He's like a bear with a sore head at the moment and to be perfectly honest, things aren't great between us.'

'Put the kettle on and you can tell me all about it.'

Bella's presence was so welcome and more than a little opportune. Rosie needed to talk and there was no one better to listen than her sage friend. They took their tea into the porch at the back of the cottage and sat in the warmth of the sun looking out over the garden. Noah slept peacefully beside them in his Moses basket. Rosie described Mike's mood of the last few days, surprised to realise that it was only the fourth day since the fire. Bella listened without interruption until Rosie finished by relating the account of their argument about Lisa and Mike's accusations.

'And are you jealous, Rosie?' Bella wasn't one to mince her words.

'No, of course not! Perhaps resentful might be a more appropriate way to describe how I feel. It's as if he's consulting Lisa about the future of the garden – our future – and not me, as if I'm no longer a part of it. When Noah was born, I missed working there and the conversations with Mike about the day-to-day trivia, but now it seems he's replaced me with Lisa.' Rosie paused and considered her own words. 'Maybe it is jealousy in one respect although there's nothing romantically going on between them, or at least I hope there isn't!'

'He'd be a bloody fool if there was! Mike loves you – he

wouldn't be so stupid as to risk losing you. And you've both been under so much pressure lately, it's bound to come out in frayed tempers and arguments. Hang in there, sweetheart, you'll get through it and be all the stronger for it.'

'Bless you, Bella – and I've been so busy rabbiting on about my problems and I haven't even asked how you are, or more particularly if you've given Stuart an answer yet?'

'Well, that's one of the reasons for my visit today. I want you to be the first to know – I said yes!' Bella's face betrayed her happiness and Rosie jumped up to hug her friend.

'Oh, wow. That's wonderful news, I'm delighted for you both! You didn't take long to decide then?'

'No, I took your advice and decided to grab my chance of happiness before he changed his mind! Though it does seem a little silly getting engaged at my age.'

'Nonsense, age has nothing to do with it. So, when's the wedding?'

Bella's face was radiant. 'We've nothing to wait for – Stuart has a lovely bungalow in the village. You'll love it, Rosie, the garden's amazing. He's perfectly happy for me to continue working although I think the time's come to cut down on my hours. I'll enjoy turning the bungalow into our home and Olive's quite happy to manage the Pantry for me. She appreciates the responsibility and loves getting me out of the way, like today!'

'I can't tell you how pleased I am for you and for Stuart, he's a very lucky man!'

'Exactly what I keep telling him! It's all happened suddenly but we think a November wedding might be good and then we'll go away somewhere hot and sunny for our honeymoon. You will be my matron of honour, won't you?'

'Oh, Bella, I'd be delighted. With any luck this arrest issue will be sorted out by then so it'll be a real celebration.' Rosie was thrilled to think she'd be part of Bella's big day, yet as ever, at the back of her mind was the possibility that she might be convicted of murder before then. 'I'm reluctant to change the subject but has Stuart heard anything from the police?'

'No, sweetheart, he hasn't but when he does you'll be the first to know even before he tells me, and I do know he's been on to them several times, insisting they share any evidence they might have. And he also has a healthy respect for DI Harris – I think they've met socially on a few occasions and Stuart says the man's a good police officer and an honest man. You couldn't have anyone better looking into the case.'

Rosie nodded. Perhaps her view of DI Harris was coloured by his interview of her. It was undoubtedly a harrowing experience but did he really believe the account he put to her, or was he just doing his job?

Noah began to stir and became the focus of their attention. Bella bounced the baby on her knee enjoying holding his solid little body and hearing his laughter. 'You'll be such a big boy by November,' she told him. 'What will you wear for Auntie Bella's wedding?'

Before Bella left, Rosie called Mike down to tell him the good news. He dutifully congratulated her and asked all the right questions yet Rosie could tell he was itching to get back to his phone and laptop. She rolled her eyes towards the upstairs as she walked Bella out.

'Don't fret, sweetheart. He loves you but he's stressed and maybe all this frantic planning is his way of dealing with things. Some people bottle things up, others get angry, this could simply be Mike's coping strategy.'

Bella kissed her friend goodbye and drove away leaving Rosie with a heavy heart. Bella was a good friend; Mary and Jim had been brilliant too but what she longed for most was her husband's comfort which presently seemed far out of reach.

CHAPTER FORTY-THREE

Tuesday felt like a waiting game. Mike again kept his head buried in his laptop, claiming to be preparing for the insurance assessor but Rosie worried it was a ploy to avoid her. They hadn't discussed anything of importance since their argument on Sunday and the mood had seeped into Monday, transmuting into sullen silences.

Neither Rosie nor Mike wished to continue the dispute but it was there, hanging almost tangibly between them. Perhaps when the insurance assessor came the following day and they knew precisely what the pay-out would be they could address the issue of their future again. The situation couldn't be ignored indefinitely.

First thing on Wednesday morning Mike left for the market garden, claiming a need to check over some paperwork before the assessor arrived. Rosie sighed; Mike didn't say if Lisa was meeting with them and she didn't ask, fearing the answer. Contenting herself with feeding and bathing Noah, Rosie tried to steer her mind away from their troubles.

Within half an hour of Mike leaving, Rosie was surprised to hear Ben barking downstairs. Someone must be knocking at the door although she wasn't expecting visitors. Picking up a fresher-smelling Noah from his changing mat she carried him downstairs, jiggling him on her hip as they bounced along.

'Hush, Ben, come away!' Rosie pulled the excited dog from the door with her free hand and opened it to find Lisa standing on the step. Glancing over her shoulder she noticed that her friend's Mini wasn't there; Lisa must have walked up from the village.

'Hi there. This is a surprise, come in and I'll put the kettle on.' Rosie stepped back and Lisa followed her into the kitchen. She had her answer now; Lisa wasn't meeting with Mike and the insurance assessor and the relief brought a smile to Rosie's face.

'Shall I take him?' Lisa reached out her arms for Noah.

'Oh, thanks. He's been a bit grizzly this morning, I think he's missing having Mary and Jim around. He's been thoroughly spoiled with all the extra attention.' Rosie passed her son over to Lisa and went to make the tea. 'If you were hoping to see Mike he's meeting with the insurance assessor this morning at the market garden – he's only just left and will probably be a couple of hours. I'm surprised you didn't see him if you walked. There's nothing wrong with your car, is there?'

'No, the car's fine. I needed to walk for this particular visit and no, I didn't see Mike.'

Rosie was a little puzzled. Lisa seemed somewhat preoccupied, not her usual chirpy self. 'Tea all right, or would you prefer coffee?'

'Tea's fine.' Her reply was strangely flat, monotonous and Rosie got the impression her visitor was angry about something yet holding back. Lisa held Noah without the usual affection she showered upon him and the baby began to grizzle again. Rosie wasn't inclined to ask Lisa if anything was wrong, fearing it may have something to do with Mike and the partnership issue, a can of worms she didn't want to reopen. Instead, she placed a mug of tea in front of Lisa and lifted Noah from her.

'I hope Mike's happy with how things go this morning. He's been quite moody of late, keen to get on with things at the garden but frustrated that not everything's going his way. And this little man's tired again. He had me up twice in the night so I think he needs another nap.' Rosie laid him down in the Moses basket in the alcove, where he grizzled for a while longer, sucking furiously at his fist before eventually giving in to sleep and snoring gently.

'It's not surprising that Mike's down, is it?' Lisa almost spat the words out.

Rosie was shocked by her tone. It was most unlike her. 'What do you mean?'

'Look at all the trouble you've brought to his door, trouble he could do without. Is it any wonder he's depressed?'

'I didn't say he was depressed, just a bit off. And it's not of my doing – I didn't ask for any of this to happen.' An uncomfortable feeling was settling in the pit of Rosie's stomach – this wasn't like the Lisa she knew, the sunny disposition, the happy-go-lucky friendliness. 'Are you okay? You don't seem yourself today.' She'd never had an argument with Lisa about anything before. This was quite bizarre.

'I don't seem myself?' Lisa repeated in an unnatural high-pitched voice. 'But do you really know me, Rosie, or do you only think you do – like you know everything else. Perfect little Rosie, everyone's friend, loved by all with the answer to everything!' Lisa's voice was brittle; she was undoubtedly angry about something.

'Lisa! What's got into you? There's no reason to talk to me like that. Why have you come here? Have I done something to offend you because if so, can't we talk about it like adults?'

Her visitor remained silent, staring at Rosie who was feeling decidedly uncomfortable, wondering at the reason for such strange behaviour.

'Is this because I didn't want to enter into a partnership yet?' She was unsure what Mike and Lisa had been discussing in their frequent phone conversations. Perhaps she should have asked him, had it out with him.

'Oh, I've got a good enough reason for coming here today, a very particular purpose in fact, and it's nothing to do with the partnership, which I don't need you to agree on because it's going ahead without you!' There was a wild look in Lisa's eyes, a look which scared Rosie. And what the hell did she mean about going ahead without her? Had Mike been making promises without talking to her first? Rosie wanted this woman out of her house. Now.

'I think you should leave. Whatever you want to say can wait for another time when you're feeling more like yourself. And we'll discuss the partnership when Mike's with us, not now.' Even though Lisa was rude, Rosie was still prepared to give her the benefit of the doubt. It crossed her mind that the girl might have been experimenting with drugs – they can have a personality altering effect, can't they?

Lisa stood up and moved around the table closer to Rosie. 'I'm not going anywhere until I've done what I came to do.' Her eyes were wide and wild – there was something disturbing about her eyes, something almost familiar, yet Rosie couldn't put her finger on what it was.

Although she tried hard to sound confident and in control of what was happening in her home, a note of fear and a perceptible tremor crept into Rosie's voice as she asked, 'And what did you come here to do?'

'It wasn't simply to tell you what I think of you, although it's something of a relief not having to pretend to like you anymore, because my feelings for you are quite the opposite. I hate you,

Rosie, and always have.' Lisa spoke slowly, her voice menacing as she perched on the edge of the table, gaining a psychological advantage by being above Rosie, looking down on her.

Rosie instinctively scraped back her chair, wanting to put distance between them, fearing the girl was having some kind of mental breakdown. Noah stirred in his crib, a deep sigh and a shudder before he relaxed back into sleep. Rosie was suddenly afraid for her son, protective, although what Lisa could do to him or her she couldn't imagine. None of this made sense; what was happening here and why?

'Look, I really think you should leave.' Rosie tried to sound firm, authoritative. She attempted to stand but Lisa placed her hand on Rosie's shoulder in a vice-like grip and pushed her back down.

'I'm not leaving yet. There are things I need to do first – or rather – things *you're* going to do.'

Rosie struggled to stand, to push her away fearing she was crazy. But Lisa was determined. Her days working in the market garden had built muscle; she was younger, stronger and the fitter of the two.

In one sudden swift movement everything changed as Lisa pulled a knife from her belt, a long-bladed hunting knife of some description with a curved blade which looked terrifyingly sharp.

'What the hell are you doing?' Rosie cried out.

Is this it? Am I going to die here, with my son in the same room?

The grip on Rosie's shoulder relaxed momentarily, allowing her to jump from her seat in fear for her life. Lisa held the knife menacingly – twisting the blade so light from the early sun streaming through the window glinted on the long curved blade.

'You're going to do exactly what I say!'

'Don't do this, Lisa! You're not thinking straight. Put the

knife down, please!' Rosie tried to edge towards the door knowing escape was not an option even if she reached it. There was no way she could leave Noah at this woman's mercy.

'Aren't you listening? You should be asking me what it is you have to do.'

'Okay, fine... what do you want me to do?'

'Nothing much, Samantha. You simply have to write a letter – so why don't you sit back down and I'll dictate it for you.'

With the shift to using the name Samantha, it finally struck Rosie – those eyes – now she recognised them. Like melted chocolate – they were Gary Drake's eyes!

Rosie's body stiffened and her heart pounded as if it might burst. She trembled with fear, not only for her own life but for her baby son's.

CHAPTER FORTY-FOUR

Tom Harris sat in his cubbyhole of an office at Bedale police station and read the pathologist's report for the second time, his anger growing with every word he digested. The fury was directed not so much at the report but at himself for being manipulated, for not having the guts to go with his instinct and argue his point with the Chief Superintendent. He'd been weak and allowed himself to be swayed, yet this report blew the whole case out of the water.

The entire Frank Stokes investigation niggled at Harris from the very beginning. It was all too neat, too tidy, which in his experience meant something was wrong. The Cantrells weren't murderers; that much was apparent from the outset but he'd buckled under pressure applied from above and now he was infuriated. The evidence appeared to fit, so Harris, to his shame and although not convinced, had arrested the couple.

The detective's instinct cried out that it was far too soon in the investigation but the super was keen to look good, wrap things up quickly and make a press release to assure the good folk of North Yorkshire that there wasn't a murderer on the loose, and the police were in control. Murder in the village was rare and some idiot's joke about living in an episode of the fictitious *Midsomer Murders* television series annoyed the superintendent. But the arrest was all wrong. Harris wasn't given a chance to dig deep, he wasn't allowed enough time to explore the broader implications of the journalist's death, and now the force was embarrassed by what he could only describe as a monumental cock-up.

The DI initially wanted extra time to delve into Stokes's background; an investigative journalist made enemies on an almost daily basis with their probing questions, snide insinuations and accusations. A life of constant dirt digging meant that suspects for the man's murder were virtually lining up all over the country, on paper at least. Still, the super insisted they concentrate on the local connection, a decision for which Harris suspected the budget played a large part.

From the start of the investigation Tom Harris recognised the Cantrells' motive was weak. This book Stokes was putting together – it was pure fiction and he believed Rosie Cantrell when she denied having prior knowledge of what the journalist intended writing. Harris's counterpart in Merseyside, DI Lloyd, eventually sent over the dead man's notes which they were using as evidence to reopen the investigation into Alison Ashby's death. In all honesty, Harris couldn't see what they'd found to suspect anyone other than the girl's boyfriend. Drake had been a chancer, a habitual petty criminal known to the police since his youth, so why the sudden shift to suspect the twin sister? He couldn't comprehend their reasoning. Harris had a gut feeling that it was simply because Rosie was a person of interest in Stokes's death and by implication, a possible murderer. The Merseyside force appeared to be in the throes of a push to solve a growing list of open unsolved crimes and Rosie Cantrell was a soft target. His colleagues also showed unwarranted interest in the missing trust fund; a peg perhaps to hang their investigation on?

Harris again read Stokes's notes on an interview with Drake's mother, and concluded the woman was deranged, living in a fantasy world, and the journalist made a notation to take her account with a pinch or ten of salt. To Frank Stokes's mind, a story about beautiful evil twins may have been a good premise for a novel but if his account was to be based on fact, then Drake's mother had nothing of value to contribute.

And Tom Harris could understand why Rosie refused to participate in compiling the book – he would have felt the same and the girl had suffered enough. After the tragic loss of her parents, she then lost her sister and her trust fund in the cruellest of circumstances; was it any wonder she moved away to begin a new life? Having Stokes contact her again after so long must have been a shock yet not something any sane person would solve by murder, and the detective was convinced that Rosie Cantrell was sane.

Then there was the evidence. Harris thrived on evidence but he liked it to be irrefutable. If the motive was weak, the evidence was also lacking. Or it was until the search of Hilltop Cottage. Again this was a premature move, driven by the chief superintendent. Instead of going in heavy-handed, Harris would have chosen to go to Liverpool and liaise with his colleagues – to delve further into Stokes's life and work. Yet against his better judgement Harris had deferred to the super, arranged a warrant and initiated the search. How the super had crowed when they found the blood-stained jacket – he even agreed to fast track the forensics – to hell with the budget – his words, not Harris's.

But it was all too neat, too easy, and when Emma Russell had found a knife missing from the kitchen drawer the DS thought all her Christmases had come at once. It appeared even his sergeant was satisfied the Cantrells had conspired in Stokes's murder. Her mantra was that the obvious answer was usually the right one – Harris often wondered what they taught detectives at Henley these days.

Could she not see that no one in their right mind would use their own knife to commit murder and subsequently admit the set should be six, not five? And who would wear a jacket to stab someone, then casually hang it back up in the cupboard under the stairs? Everyone knew you threw knives into the river and burned every item of clothing you'd worn; people watched the TV these days, didn't they? What was it Emma said – it could all be a double bluff? She hypothesised that the Cantrells wanted them to find the knife and jacket because they would think the police wouldn't believe they'd be so stupid as to leave them in such obvious places. His sergeant's theories left him dizzy, her reasoning often became too complicated for him to understand.

Harris had believed Rosie's story from the beginning. And regarding the jacket, well, it was a heavy denim affair and the weather was scorching that day so he had no problem accepting that she'd not worn the jacket for weeks.

Perhaps Mike Cantrell hadn't been as circumspect as he could have been. Not telling them or his wife about his later meeting with Stokes wasn't the cleverest of moves, yet things were travelling at pace by then. Harris understood the omission. Having a previous conviction for assault didn't benefit his case but the man had proved himself since his younger days. Mike was a family man now, a responsible member of the community and a hard worker. Why would he risk everything he'd worked so hard to build up?

But by far, that day's pathologist's report was the most persuasive factor in convincing Harris they'd got it spectacularly wrong, leaving them up the creek without the proverbial paddle. As the cause of Stokes's death was undoubtedly the knife wounds to the chest, the chief superintendent refused to fast track the autopsy. If only he had. Stokes's body lay in a drawer in the mortuary in a queue for too long, and now Harris held the findings in his hand. He was an angry and frustrated man.

The knife wound punctured Stokes's left lung and nicked the left coronary artery, disrupting blood flow to the heart. There were two entry wounds, so apparently whoever killed him wanted to ensure he did not survive, but the startling sentence and the one which angered Harris above all, was the one describing the blade. The pathologist categorically stated that the blade was a *hunting knife, four centimetres wide, with a curved blade.* Harris didn't have to look at the files to know the knife they'd found near the scene of the crime, the knife missing from the Cantrells' kitchen drawer, was a short straight knife of no more than two centimetres wide.

This new evidence confirmed the couple's innocence and Harris's more recent train of thought that Frank Stokes's murder was not about the man himself. It was all about Rosie Cantrell. Someone was framing her – the blood on the knife and the jacket – and whoever was doing so was prepared to kill an innocent man to ensure Rosie suffered.

Harris remained convinced the answers he was seeking lay in Rosie's past connection to Frank Stokes. Running his fingers through his hair and sighing deeply, the DI tapped on his computer, settling down to go over every single piece of information they'd gathered over the last three weeks.

Two hours later Tom Harris reached his Eureka moment. Pulling out his phone he called his sergeant and told her to meet him in the car park ASAP. They were heading to Thursdale, and he only hoped it wasn't too late.

CHAPTER FORTY-FIVE

Rosie was terrified. How had she not seen it before. Those eyes – this was – Lisa must be – Gary Drake's sister! Rosie could barely think straight. This woman was crazy, waving a knife and talking about writing a letter! How could she get herself and Noah out of there safely? It was her own stupid fault that Lisa was between her and her son; how could she have let it happen?

Noah slept on, blissfully unaware of the danger around him which was exactly how his mother wanted to keep it. Could she get the knife – dare she even try? Rosie mumbled a silent prayer to the god she'd neglected since her childhood, begging for help, for divine wisdom.

Perhaps the best chance was talking her way out of the situation although Lisa seemed beyond rational. Would she listen to reason?

'Lisa, this isn't going to end well for either of us. Will you put the knife down and we'll talk about it? Whatever the problem is we can sort it out without violence.' Rosie tried to keep her voice even yet not patronising, and moved to sit back at the table to show her aggressor she was willing to talk.

To Rosie's surprise, Lisa threw back her head and laughed. 'You really don't get it do you, Samantha? This can't be resolved with a cup of tea and a chat. It's too bloody late – he's dead and you killed him and now you're going to pay for it!'

'But I didn't kill him. The police have got it wrong.' Rosie was confused. When Lisa pulled the knife she'd thought that for whatever reason it must have been her who killed Frank Stokes – yet now Lisa was accusing Rosie.

'I'm not talking about the journalist! He's irrelevant! Think, Samantha! Go back ten years; surely you haven't forgotten?'

She could never forget and suddenly it all began to click into place – Lisa thought Rosie had killed her brother!

Rosie looked away, frantically thinking of something to say to appease this troubled woman. 'Look, I didn't kill your brother. He went to prison, he died there.' Rosie stammered the words but it was the wrong thing to say.

Lisa was suddenly beside her with the knife at her throat. 'And you put him in that stinking prison! You and your precious sister – you led him on, let him think you cared for him and then tried to make a fool of him!'

Rosie didn't know where Lisa's version of events was coming from and silently reasoned that arguing the point might go against her, so, trembling and in fear for her life she asked, 'What is it you want from me?' Her whole body was shaking. The only certainty of this bizarre situation was that it was not going to end well.

'That's better.' Lisa laughed, a witch's cackle. 'I want everything, *Samantha*! Let's get down to business, shall we?' From her pocket she took out a small brown bottle and shook it. The rattle told Rosie there were pills inside. 'You're finished, all washed up and at the end of your tether. Poor you! So much pressure – you couldn't face living anymore. No one will be surprised that you've decided to take your own life. It's understandable. The weight of guilt you're carrying for murdering that poor journalist; the shame you've brought upon Mike and Noah. Yes, it's all perfectly reasonable.' Lisa smirked as the colour drained from Rosie's face; the utter horror of her situation dawning on her.

'Don't worry, it'll be quite painless, I promise! Although Gary's death wasn't painless. They beat him to a pulp, did you know? His beautiful face swollen, ripped apart by those animals. So actually I'm doing you a favour here, letting you slip away painlessly. You don't deserve my kindness.'

'I won't do it!' Rosie couldn't capitulate; if she was to die she'd at least go down fighting. Lisa's eyes shone and she laughed as if relishing the whole scenario. Moving swiftly towards Noah's crib she reached him in seconds, pressing the knife against his soft pink cheek. The child slept on with only a whimper, as if dreaming.

'Please, don't hurt him!' The desperate plea of a mother who would risk her own life but not her child's.

'It's in your hands. It's you – or Noah.' Lisa's face was glowing. She was actually enjoying the drama of the situation, on some kind of an adrenaline high.

Hot tears streamed down Rosie's face. 'Okay, I'll do whatever you say! What do you want me to do?' There was no choice, no way she could risk her son's life. Any mother would die for her child and it appeared this is what she must do. It was her only option.

'Good, I knew you'd see sense in the end. Now, find some paper and a pen, and to make it easy for you I'll even tell you what to write.'

Rosie moved slowly to the dresser and with trembling hands took out a writing pad. Glancing at the clock she was dismayed to see it was only an hour since Mike had left for his meeting. He wouldn't be back anytime soon and no one else was likely to call on her on a Wednesday morning. If it weren't for Noah she'd fight; even if she died in the struggle it would be better than letting Lisa win. But the young woman was astute, cunning, and knew Noah was her weak spot, her Achilles heel. Yes, Rosie would kill herself rather than allow her son to be harmed and it appeared this was what she must do. Returning to the table she almost fell into the seat, feeling physically sick, she thought she might vomit.

Lisa's eyes were wild, excited. She kept the knife pressed to Noah's face. 'Well done. I knew you'd be reasonable. This will be the last letter you write, Samantha, so we'll make it a good one, shall we? It's a confession to murder – and also your suicide note for poor Mike. Can you imagine how he's going to feel when he learns you were capable of murder, that you killed the journalist and allowed suspicion to fall on him? Your husband will need someone to comfort him in his distress – but don't worry, Samantha, I won't let you down. I'll look after him for you! Mike will turn to me for solace and with you out of the way, he'll be all mine.'

Lisa's expression was pure evil, her face flushed, excited. 'And this poor motherless babe? No worries there either. I'll be a good stepmother, don't you think? When he's old enough to understand I'll tell him the truth. I'll make certain he knows his mother was a wicked murderer! *Now write!*'

Lisa had clearly put much thought into this 'confession' and the words tumbled from her mouth almost too quickly for Rosie to write them down. A sinking feeling overwhelmed her at the hopelessness of her situation. While Lisa stood with the knife still pressed on Noah's face there was nothing Rosie could do; any move might cause this madwoman to kill her baby son, her beautiful innocent child!

The letter expressed Rosie's regrets, especially at implicating her husband who was entirely innocent of any crime. Lisa had thought of everything, exonerating Mike to free him up for her to make a move on. By the time the words were written, Rosie's tears were dripping onto the paper. Surely her life was not going to end in this way at the hand of such an evil woman.

Please, God, I'm begging you to help me!

'Aw, what a lovely touch, a tear-stained confession. Maybe it will help everyone to think more kindly of you when they learn you're a murderer!' Lisa was well into her stride, undoubtedly enjoying the pain and anguish she was causing. 'And now the tablets, Samantha. The whole bottle! You'll slip into a nice peaceful sleep and I'll not have to look at your smug face again!'

Perhaps Rosie could keep her talking, put off the final moment? 'Why do you hate me so much, Lisa?

'You know why. It's your fault Gary's dead. He was my big brother, my hero when I was growing up and you took him away from me! It seems only fitting that I'm taking everything which belongs to you; Mike, Noah, the market garden. Now get on with it!' With her free hand Lisa slid the bottle across the table.

Rosie picked it up slowly and looked at it. It had her name printed on the label; an old prescription the doctor gave her when she couldn't sleep after Noah was born. Lisa had thought of everything.

If Rosie wanted to save her son there was no way to escape her own death.

CHAPTER FORTY-SIX

Emma Russell yawned; she'd had a late night. 'So, what makes you think this Lisa Edwards is involved with Stokes's murder?'

Harris wondered why his colleague chose to go out drinking midweek, she should know better. 'I'm not a hundred per cent sure but I think Lisa could be Gary Drake's sister.'

'That's a bit of a stretch isn't it, boss? I mean, we've already arrested the Cantrells and the evidence against them is pretty conclusive.'

'Read the file,' Harris barked. 'The evidence is screwed up – the knife we found was planted – the pathologist's report proves that it couldn't possibly have been the murder weapon!' Why, he wondered, did his sergeant always want to travel the easy road, laziness maybe? He kept his anger in check and remained silent while she read the document.

'Okay, but this still doesn't explain why you think Lisa Edwards is involved even if she is Drake's sister?'

'If I'm right she's wreaking revenge on Rosie, whom she blames for her brother's death. It's a bit of a hunch, I know, yet having been back through every interview, every conversation, I'm convinced we've been looking at this case from the wrong angle. Yes, finding a motive is essential but in this case there was no real motive to kill Stokes. True, the man made plenty of enemies in years gone by but he was on the way out, no longer a serious threat to anyone. And this book of his wasn't a real motive. I think he was a pawn, a tool to get at Rosie Cantrell; she's the real victim here. Start at the very first interview with the Cantrells – look, it's all in the file!'

Harris wanted his sergeant to pay attention, to see what they'd missed in their hurry to get a conviction. 'The two PCs who visited them when Stokes was first reported missing – Mike Cantrell told them Stokes claimed to have another appointment in the area – can you see?'

'Yes, but there are no details of who it was with.'

'Exactly! It was a lead we should have followed up, and I'm ashamed to say we didn't. How likely was it that Stokes was meeting with someone in this area who was entirely unconnected to his current project, his precious book about Rosie? Could his meeting have been with Lisa? Could she have made contact with him, or him with her? Now turn to Stokes's own notes on this proposed book. He records a meeting with Drake's mother, a woman he wasn't particularly impressed with. I checked out the Drake family and found out there was a younger sister so I'm sure Stokes did too, and he'd want to interview her for sure.'

'Is that all?' Emma sounded unconvinced. 'It's not much to go on, is it, boss?'

'But for Stokes to be seeing someone else in the area, and if that someone was connected to the book, it could have been Drake's sister. Maybe Lisa too had discovered Rosie's new identity and had her own plans for revenge – which, by the way, is a pretty powerful motive. So, if we add a sister into the equation and look for a suitable candidate in the area, Lisa Edwards is the most likely fit.'

Emma said nothing.

Harris glanced sideways at her face and knew she was still sceptical. 'Look, someone's framing Rosie. The knife from her kitchen with Stokes blood; the stained jacket – it has to be someone close to them who could gain access to their home. It's a small community. Most of the residents have been there forever but Lisa's an incomer. She appeared in the village out of nowhere and was conveniently available to work for the couple when they needed help. She's also the right age. It could be a coincidence yet this girl's in an ideal situation to ruin her employers' lives.'

'Okay, it's a theory but don't we need proof?' Emma conceded.

'Yes, which is why we're going to visit Rosie Cantrell to see what she can tell us of this girl and then pay a call on Lisa Edwards herself, something we should have done long before now.' Harris could tell from his sergeant's silence that she was still unconvinced. 'Look upon it as investigating a new line of enquiry; a new lead. We're going back to square one with this, Emma, and due to the revelation of the pathologist's report, we no longer have the murder weapon. So why don't you get on your phone and do a bit of digging? You could start by googling Lisa's name and then have a look on those social media sites which all you young folk love so much. Try her surname as Edwards and Drake.'

Emma was happy to comply and tapped away on her phone. Neither were uncommon names but the DS failed to find anyone of the right age and description. As they neared their destination she'd come up with nothing on the most popular social media sites either.

Harris frowned. 'Isn't that a little suspicious in itself?'

'She could just be a private sort of person?'

'Are you on any of these sites or your friends?'

'Yes, I suppose...'

'Then let's keep an open mind, shall we?' He changed down a gear as they approached the track to Hilltop Cottage.

CHAPTER FORTY-SEVEN

Rosie's heart pounded as the sound of a car startled Lisa, shifting the young woman's focus to the window and fleetingly away from Noah.

'Are you expecting anyone?' she snapped.

Rosie shook her head, trying to keep her nerve.

This could be my one and only chance! An answer to prayer.

The car drew up outside and the engine cut out.

'Don't answer the door! Whoever it is can't see us from the window – stay still and quiet or you'll regret it!' Lisa's voice was icy; her hand still pressing the blade against Noah's little face, yet Rosie thought she detected a hint of uncertainty in her tone.

If whoever it is knocks, there may be an opportunity...

Two car doors slammed and Rosie's hopes rose – two visitors were far better than one in this instance. It wouldn't be Mike. It was far too early for him to be home and he would be alone. The only visitor who might possibly arrive unannounced was Bella, but it was unlikely to be her.

For a moment time stood still. The air was heavy and Noah's snuffly breathing sounded loud, exaggerated in the silence. Rosie prayed for the visitors to knock.

They did – and as Rosie expected, Ben burst into life, barking frantically, spinning around chasing his tail in excitement and anticipation.

Now, Rosie – it's now or never!

Noah woke at the noise and cried. Ben's barking always disturbed him, and Rosie watched in horror as Lisa covered his mouth with her free hand.

'No!' She screamed and leapt from the chair, reaching for Lisa before thinking through the ramifications of her actions. Lisa, momentarily startled, looked away from the baby to Rosie who launched herself at this woman – this threat to her child.

'Mrs Cantrell! Open the door. It's DI Harris here!' The detective was shouting, banging again on the door, aware that someone was inside, but Rosie was oblivious, single-minded in her attempt at saving her son.

Lisa took her hands out of the crib to fend Rosie off – Noah could breathe again and screamed even louder than before.

The door rattled. DI Harris was trying to batter it down to get inside.

Rosie saw the knife raised in the air and lunged for Lisa's arm. Her body weight knocked the woman off her feet and the two fell to the floor, the knife still in Lisa's hand. But Rosie held on to her wrist, banging it frantically on the stone floor in an attempt to get her to drop it.

Suddenly a black-booted foot appeared from nowhere and pinned Lisa's arm to the floor. Rosie looked around, breathless, to see DS Emma Russell pulling handcuffs from her belt. The sergeant had entered the cottage through the back door and roughly rolled Lisa over onto her stomach and snapped handcuffs on her wrists.

Rosie scrambled to her feet and ran straight to her son. She lifted him gently from the crib and cradled him into her shoulder whispering soothing words, as much to herself as to Noah. Her breathing rapid, Rosie held her son close.

Is it over? Could this nightmare finally be at an end?

DI Harris was in the room now too, assisting his sergeant in dragging a struggling Lisa to her feet. With the woman restrained, he turned his attention to a trembling Rosie and Noah.

'Are you okay?' He sounded winded.

Rosie nodded, unable to speak and the detective pulled out his phone to ring the station for back-up.

DS Russell marched Lisa outside where she waited with her prisoner secured in the back of the DI's car.

'Shall I ring Mike for you?' Tom Harris offered and Rosie nodded again, still rocking her son who had ceased his screams and was sucking furiously at his fist.

Harris said very little on the phone, simply that there'd been an incident and his wife needed him at home immediately. Ending the call, the detective then asked if he could get anything for Rosie who cradled her son on the sofa and could only answer with a shake of her head.

Mike arrived moments after the back-up police car, stunned and perplexed to see Lisa in handcuffs being placed in the back seat and driven away. He ran into the cottage. At the sight of her husband, Rosie burst into tears and the DI moved outside for a few moments to allow them some privacy and to speak to his sergeant.

Returning shortly, Harris summarised the morning's events as concisely as possible. The biggest shock for Mike was discovering that Lisa had been the one to cause all their troubles – that she was Gary Drake's sister and Frank Stokes's murderer. There would be time to hear more later.

DI Harris looked from Mike to Rosie. 'I have to go now but I strongly recommend you see a doctor, you've had quite a shock.'

'No, I'll be fine – and thank you so much – if you hadn't come...' Rosie finally managed to speak but as she tried to express her gratitude, thoughts of what might have been almost overwhelmed her.

'I still don't understand why Lisa would do this,' Mike said.

'Perhaps this isn't the time to go into specifics. You're safe now and please accept my apologies that it took us so long to get this right, and for all you've gone through, unnecessarily as it happens. I'll need to take a formal statement about this morning's events but not now. I'll get back to the station and be in touch later today when I'll be able to tell you more.' DI Harris left Hilltop Cottage and when the door closed behind him, Mike took Rosie in his arms.

'Oh, Rosie, I'm so sorry! I've been such an idiot these last few days when I should have been supporting you. Can you ever forgive me?'

The look in her eyes gave him his answer as she put her finger on his lips to silence him. 'We've both been fooled. There was no way we could have known Lisa was behind all of this and I don't have the words to describe how I'm feeling. As the inspector said, we're safe. We'll talk more about it later.'

Rosie held Noah so tightly he was beginning to wriggle and she was gripped by a sudden desire to laugh. But she didn't. Instead, she allowed Mike to take Noah from her while she finally gave way to the hot tears welling up inside her.

Rosie knew it wouldn't be easy to recover from the morning's ordeal. What she'd been through was even more horrendous than the events surrounding Ali's death. It would take time and possibly professional help for both her and Mike. She shuddered to think about what might have been. Eventually Rosie would share the minutiae with Mike; talk it out of her system.

One thing she knew for sure was that there'd be no more

running away. This time she hadn't lost everything; there was still her husband and Noah, Mike's family and some very good friends. Rosie was grateful to have a glass, and that glass was now at least half full. She felt very blessed and thankful that her prayers were answered.

CHAPTER FORTY-EIGHT

A few hours, but a lifetime since her ordeal, Rosie heard a car pull up outside Hilltop Cottage. This time Rosie hurried to the door, hoping it was Tom Harris and anxious for news. The detective formed a weak smile as he entered, his long face otherwise expressionless. Rosie didn't offer coffee although they could probably all use some, craving facts above caffeine. The detective took a seat in their lounge, cleared his throat and spoke slowly.

'I'm sorry to have put you through all this, Mrs Cantrell, but we're confident it's finally over.' He paused and again attempted another smile, obviously something he was unused to doing.

Rosie let out a sigh and sank back into the sofa next to Mike who snaked his arm protectively around her shoulders. As the tension left her body an overwhelming desire to curl up in that very spot and sleep for hours suddenly overcame her. Tom Harris's words were a welcome comfort and she finally allowed herself to believe the ordeal of the last few weeks had ended; the nightmare over. Yet Rosie needed answers before sleep and nodded for the DI to continue.

'I know you've already worked out that the young woman

you know as Lisa Edwards is actually Lisa Drake. She was fifteen when her brother Gary died, an impressionable age to lose the brother she adored and who could do no wrong in her eyes. I dare say she felt the loss keenly.

'It appears Drake used his sister in his plan to defraud you of your trust fund. Lisa's been very open with us, admitting everything, which will undoubtedly help in unravelling her and her brother's crimes.'

Rosie hadn't considered the trust fund until the detective mentioned it; it had been the least of her worries. Instead she thought fleetingly about the young Lisa, only fifteen and faced with her brother's imprisonment and subsequent violent death. Rosie hadn't been much older when her parents died and remembered the unbearable pain of loss, the realisation of never again seeing those she'd loved so much. Had Lisa felt that way too?

DI Harris continued. 'Shortly before your sister died, Drake solicited Lisa's help in hiding the money, opening an account in her name under the guise of it being a lottery win on which he wished to avoid tax. Lisa seems unaware of her brother's long-term plans although he did tell her he was going abroad for a while, alone.'

'So he *was* just using Ali – he wanted the money not her.' Rosie's voice trembled as Drake's true purpose was confirmed, regret and sadness enveloped her but she swallowed the threatening tears and listened as the detective continued.

'Lisa kept her brother's secret even when she realised the money wasn't a lottery win, not even telling her mother. Looking for someone to blame for her brother's death Rosie became the target, Rosie, undeservedly so, and she vowed to seek revenge. Naturally this was impossible at such a young age but Lisa guarded her secret patiently, all the while planning to avenge her brother's death until eventually she was in a position to act.

'It appears she left home after completing her schooling, her relationship with her mother was no warmer than Drake's, and she spent some of the money supporting herself while employing a private detective to find you.

'When you were eventually located she followed you to Thursdale, purchased a property and again bided her time until the opportunity of working for you presented itself. It appears her plans were somewhat fluid at the time; Lisa possesses endless patience and settled in to wait for the chance to bring about your downfall. Although content to play the long game, when she heard of Frank Stokes's renewed interest in you from her mother, it seemed to be the perfect opportunity for payback. It's not clear if Lisa decided to murder him from the outset although she has now confessed to killing him.'

Rosie sighed. Although shocked at Lisa's callousness, the detective's words were balm to her soul, this was what she'd longed to hear – the police had found the real murderer and she was no longer under suspicion.

DI Harris continued. 'Lisa made herself indispensable as an employee and wheedled her way into becoming a personal friend to you both, someone you would never suspect. This placed her in the perfect situation to frame you for Stokes's murder, Rosie. She's also admitted to causing the damage at your market garden, though quite where those plans fit in, I'm not entirely sure.'

Tom Harris paused and Rosie decided coffee would now be appropriate – she certainly needed something and as drinking the large glass of wine she craved in front of the detective didn't seem fitting, Rosie went into the kitchen to make coffee.

'I think I can enlighten you as to her reason for the fire,' Mike explained. 'Lisa offered to invest in the business; to become a partner, knowing we were struggling financially since Noah came along and Rosie could no longer work with me. We initially declined the offer so possibly Lisa decided to give me a little push in that direction. I'd recently accepted her offer of investment and was on the point of drawing up an agreement.'

'Ah, yes that could explain it. As to Lisa's final goal perhaps the words she spoke to your wife are telling – she intended to steal Rosie's life – the business and perhaps also yourself and the baby?' DI Harris paused for confirmation but was met with silence as Mike's face burned with shame. Harris deftly changed the subject as Rosie returned with the coffee.

'How we came to suspect Lisa is partly thanks to our colleagues in Liverpool. They followed the money trail in their investigation, a line of enquiry in which they erroneously suspected yourself, but eventually led them to Gary Drake's family. They also passed on Frank Stokes's notes on his proposed book which mentioned the existence of a younger sister. Sadly we should have followed this lead sooner, yet with so much evidence pointing to you I'm afraid we opted for the more obvious route.'

Rosie felt a pang of shame at the ill feeling she'd harboured towards Theresa Lloyd who'd initially suspected Rosie of stealing her own trust fund and even of being complicit in Ali's death, yet the woman had only been doing her job. After passing round the coffee, Rosie settled down to listen to the rest of DI Harris's explanations.

'We've been in touch with our colleagues in Liverpool to appraise them of recent developments and I'm pleased to tell you that they've closed the investigation into your sister's death. You're no longer a person of interest. But getting back to Lisa, she's been quite open about the logistics of her plan. Having made contact with Stokes on discovering he was looking for you, she arranged to meet him in Thursdale after his visit here, with the promise of helping persuade you to co-operate with his book. However, Mike threw a spanner in the works by arriving at the pub prior to their rendezvous, so her plans took a different direction. When Mike left, Lisa waited for Stokes to come out and took him to the woods where they could talk without being seen together. Instead of fulfilling her promise, Lisa murdered the man.' Harris took a swig of his coffee, his sensibilities apparently untouched by the horrors of a cold-blooded stabbing while Rosie was feeling decidedly queasy.

Smacking his lips, the DI continued. 'Initially we suspected you, Mike, having been seen in the pub and with no alibi for the time immediately afterwards, but that wasn't Lisa's intention. Instead she wanted the blame to fall on Rosie and so broke into your home to "borrow" your jacket which at some point she smeared with Stokes's blood before returning it for us to find at a later date. It appears when she visited Rosie on another occasion Lisa had also stolen one of your knives, an event which went unnoticed by yourselves until we searched the cottage.'

Mike's face coloured. 'It's incredible how callous she's been while all the time pretending to be our friend. How two-faced can you get?' Rosie watched him, understanding a little of how he must feel at being taken in by Lisa.

'With her full confession, Lisa will be remanded in custody until sentencing in a few months. There'll be multiple charges and quite honestly, I don't envy the CPS in having to sort this one out. I'm afraid although she's confessed to keeping your trust fund, she's been living on the money so some of it may not be recovered. However, her house will be sold under the proceeds of crime act and the money returned to you but it will take time.' With his explanation complete Tom Harris finished his coffee and stood to leave.

Mike was the first to speak. 'Thank you for everything. If you hadn't worked out Lisa's part in all of this, she might have got away with it and I could have lost Rosie. We'll be forever grateful.' He spoke for them both.

Tom Harris smiled as he turned towards the door. From the couple's reaction it was clear the money was unimportant – getting their lives back was paramount. This case hadn't been Harris's proudest moment and he berated himself over missed clues and not having trusted his own judgement, but the outcome was satisfactory. The couple were safe and free to rebuild their lives; he would take comfort in both that and seeing Lisa Drake convicted of her crimes. There was little more for which a detective could hope.

EPILOGUE

I t was November and Rosie stared at the image of her friend in the full-length mirror. 'You look beautiful, Bella. Stuart's a very lucky man.'

Both women were experiencing bittersweet emotions. Bella, with thoughts of her first husband, was suffering wedding day nerves, wondering if she was doing the right thing, until her matron of honour reminded her how much she loved Stuart. Rosie was still finding it hard to believe her life was back on track – she was slowly learning to stop continually looking over her shoulder and jumping at unexpected noises.

Rosie shuddered, then smiled at her friend, determined to do her best for this loving and generous lady. 'Hey this is your special day and we're going to enjoy it, that's an order! Now let's get a wriggle on, you're already five minutes late and we don't want Stuart to think you've changed your mind.'

The day was an uplifting and validating experience, and by its conclusion it became clear to Rosie that this was a turning point for her as well as Bella, a fact which was confirmed over the following year.

'Sorry, love, it's a bit cold!' The young maternity nurse laughed as she smeared gel on Rosie's abdomen. At around nine weeks pregnant this was Rosie's first scan and Mike, sitting beside her was attempting to keep a wriggling eighteen-month-old Noah on his knee while looking expectantly at the screen.

'Baby!' Noah babbled the latest addition to his vocabulary and reached out towards his mother. Mike tugged him back, turning to glimpse the grainy image.

'Yes, baby!' he repeated before noticing the frown on the nurse's face. 'Is everything okay?' he asked tentatively.

'Erm, yes, I think so. Can I ask if either of you have twins in the family?'

Rosie beamed. 'I'm a twin.'

The world was suddenly an exciting place. Mike squeezed her hand. The scan was welcome news and she couldn't wait to share it with their friends and family. Unlike Noah's arrival into the world this was very much a planned pregnancy, a new start with a new baby, only now it appeared there was two – double the delight!

Looking back on the horrendous time when Alison died, it was only now that Rosie could understand her own extreme reaction. Running away and changing her name was at the time the only way she could cope with the unbearable distress. The ensuing years were primarily spent in trying to forget – to bury the pain in the darkest recesses of her mind and resolutely refusing to dwell on those bitter memories. It wasn't an entirely successful strategy, for as well as denying the painful memories, Rosie had inadvertently blocked the happy ones too.

In her staunch denial and determined attempt to erase the pain, she also lost the joyful years of her childhood, the closeness of family, all those things which had previously grounded her and moulded her into the young woman who was Samantha Ashby. Perhaps if she'd allowed them to, those happy memories would have eased the pain of missing her family. Rosie would never know. *If only* are two of the saddest words in anyone's vocabulary.

One of the first things Rosie did in the days following Lisa's attack was to drag out the box from the back of the wardrobe, open it and share the contents and memories with Mike. Her childhood photographs now brought much-needed comfort and she vowed never again to deny her family's existence. Those beautiful images she'd hidden away for so long were finally prominently displayed in Hilltop Cottage for all to see and Noah would grow up under their gaze, learning of his family and what wonderful people they were.

Frank Stokes's death was an event the Cantrells would never forget and a time which tested their marriage to the limits. Only when the police discovered the truth and Lisa was unmasked as the real killer could the process of recovery begin. Mike and Rosie talked for hours after Lisa's arrest – apologies and regrets expressed by them both and they vowed never again to allow secrets to divide them. It would take time to recover from the trauma but together they would survive and rebuild their life.

Nothing could make up for the horror and suffering of those weeks, yet one or two surprises eased their way and made life a little more comfortable – not least of which was the recovery of Rosie's elusive trust fund.

The couple had assumed that after almost ten years most of the two million pounds would be gone and therefore were surprised to learn that most of it remained and would be returned to them, largely due to the increased value of Lisa's cottage. Rosie didn't hide the fact the money was welcome – it was her birthright, her entitlement, and it enabled them to rebuild the market garden and renovate Hilltop Cottage. Yes, Rosie had been glad to escape that harrowing morning with her life and the money was simply a bonus but one that enabled them to do so much, not least of which was to have another baby – or two as it happened.

Lisa Drake was charged with multiple crimes including murder, attempted murder, arson and fraud. Due to her confession a lengthy trial was avoided and at her sentencing hearing, she was given a life sentence with a recommendation to serve a minimum of fifteen years.

Mike and Rosie were relieved it was over and they could throw themselves into rebuilding their market garden and their relationship.

Staying in Thursdale was never in question. Apart from Ginny Yarrow, the villagers in general had been supportive, rallying round after the fire and refusing to believe Rosie and Mike could in any way be connected to a murder. When the truth was revealed and the shock of Lisa's deception made public, messages of encouragement and offers of help overwhelmed the couple. If anything, the Cantrells were more a part of the village than ever before and so it remained their home, their happy place.

The events of late summer 2019 produced a ripple effect, focusing the minds of those involved on what was important in life. Mike's parents, supportive throughout, decided to relocate nearer to their family, recognising they were missing out not only on seeing their son and his wife but also on Noah's childhood years.

Jim took early retirement from his driving job, intending to work with his son in the market garden, much to Mike's delight, and the Cantrells senior found a bungalow in Thursdale which suited them perfectly. Mary chose not to search for another job, hoping instead to become a more hands-on granny, with her daughter-in-law's full approval.

On Rosie's first meeting with Ginny Yarrow after the truth was revealed, the woman waddled towards her, smiled and had the audacity to say, 'I always knew you weren't involved in such an awful business.'

Rosie smiled sweetly and thanked her. Life is too short to hold grudges.

THE END

NOTE FROM THE AUTHOR

Thank you for reading *The Deception* which I hope you enjoyed. I'm occasionally asked if I know the ending of my novels before I begin writing and almost always the answer is no. The characters have a habit of surprising me, of taking over their own destiny, and each story evolves and changes beyond my original ideas. It's to be hoped this makes them more interesting and less predictable.

The title of this book has changed several times during its writing. The word 'deception' seemed fitting as the story is littered with deceptions great and small. Rosie deceived Mike – but was it any different to the way Mike deceived Rosie? Frank Stokes made a habit of deception. Alison deceived Samantha, and Gary Drake was the greatest culprit of them all.

Is deception ever justified? We must decide for ourselves. As in the quotation from Sissela Bok, *"While all deception requires secrecy, all secrecy is not meant to deceive."*

To read more of my work, please visit my Amazon author page, Facebook author page @gillianjacksonauthor, follow me on

Twitter @GillianJackson7 or visit my website, www.gillianjackson.co.uk.

ACKNOWLEDGEMENTS

My thanks as always to my husband and family for their love and support during the hours I spend writing. And to the team at Bloodhound Books for their amazing help in getting this book out into the world, this is my third book with Bloodhound and with each one I learn more from these dedicated professional people. I truly appreciate their advice and guidance throughout the process.

A NOTE FROM THE PUBLISHER

Thank you for reading this book. If you enjoyed it please do consider leaving a review on Amazon to help others find it too.

We hate typos. All of our books have been rigorously edited and proofread, but sometimes mistakes do slip through. If you have spotted a typo, please do let us know and we can get it amended within hours.

info@bloodhoundbooks.com